I0710219

ALL FIRED UP
GREEN VALLEY HEROES BOOK #7

ALLIE WINTERS

Copyright

This book is a work of fiction. Names, characters, places, rants, facts, contrivances, and incidents are either the product of the author's questionable imagination or are used factitiously. Any resemblance to actual persons, living or dead or undead, events, locales is entirely coincidental if not somewhat disturbing/concerning.

Made in the United States of America

Print Edition

ISBN: 978-1-959097-90-7

Chapter One
MADELINE

"What the hell?"

I stare at my computer screen, the rows of syntax blurring together as I rub my eyes.

Why is this code duplicated in so many spots? Who wrote this? A trained monkey?

They weren't trained well, apparently.

I'll have to spend a while creating a function to refactor it, but it'll be worth it in the end. The senior developer will have my head if I turn in this project with the code looking like this.

The loud drone of the vacuum in the living room snags my attention, and my lips purse, annoyance at my mom rushing through me. How many times have I asked her to keep it down during the day? I'm trying to work.

As I push away from my desk and grab my headphones off the bedside table, I briefly fantasize about a place of my own. One with complete silence all the time. Decorated nicely, too. I'm a simple girl with simple wishes.

But where would that leave Mom? She already somehow managed to end up on the brink of foreclosure when I was in college. If I hadn't moved back here and taken over the bills, who knows what would have happened to her?

Thank God I can work from home, because Lord knows there aren't any web development jobs in Green Valley, Tennessee.

I put my noise-canceling headphones on and settle back in, ready to tackle this code, when my door bursts open and Mom waves a flyer in front of my face, smiling.

"Have you seen this?" she asks, her voice muffled, and I reluctantly take off the headphones.

"Maybe if you stop waving it around, I'd know what you're talking about," I mutter. I do my best to push my annoyance away, but some days are better than others. Mom can be an . . . acquired taste.

"Oh, stop it, sourpuss," she says, no heat behind her words. "I saw this on the bulletin board at the Piggly Wiggly."

I take it from her and quickly scan the paper. "Oh, that," I mumble, a nervous thrill running through me. I saw this same flyer at the library last week. "What about it?"

Mom's smile grows wider. "Well, it's wonderful, is all. Your father would be tickled pink at the town putting out a call for volunteer firefighters."

The familiar ache in my chest at the mention of Dad burns for a moment, then disappears. You'd think after eleven years it'd go away.

"Oh, he'd have so many ideas," she rambles, and I tune her out for a moment. I'm glad she's able to talk about him now like this. It's a hell of a lot better than when she could barely get out of bed after his death. But if someone doesn't stop her, she'll keep talking forever.

"Yeah, I saw this the other day," I interrupt, holding the flyer up.

She sits on the edge of my bed, facing me. "So, are you interested?"

I will myself not to react, even as my index finger finds the loose string at the hem of my shirt and starts twisting. "Why would you think that?"

She gives me a signature Mom look and the corners of my lips twitch at her deadpan stare.

"It's a volunteer thing," she says. "It'd be perfect for you."

I resist the urge to rub at the back of my neck.

"I know you were disappointed you weren't accepted before."

I let out a sigh. "That was seven years ago. And Chief McClure was right to turn me down." I had no business trying to be a firefighter fresh out of high school.

Mom huffs. "He still should have given you a chance. Firefighting runs in your family's blood."

I smirk at her insistence. "I could barely do a pushup back then."

Not that I'm much better now. I think my record is five in a row.

"Well, you can do them now. There are lots of women firefighters out there nowadays. You should try again."

Not in Green Valley, though. It's still a boys' club. And though I do the occasional workout video at home, I have no delusions I'm up to the extreme physical fitness standards of a firefighter.

"Besides, there's not as much pressure now," she continues. "It's a volunteer thing."

Yeah, I heard her the first time.

She stares at me, waiting for a response, and I internally groan, knowing she won't give up. "I already thought about it," I admit. Seeing that flyer last week brought up a lot of old feelings about wanting some kind of connection to my dad again. To do something he'd be proud of. Something he'd dedicated his life to.

"So you're going to try out?" she asks with glee, as if it's already a foregone conclusion.

God, she's relentless.

"I'll go on Saturday and see what it's all about. But no promises," I add when she claps her hands together.

She sobers somewhat. "I think you'll find a lot of fulfillment in it." She reaches out and smooths a hand over my hair. "Your father would be so proud of you."

That ache in my chest flares to life again, lingering. I give her a half-hearted smile and tell her, "I have to get back to work now."

Her hands flutter and make a shooing motion. "Oh, you and your work. Isn't that supposed to be a perk of working from home? That you can stop and chat with your mom every once in a while?"

I keep my mouth shut. When the chats are every fifteen minutes, it's not so much of a break as a second job. I've had to start making up virtual meetings just so I can get some peace and quiet for a while.

"All right, let me know how it goes on Saturday. I have my fingers crossed for you."

I welcome the silence of the room at her departure, my gaze gravitating toward the paper she left. They must be in need of volunteers if they put this out. I dog-ear the corner, indecision warring within me. Yeah, I told Mom I'd go, but that was to get her off my back.

The memory of me, fresh-faced and naive at eighteen, going down to the fire station to ask if they were hiring, returns. Grizz Grady had snickered into his palm, but Chief McClure hadn't. He'd taken the time to gently explain what the tests were like, with the unspoken implication that I wouldn't pass. I'd thanked him for his time and gone and cried in my car. It was a last-ditch effort to stay in Green Valley instead of heading off to college, afraid of leaving Mom alone.

Looking back, though, I'm glad he'd steered me away from it. I make great money now as a web developer, enough that I don't have to worry about Mom falling behind on house payments again. Sure, a part of me still remembers wanting to grow up and be a firefighter like Dad. He'd been in line to be the chief of his own fire department one day. Before he died. Before we had to move to Green Valley because Mom couldn't keep it together. If not for Aunt Lucy, I don't know what we would have done.

I push those thoughts aside and stare at the paper again. The fire department's phone number is at the bottom of the page, along with the line, *Call for more info*.

Glancing over at my phone, I pick it up, and before I lose my nerve, I call.

* * *

AM I actually going in there?

I smooth my palms over my pants, getting rid of the dampness that keeps popping up, and stare at the firehouse through the windshield. The two-story brick building appears simple enough, nothing to be nervous about. Hell, the flowers planted along either side of the path that leads to the front entrance appear downright inviting. But tell that to my churning stomach. What if they laugh me right out of there?

The woman on the phone had been perfectly pleasant, answering all my questions with no hint of dismissal. It had surprised me at first they'd had a female firefighter on staff, until she'd said she was the office manager. She'd told me the only way I'd know if I could pass the physical fitness test was if I tried. It was a diplomatic answer and one I couldn't fault her for. With too many people sue-happy nowadays, they probably didn't want to open themselves up to a lawsuit for denying a woman the chance to try out.

Is a part of me looking for an excuse not to try?

Shame rushes hot and heavy through me for a moment, thinking how disappointed Dad would be in me for not giving it my all.

Loud music interrupts my thoughts, and a Ford Mustang pulls into the lot, parking at the end, away from everyone else. I blink, surprised at who exits.

It's Hunter O'Connor.

Not exactly the hometown hero, firefighter type. I mean, body-wise, yes. There's no denying that. The guy's got muscles that definitely don't exist on me. But his dad and brother are Iron Wraiths, and very much not model citizens. Not the kind of family who becomes volunteer firefighters.

He looks toward me as he passes by and I jerk my head in a different direction, my heart pounding out of nowhere. Did he know I was looking at him? Not that it matters if I was. I'm allowed to look. It's a free country.

Jesus, why the hell am I arguing with myself about this?

Once he's an appropriate distance ahead, I force myself to get out of the car and head toward the open bay where a small group is gathered. Chief McClure is next to the gleaming red fire engine, with Grizz Grady beside him. Guess he still works here, too.

Opposite him is Harry, the cashier at the Piggly Wiggly who always tries to make small talk. There's also a guy in his early thirties I don't recognize, and Hunter. I avoid all of them and sneak to the back of the group.

"We're waiting on two more," Chief McClure says. "They said they'd be here."

I nod, still not looking, even though I think he was addressing me. My heart is pounding again, sure everyone is staring at me, wondering why I'm here.

I'm not even sure anymore why I am.

Someone sidles up next to me, but I don't have to turn my head to know who it is.

"Madeline Woodward," Hunter says in a deceptively soft voice. "What's a girl like you doing here?"

To be a firefighter, I think, but I don't say the words aloud. They sound so stupid.

"I thought you'd left this hellhole," he says when I don't reply.

I wet my lips as all the moisture recedes from my mouth. "I moved back a few years ago. After college."

"Hmm," he draws out. "Willingly?"

I glance at him, the harsh planes of his face, the cut of his jaw beneath the dark stubble, those intense hazel eyes boring into me. Has his gaze ever been on me before? Did he ever look at me in high school? To be honest, I'm half-surprised he remembers me, especially since I didn't grow up here. He was also a year ahead of me, up until senior year, at least.

An image of the first time I saw him flashes through my mind, him making out with Lydia Marino under the bleachers. I'd stumbled upon them, freezing when I realized what I was seeing, but unable to look away. I'd never seen anything so . . . passionate before. But when his hand had pushed under her shirt, molding over her breast, I'd snuck away, the two of them none the wiser.

My cheeks heat. Can he tell I was thinking about him? Oh, wait. He asked me a question.

"My mom needed me here."

He makes a sound of dismissal. "Oh, a do-gooder. Is that why you're here? So you can save the town, too?"

My cheeks flush hotter as I finally fully look at him.

He gives me a once-over, but there's disapproval in it, and he smirks. "Can you even lift the hose?"

My shoulders tighten at his rude question. He's got a point, but who is he to question me outright to my face?

"Can you pass the written tests?" I shoot back before I can think better of it. If I remember right—and I definitely do—he'd barely passed high school. He'd been held back a year and had to graduate with my class.

His smirk doesn't drop, but something flashes in his eyes.

Two of the Clewis brothers jog up to join our group and Chief McClure claps his hands together.

"All right, guess that's everyone," he says. "Glad to see we've got some interest from the community in our volunteer firefighter initiative. This is a program I've wanted to do for a while, and our lieutenant, Buck Rogers, helped us get some state and federal grants to get it going. He's not here today, but he will be tomorrow."

He pauses and looks at the six of us. "Everyone here should recognize me. I'm Carter McClure, the fire chief of Green Valley. Next to me is Grizz Grady, our fire captain. We're going to outline our plan for how this training will run, and I'm warning you now it's going to take up most of your weekends for the next couple of months."

He surveys us steadily, as if taking our measure, and I resist the urge to rub my arms as goosebumps wash over me. "We understand everyone here works full-time, so it'll be a mix of instruction and skill demonstrations on Saturdays and Sundays. You'll also be expected to study on your own to get up to speed since we have limited time on the weekends. We appreciate your time and commitment, but we also only want people who are serious about this."

His gaze lingers on me and Hunter in the back, but I can't tell if he's looking at both of us or just one.

Hunter raises his hand. "You need to be pretty strong to do this, right? To carry people out of burning buildings and stuff?"

It's obvious who his question is referring to as the other men in front of us turn to stare at me.

My armpits grow damp. Shit.

Chief McClure says, "There is a physical component to it, yes. It'll be one of your final exams."

Fine. Hunter wants to play that game? I raise my hand. "There are also written tests, right? Testing your math skills, reading comprehension, situational judgment, memory, things like that?"

I already know the answer. I'd done my research.

The chief responds that there are and goes over some of the areas that will be tested, but I'm paying more attention to the way Hunter's face pales. Whoa. Are the tests that big of a deal to him?

He glances at me, something like shame crossing his face before it disappears and he sneers. He moves away from me and toward the front of the group, leaving me alone in the back.

I cross my arms, not liking the unsettling mixture of guilt and anger brewing in my gut. He's the one who started it, not me. And I'm not wasting another minute thinking about him. I've got bigger fish to fry than Hunter O'Connor.

Namely, how the hell I'm going to become Green Valley's next volunteer firefighter.

Chapter Two
HUNTER

My gaze tracks Madeline across the parking lot as she opens the door to a newer-model Camry and gets in. Fucking tryhard. She hasn't changed at all since high school.

She'd answered all of Chief McClure's questions he asked the group about fire safety, trying to be teacher's pet once again. What, being valedictorian and going away to college on some fancy scholarship wasn't enough for her? I'd assumed she'd gone on to work at NASA or something ridiculous, not come back here to Green Valley. Where's she been hiding the last few years?

She has no business trying to be the best at fucking firefighting, too. Come on already. Why's she even here? The girl's so slight, she looks like she can barely lift a pencil.

Her car doesn't leave the lot, so I assume she must be eating in her car like I am during our lunch break. Probably because no one wanted to sit with her inside. Because no one wants her here.

I don't want her here.

The memory of her from all those years ago barrels into the forefront of my mind, her begging our economics teacher to pair her with anyone besides me for our end of term project. I push the thought away, along with the hot wash of shame that comes with it.

Is she going to pull the same shit here, too? Refuse to partner with me for those training exercises McClure was talking about? I'm not going through that again. What the girl needs is to be taken down a peg.

My gaze lands on the passenger side floorboard of my car and the bag filled with the fake roaches I'd pranked my brother with on April Fool's Day. A smile spreads over my face as I set my sandwich down and retrieve the bag.

Chief McClure and Grizz set out all the turnout gear earlier that we'll practice putting on after lunch, and they'd specifically placed hers at the end with the smallest sizes they had available. If a couple of these plastic bugs were to find their way into her boots . . . who would even know how they got there?

After scarfing down the rest of my sandwich, I casually make my way back inside, making a quick pit stop in the empty bay where our afternoon session will be, then to the small downstairs break room, where Harry is finishing up his lunch. I sink into the armchair over in the corner and pull out my phone, praying Harry doesn't strike up a conversation. He can't keep his mouth shut on a good day.

When our lunch break is over and we're gathered in what the chief calls the apparatus bay, it takes everything in me to not look over at Madeline. Don't want her suspecting anything.

"Our turnout gear is made with Nomex," Chief McClure tells us, "which can withstand temperatures of up to sixteen hundred degrees. It can also only be cleaned by a special process, so don't go sticking it in a regular washer or you might ruin it."

Grizz takes the reins next. "You've got your coat and pants, your fire hood and helmet, your gloves, and your boots. The whole set weighs about forty-five pounds, and once you add on tools, lights, radios, et cetera, that extra weight goes up, so be prepared for that. Now I'm going to show you the correct way to put everything on, then you'll practice."

After his demonstration, we're given the go-ahead to put ours on. I bide my time and savor the sweet sound of Madeline's scream a few minutes later.

Everyone looks at her over in the corner of the bay where she's run away, her light brown hair disheveled, her cheeks stained with a fierce blush. She points toward her boots. "There are roaches in there."

Chief McClure frowns, probably ready to tear this bay apart to find where the offending insects are coming from, but I walk past him and give a put-upon sigh.

"Seriously?" I say to Madeline. "I'll take care of it."

I keep my grin to myself as I pick up the boots and walk out of the bay and around the side of the building to a grassy area. I empty the fake roaches into my palm and stick them in my pocket.

But when I turn around, I'm not alone. Whoa, how'd she sneak up on me like that without me hearing?

"What are you doing?" Madeline asks, suspicion in her voice.

I open my mouth to respond, but nothing comes out. Did she see what I did?

"Did you put those bugs in your pocket?" she asks.

Well, shit. Still, I'm not fessing up.

Her gaze narrows, the deep brown of her eyes piercing me. "Were those fake? Did you plant them there?"

"What are you, Nancy Drew? Forget about it."

I move past her, but she grabs at my forearm, her fingers soft and delicate. Not the hands of a potential firefighter.

I look down at her hand on my arm pointedly until she removes it in a hurry.

"Don't mess with me," she warns, and I nearly laugh.

"Or what?" I step closer, aware of the size difference between us. I'm not exactly looming over her, intimidating her with my size . . . But I'm also not *not* doing that.

She doesn't answer, probably because she realizes she doesn't have a leg to stand on.

"No one wants you on this team," I tell her. "You realize that, right? No one wants a know-it-all whose only skill is to play teacher's pet. That won't help in a fire."

Her nostrils flare. "You don't know anything about me. And why are you here, anyway? On some kind of recon mission for the Iron Wraiths? You going to steal the fire engine for their chop shop?"

What does she know about that? "I'm not part of the Iron Wraiths," I grit out.

"Right." There's clear disbelief in her tone. "Just the rest of your family is. But not you. That'd be ridiculous."

I'm silent, unable to refute her words. They're true. And also the exact reason I'm here.

"You didn't answer my question," she says. "Why are you here?"

To be different from my family. To change how people see me. To maybe do something meaningful with my life for once.

Not that I'm telling her any of that.

"None of your business."

I walk away, leaving her there, and return the boots inside, muttering, "All good now."

When she joins us again, I half expect her to tattle on me, but she doesn't. She only quietly puts on the rest of her gear, and I do the same.

McClure talks more about the turnout gear, but I can't pay attention, waiting for Madeline to say something. To demand I empty my pockets. To ask for me to be kicked out of the program. Is she messing with me? Playing a trick of her own? Or is she really going to keep quiet?

No, I need to focus on what the chief is saying. It's so much easier trying to remember things I hear than having to read about it later. How serious are these tests going to be that he mentioned earlier? Me and tests have never exactly got along. The letters always seem to move around on the page.

After we're finished and remove our gear, we're assigned lockers inside and given a tour of the building. I do my best to memorize the layout, especially if I'll be here every weekend for the next couple of months. By the end, I'm feeling cautiously optimistic.

The only thing is, how long will it take before my family finds out I'm doing this? Word spreads fast in Green Valley, but at least they don't have much contact with law-abiding citizens like the fire chief. He won't be the one to tell them. Still, they're going to find out eventually and I need to come up with a better reason for why I'm doing this, one that they'll accept. One that's not because I don't want to be like them.

I linger inside the fire station after we're dismissed for a bit, not wanting to run into Madeline in the parking lot. Not that I'm afraid of her or anything. I just don't want her making some big scene by accusing me of anything in front of everyone. It was a harmless prank. She didn't have to get her panties in a wad about it.

When I finally return to my car, there's a note under the windshield wiper, and I pull it out, frowning.

Sorry about hitting your car. My bad!

Below it is an out of state number.

What the fuck? I parked in the corner specifically so no one would go near my car. And why was anyone else even over here? Who's parking at the fire station?

The urge to flip out is strong, but I don't. Two of the other guys are still chatting by their cars, plus Madeline is still over there.

Whatever. I don't have time to worry about her right now. I need to figure out where this car hit me and what kind of damage we're looking at.

I inspect every inch of my car, but can't find anything. What am I missing? If the damage wasn't obvious, why would someone even leave a note?

Pulling out my phone, I dial the number, but a recording picks up.

"Oh, hello there. If you're hearing this message, you've made a woman feel unsafe and/or disrespected."

There's more, but my gaze is stuck on Madeline across the way, looking at me through her open window, a Cheshire cat grin on her face. Did she . . .

I crumple the note in my hand and she laughs, then gives me a little wave and drives off.

So she wants to play it like that?

Game on.

Chapter Three
MADELINE

As I pull up to the fire station's parking lot Sunday morning, I have to admit I feel a bit like a badass. The shock on Hunter's face yesterday as he realized what I'd done was priceless.

His car isn't in the same place today, though. It's not anywhere. Did I actually scare him off? Well, good for me. He had no business being here.

So why is there this weird sense of . . . disappointment in the pit of my stomach?

I push that aside and head in, finding a man around my age in the bay laying out an array of tools and equipment.

"You must be Madeline," he says, pausing to hold a hand out for me to shake. His eyes are incredibly blue.

"H-hi," I stammer, unsure how my reputation precedes me as I return his handshake. "How do you know who I am?" I don't recognize him, so he didn't go to school here.

"Lucky guess. And you're the only woman in the training program."

"Oh, right." Duh. Context clues, Madeline.

A phone rings off in the distance and he excuses himself, muttering something about how no one else answers the phone in this damn place on the weekends.

There's a prickling along the nape of my neck, and I turn around, finding Hunter about ten feet away. His dark hair is casually messy in that artful style male models seem to sport, though I doubt he spends hours in front of the mirror to achieve the same look.

"Still being teacher's pet, I see," he says, half smirking, half frowning.

That's the second time he's called me that. "What makes you think I'm a teacher's pet?"

He rolls his eyes and crosses his arms over his broad chest. "Have you already forgotten high school?"

My brows knit. "I wasn't a teacher's pet. I barely even talked back then." Not that I do a whole lot of that now, either. Except with . . . him, it seems.

"Well, you didn't have to talk to have the teachers thinking the sun shined out of your ass."

I can't help the flush that burns across my face. What is he talking about?

"Sounds to me like you're jealous." It's the only semi-witty response I can come up with at the moment.

His jaw tightens briefly before he smirks again. "Whatever you tell yourself."

He saunters away, leaving me standing awkwardly by myself by the table of power tools. I'm not sure who that point went to. Not that there's a score, per se.

But there kind of is.

Twenty minutes later, the group gathers in front of our instructor, Buck, as he explains what the tools in front of him are used for, and I thank past Madeline for reviewing the chapter in our textbook already. Otherwise, I'd have no idea about some of this stuff. A pike pole? Halligan bar? They'd sound made up if I wasn't looking at them in front of me.

After going over the forcible entry and structural firefighting tools, he moves on to the gas-powered ones.

"Anyone know what this is?" Buck asks us, holding up a rescue saw with a gleaming silver circular blade.

"It's a saw," Harry says, going for the obvious.

Buck chuckles. "I meant what kind."

There's a lot of shuffling of feet and no answers, until I raise my hand and say, "It's a rescue saw. They can also be called concrete or quick cut or rotary saws."

"Right. Someone did her homework."

Hunter pointedly looks at me, but I avoid his eye, not wanting him to call me a teacher's pet again. It's not my fault no one else answered.

Buck shows everyone how to turn it off and on, then gives one of the guys a chance to try it himself as he continues to tell us what they use the saw for in rescue operations.

"And this," he says, moving on, "everyone should know is a chainsaw. We use the Stihl brand for consistency with all our saws. Anyone want to try her out?"

"I think Madeline should," Hunter pipes up. "Since she knows so much about saws."

All eyes turn to me and a quiet snicker sounds from someone.

Buck makes a *be my guest* gesture toward the chainsaw. Wait, he's not going to show me how to turn it on and off first? He did it for the other guy.

I hesitate then admit, "I've never used one."

Buck nods agreeably and motions to Hunter. "You want to give it a try?"

One of the Clewis brothers slaps Hunter on the back. "You should be a pro, mill boy."

He works at Payton Mills? The image of him as a lumberjack pops into my head, with a red flannel and rolled-up sleeves to show off his forearms. His muscles flex as he swings an axe, and he wipes away a bead of sweat that trails down the side of his face, his gaze smoldering.

I blink, getting rid of the image. Why am I thinking of him like that?

Another image pops into my head of him making out with Lydia under the bleachers back in high school and I rapidly blink that away, too.

Stop that. I'm supposed to be paying attention.

Hunter places the chainsaw on the ground, flips a switch, and moves the lever on top, then with one hand bracing the machine, he pulls a cord. The engine turns over and he moves the lever again.

"You want the chain brake off?" he asks Buck, who shakes his head.

Hunter turns the chainsaw off but doesn't look at me to gloat as he returns to his spot in the group.

"You want to try it now?" Buck asks me.

Oh, crap.

I nod, knowing I can't refuse in front of the group, and wipe my damp palms on my pants.

I bend and flip the switch, then move the lever to the same spot Hunter did. Okay, here goes nothing.

Pulling the cord, I brace myself for the kick of the engine, but nothing happens. There's another snicker from behind me.

"It can take a few tries to catch," Buck says kindly.

I try again and nothing. Then a third time. Bupkis.

I swallow back the hot frustration in my throat and thank whatever higher power there may be that it finally roars to life on the fourth try. Otherwise, I was going to have to curl into a ball and die.

After shutting it off, I slink back to my spot and avoid answering any more questions for the rest of Buck's lesson. When he releases us for lunch, I get my purse from my locker and hightail it to my car, wanting to decompress with some fast food during our break.

Why did Hunter have to call me out like that for answering a question? He should have been the one to answer since he works at a freaking sawmill.

I reverse out of the space and slam on the brakes, screaming, when there's a loud burst of sound behind me. Was that my car? It was too close to be anything else.

I get out and puzzle at the fragments of what looks to be a balloon right by my rear tire. What the hell?

Glancing up, I find Hunter in the same spot from yesterday, leaning against the driver's side door of his Mustang with a shit-eating grin on his face. That fucking—

I march over there, relishing the way his eyes widen, and stick my finger in his face. "Did you do that?" I ask, pointing at my car. I'm still not sure exactly what he did, but it had to be him. Who else could it be?

He shrugs, way too casually to be real. "You wanted to mess with cars."

My mouth opens, but nothing comes out. Damn. He's right. I did mess with his car. Well, not really, but he thought I did at first. If I was smart, I would have fled the scene of the crime. Also, I shouldn't have left that phone number. It could have remained a mystery forever. He'd never have suspected me otherwise.

But I was vain enough to stay behind and watch him. To make sure he knew I was the one who pranked him. Stupid ego.

The difference is, he messed with my car for real. Not that it's damaged, but that's not the point. I didn't actually do anything to him, and it was only in retaliation for his roach trick.

This means war.

I grind my teeth and walk away, mindful of the Clewis brothers also in the parking lot watching us. My appetite is gone now, so I head back inside the firehouse and straight to the clipboard where everyone wrote down their contact information yesterday, in case we need to get hold of each other. Copying down Hunter's email address, an evil grin spreads over my face. I'm going to sign that fucker up for every spam site I can find.

And this time, he'll have no clue it was me.

Our afternoon lesson involves Buck showing us how everything is organized on the fire engine, and we have to crowd close so everyone can see. Somehow, I end up next to Hunter, but it'd look too weird if I asked to switch spots with someone else, so I suck it up. A part of me wants to rail at him, to tell him what a jerk he is, to demand he leave me alone. But another part can sense his body heat standing this close, warming me. Can smell the subtle scent of his cologne, something intoxicating I want to get a deeper whiff of. I've always had a thing for men's cologne.

He shifts and touches my arm, then jerks away, giving me a look I can't interpret, like I shocked him. What's his problem? He was the one who moved, not me.

I angle my body away from him and ignore the spot on my arm that's tingling. I need to be focused on what Buck's saying, not hyper-aware of Hunter next to me. This is potentially life-or-death information. I need to learn.

And forget about stupid boys.

Chapter Four

HUNTER

After training, I go home and shower, washing away the day. My brain is sluggish, like it's too full of all the information Buck threw at us. I have to remember everything, though. I have to pass those tests at the end of our training. All of this will have been for nothing otherwise.

Well, maybe not for nothing. I got a good rise out of Madeline today. She should have known better than to mess with my car yesterday. It's her own fault she didn't suspect I'd try anything with hers today. And, if she was paying attention, she would have easily seen the balloons I'd wedged behind her rear tires. It's not like I could hide them.

She'd stormed over to me, fire in her eyes as she confronted me. But what had surprised me most wasn't the satisfaction I'd got from seeing her like that. It was the edge of . . . arousal that had come along with it. I wanted to see her like that again. Hot and bothered without that buttoned-up control she keeps so tightly bound around herself.

I scrub a hand down my face. I'm a sick fuck, but what's new?

Besides, these little pranks aren't intimidating her into quitting. What I should do is drop it and ignore her for the rest of the training.

But that doesn't stop me from imagining other pranks I could pull on her.

Nothing dangerous. And nothing that would get me caught. I don't want to get kicked out before this has even really started.

Speaking of, if I'm being serious about this, I need to look at that textbook they gave us. The thing is like a brick, but Buck said it was important. We're supposed to read chapters one through four to catch up on what we went over this weekend, and ideally up to chapter eight so we have an idea about what we'll be doing next weekend.

Eight fucking chapters in one week? There's no way. I'll be lucky to get through one.

I bet Madeline will finish the whole damn textbook tonight. For fun.

Cracking open the spine, I settle in on my couch and find the first chapter, but the letters skip around as usual. Sometimes reading out loud as I really focus on the words helps, but it's slow going. I don't get how it's so easy for other people.

Guess they're just not as stupid as me.

After fifteen minutes, the familiar headache that forms has me wincing, and I slam the book shut. It's not because I was trying to read. It's because I keep comparing myself to Madeline. And obviously, I come up short.

One thing I can excel at, though, is the physical training. I'd work out now but I just showered and I'm due at Mom and Dad's in twenty minutes. I eye the textbook again and end up leaving early rather than torturing myself.

Being in my childhood home is a different kind of torture, though. Mom greets me with her gravelly smoker's voice and ushers me inside, and I brace myself for her to bring up the firefighting training. She has to have heard about it from someone by now.

She doesn't say anything, though, and after a few minutes of her normal peppering me with questions, I breathe a sigh of relief. She would have brought it up by now if she knew.

A timer dings in the kitchen and she shoos me away to the living room, urging me to talk with my dad and brother who are watching a hockey pregame show. Dad already has a Natty Ice in his hand, his preferred beer. Why he likes that shit is beyond me, but whatever gets him buzzed the quickest is all he cares about.

"How's work?" Dad grunts, his gaze never leaving the screen.

"Fine." I slump onto the lumpy couch cushions, avoiding the puke stain still there in the center from when I had a stomach bug nearly twenty years ago.

That's the extent of our conversation, and I sit there, staring at the screen but not really seeing anything until Mom calls us for dinner.

Dad makes a big fuss about missing the start of the game, but shuts off the TV after she asks for a second time.

"We eat in front of the TV every night," he grumbles. "Why do we have to eat at the table tonight?"

"Because Hunter's here," she chides softly.

"You act like you never see the damn kid."

Kid? I'm twenty-six.

Mom reaches out and brushes a hand over my shoulder. "You should come over for dinner more often."

If it was only her, sure. But it's not.

My brother, Nate, sits down across from me at the dinner table and tucks his long, greasy hair behind his ears, revealing a bruise around his temple.

"What happened to you?" Mom asks him as she sets a casserole dish on the table. Looks like Tater Tots smothered in cheese with chunks of cooked ground beef.

Yum.

Nate shakes off her concern. "Nothing," he mumbles, letting his hair hang forward in his face.

Dad lets out a bark of laughter. "Boy was getting a little too big for his britches. Wolf had to put him in his place."

Nate stays grim-faced.

"Hunter, when are you coming out to the Dragon with us?" Dad asks, settling in his chair and scooping a heaping portion of casserole onto his plate.

Their dumb biker bar? Yeah, no thanks. Especially if their dealer is messing people up.

"I've been getting a lot of overtime at the mill," I tell him, avoiding his eye. "I'm dead tired at the end of the day."

"You working weekends, too?"

I shrug. "Yeah."

Just not in the way he thinks.

"You know, that invitation to join the Wraiths doesn't last forever."

Shit. This again? "I know."

"Catfish has been asking me about you."

I scoop the Tater Tots onto my plate and feign nonchalance. "Has he?"

"Yeah. And you're making me look like a real jackass when I have to tell him I don't know what's holding you up."

I make a noncommittal sound and take a huge bite so I don't have to respond.

"You going to answer me, boy?"

Guess it doesn't matter how old I am. Or that I haven't lived here in years. I'll always be *boy*.

Mom's glaring at me from the other side of the table to answer him.

"I'm not really interested," I say as diplomatically as I can.

Mom's face crumples as Dad's darkens.

"I'll tell you what you're interested in," Dad threatens, tossing his fork onto his plate.

"Can't we just have a nice family dinner?" Mom asks, interjecting herself into the conversation. "One night where we don't get into it?"

She lays a hand on her husband's arm, but he shakes it off immediately, pointing a finger at me. "I'm tired of this boy's disrespect. You're stupid enough as is. The least you could be is respectful."

Respect what, exactly? Him? The man who hasn't held a job in twenty years and deals drugs part-time for the Iron Wraiths? That's what I'm supposed to respect?

I itch to say all that, the words bubbling to my lips, but Mom would have my hide. And then, after I leave, there's a good chance Dad would have her hide, too. He hasn't tried it again with me after my seventeenth birthday, when I finally matched him in height, but Mom is half a foot shorter and a good fifty pounds lighter.

"Sorry," I mutter, keeping the peace for Mom.

"Anything exciting happen at the Dragon last night?" Mom asks, desperately trying to change the subject.

Dad gives me one last glare and lets himself be distracted, eventually laughing about something Pete Lundy did that involved him breaking a barstool.

Nate and I are both silent throughout the rest of dinner, and when Dad finally finishes and returns to the TV to watch the Predators play the Rangers, I gather the dirty dishes and bring them to the kitchen.

"You don't have to do that," Mom says, bustling in behind me with the leftover casserole.

"I'll do the dishes," I tell her, turning on the sink faucet to let the water heat up. "You can take the night off." Lord knows no one else would offer to do anything for her around here.

"You should go spend time with Dad."

A snort of laughter escapes me. "He's watching hockey. Besides, all he's going to do is guilt-trip me about not joining his precious club."

I put in the stopper and dish soap, then let the sink fill with water, watching it bubble up.

Mom sighs as she gets out the plastic wrap to put over the casserole dish. "It hurts him that you haven't joined the Iron Wraiths yet."

No, it hurts his ego. Like he said at dinner, he's got the top guys breathing down his neck about it. Why any of them are concerned about me, I have no idea.

"He wants to share that part of his life with his sons," she continues. "It's important to him."

"He's got Nate."

"He has two sons," she says. She studies me for a moment, then sighs again and opens the junk drawer to pull out her cigarettes and a lighter. She lights one and inhales, then blows the smoke away from me. "I don't get why it's even such a big deal to you. You grew up around the Wraiths. You know them all."

And that's exactly why I don't want any part of it. They're a bunch of lowlifes.

"You think you're better than us or something?"

I glance over at her, her gaze steady on me.

"No," I mumble, grabbing a dishcloth from underneath the sink and piling the silverware and plates into the hot water.

"Then why can't you do this for your family?"

I bite back the question of what in the hell they've ever done for me, because that's sure to open a can of worms.

"The Iron Wraiths don't need me. Especially since I won't deal for them."

Both Nate and Dad have already had too many run-ins with the law. It's only a matter of time before something real happens.

"Not everyone deals," she argues. "Your dad and brother don't."

Yes, they do. She just refuses to accept the truth. How does she think they bring money home? What bullshit excuse are they giving her?

I'm silent, ignoring her stare until she gives up and puts out her cigarette, then takes the wet dishes from me to dry.

After we're finished, I give her a brief hug and tell her I have to go, denying her protests about how I just got here.

"Let me at least give you some casserole to take home," she offers.

I control my wince. "No, it's fine. I have plenty of food at home."

Before I leave, I stop by the bedroom Nate and I used to share before I moved out.

"You okay?" I ask him, motioning to his temple.

He pauses the video game he was playing and rolls his eyes. "Yeah."

"Why's Dad on my case again?" We'd had a huge blowup a couple of years back. I thought we were done arguing about it.

"The Wraiths have lost a lot of people lately. We need new recruits."

That's because the criminal dumbasses keep getting locked up.

"When are you going to get a real job?" I ask him. The man is twenty-eight and still living at home and dealing part-time.

"When you finally get laid."

"Fuck you," I tell him, laughing.

He grins. "Quit busting my balls, then."

"Yeah, whatever."

I leave, waving a hand to Dad in the living room, not that he notices, and drive home, my hands flexing on the steering wheel the whole way. So he's starting up with the whole joining the Iron Wraiths thing again? When's he going to let that go?

When I get home, I force myself to read chapter one of the firefighting textbook, and though it takes me an hour, I manage to do it, cross-eyed by the end. Crawling into bed, the exhaustion leaves me as I stare up at the ceiling, wondering if I'm fooling myself with this volunteer firefighter thing. If anyone will actually take me seriously.

A grimace crosses my face remembering Madeline's dig from yesterday about my family. As if I have some nefarious purpose being there that's related to the Iron Wraiths. As if I'm not good enough.

And yet, Mom's under the impression I think I'm better than them.

Which one is the truth? Is it somewhere in the middle?

Then where does that leave me?

Chapter Five
MADELINE

My armpits are sweating. Profusely. I want so badly to lift my arms and wave some cool air under there, but I can't. Hunter could walk in at any moment.

He'd used the coffee maker in the break room at the firehouse last week, and I'm counting on him doing the same today. Otherwise, my prank won't work.

Not that I spent all week researching pranks. Not that I even got behind on my actual work at one point because of my newfound obsession. I have no idea if the spam emails are working, so I need something more concrete.

Cue the coffee prank.

I continue standing at the kitchenette counter in the break room, idly stirring my coffee that's long gone cold, but I need to look casual while guarding the creamer. No one else can use it but Hunter.

Someone enters behind me, and I glance over my shoulder, but it's one of the Clewis brothers. I really need to learn their names.

I smile, trying to seem inconspicuous, and he gives me a brief head nod before retrieving something from his locker and leaving. Thank God.

When Hunter finally shows up, my belly does a weird flip-flopping motion.

You're not going to get caught, I tell myself. He has no way of proving it was you.

Stepping away from the counter, I sit at one of the tables and sip at my now-disgusting coffee. Just act casual.

He grabs a mug from the cabinet and pours himself a cup from the coffee pot. Oh God, what if he takes his coffee black? I never even considered that possibility.

Thankfully, he opens the fridge and roots around, but what he's looking for isn't there.

"Are you looking for the creamer?" I ask, hoping my voice doesn't give me away.

He finally looks over his shoulder and acknowledges me. "Yeah."

"There's powdered creamer on the counter." I point to the tampered bottle I placed there earlier when no one was looking. The real creamer from the fridge is in my locker.

He makes a face of disgust and I don't blame him. Powdered stuff is kind of gross.

"It's actually not bad," I say, holding my cup up and taking a sip.

Now he just needs to take the bait.

He stares at me, his brows knitting. "Why are you being nice?"

I roll my eyes, cursing his suspicion. "Sorry, jeez. Don't have any, then. I don't care."

Looking down at my cup, I inwardly smile as he turns back around and shakes some into his cup.

The coffee froths and bubbles up, then spills out onto the counter.

"What the fuck?" he shouts, jumping back.

Perfect. It had taken a while to crush up all that Alka-Seltzer, but it was worth it. It would have been better if I could have filmed it, but that's okay. All I need is the memory.

I wipe the smile from my face and paste on what I hope is an innocent look as he whips around to face me.

"Did you do that?"

"Do what?"

He points to his cup full of brown, bubbly froth.

"What do you mean?" I ask. "I'm over here."

His nostrils flare and he stares at me for another moment before grabbing a wad of paper towels to clean up the mess. He dumps the cup in the sink and walks out, no coffee to be had.

The evil grin that I only seem to use when it concerns him bursts forth, then I tiptoe to my locker to put the real creamer back in the fridge and take my fake powdered creamer to stuff in my purse.

This morning's lesson is about different types of fire extinguishers and when to use each in different situations. Grizz Grady provides a demonstration and even allows us to try them out ourselves. I half expect Hunter to turn the nozzle on me as an *accident*, but he doesn't. In fact, he ignores me.

Not that it matters.

We break midday for lunch, and I grab my lunchbox out of the fridge. Hunter didn't see me put it in here so it shouldn't be tampered with, and I'm not chancing him messing with me in my car, so I sit in the break room opposite Harry. He strikes up a conversation with me about the price of eggs lately, which I assume is a hot topic at the Piggly Wiggly. Wish I'd brought head-phones now.

Five minutes in, Silas, the trainee I didn't recognize last week, comes in and interrupts us, telling me Chief McClure wants to see me. I grab the excuse with two hands, desperate to get away from this inane conversation, but the chief isn't in his office when I go and check. I wander around, but don't see any sign of him, and eventually bump into Silas again near the entrance.

"Where's Chief McClure?" I ask him.

He shrugs. "I don't know. One of the other guys said he was looking for you."

Huh. Well, it must not be too important.

When I return to the break room, a huge chunk of my sandwich is gone, with a clear bite mark. What the hell? I hadn't even started eating it yet since Harry kept talking to me.

I look up, finding Harry staring at me with wide eyes.

"I-it wasn't me," he stammers out, his gaze flicking to something behind me.

My shoulders drop. Of course it wasn't.

It's no surprise to find Hunter in the doorway as I turn around, casually resting in the doorframe. He wipes at one side of his mouth and smirks.

Real subtle.

I drop into my chair and pick up my sandwich, not wanting to show him I care that he ate practically half of it, then a thought occurs to me.

"Did you do anything to this?" For all I know, he took a bite, then smeared ghost pepper sauce or something crazy over the rest.

"I don't know. Did you do anything to my coffee?"

I eye him speculatively, but ultimately can't take the risk, and dump my sandwich in the trash. I have a granola bar in my purse I can eat later.

"He didn't do anything other than take a bite," Harry says.

Really? He couldn't have mentioned that before I threw it away?

"Way to be a snitch," Hunter mutters.

I glance at the trash can, but there's no way I'm digging through it for my lunch. He'd have a field day.

Grabbing my purse off the table, I head toward the doorway, wanting to sit in my car in peace for the remainder of our lunch break, but he doesn't budge. His stupid shoulders are too broad to squeeze past.

"What's the password?" he asks, smirking again.

What is he, five?

I give him a sickly sweet smile. "You're an ass?" I guess.

The laugh he lets out surprises me, as if he's genuinely amused. After a moment, he cuts himself off, his expression looking like he surprised himself, too. He gives me a once-over, but there's not the same disapproval from last week.

He moves marginally, giving me some room, but I'm still forced to brush against him. His warmth sends a tingle up my spine, and I shake off the sensation as I exit the fire station, not looking back.

Nothing appears amiss with my car in the parking lot. He's not smart enough to pull off two pranks in a row, anyway. Then again, he'd made me think he'd tampered with my food when he hadn't.

I need to come up with something to get him back. Something he won't expect. Something . . .

Oh, I know exactly what.

* * *

I HOLD my lunchbox carefully as I make my way inside the firehouse the next morning, uncaring if Hunter sees it's my lunch. There's a special surprise in here for him.

As I enter, though, I'm stopped by a frazzled-looking Grizz, who's carrying a . . . baby.

"Thank God you're here," he says, holding the baby out to me.

I step back, unsure of what's happening.

"Take it," he insists, wiggling the wide-eyed baby in my direction.

"What?" I ask stupidly, my brain still not getting with the program.

He physically puts the baby in my arms, until I have no choice but to hold it for fear I'll drop it.

"The baby was abandoned here," he says, and turns around. "I need to make some calls."

"Wait," I call out, panic in my voice. "I don't know anything about babies."

Seriously, I'm useless. I've never even been around a baby before. I have no siblings, no cousins, no friends with babies. I'm the last person to trust with one.

"You'll be fine!" he yells, halfway down the hall now. "You have maternal instincts."

"No, I don't!" I yell back.

A derisive noise sounds from behind me. "I'll say."

Oh, no. Not him. Not now.

"Is this a new prank or something?" Hunter asks as I turn around. "Gotta say, you're really upping your game."

"This is not a prank," I whisper, afraid someone will hear. I don't want to get in trouble, even if he can't technically prove I did anything. "Do you know anything about babies?"

He holds his hands away from him. "Whoa, whoa. You're not pawning that off on me."

The baby makes a sound of distress, its face scrunching up before it releases a wail.

No, no. It was just fine. What happened?

Hunter leans in closer. "What's wrong with it?"

"I don't know." I can't help the anxiety that leaks into my voice.

I rock the baby in my arms, but that only seems to piss it off more, its cries increasing in volume. I move it in a more upright position, trying to burp it, but that doesn't help, either. Maybe it has a dirty diaper? I don't smell anything, and I don't have another diaper to change it into, but I check, just in case. Nope, seems clean.

"It's a girl," I say aloud, only because I had no idea from looking at her which sex she was.

Hunter winces as her shrieks get louder, echoing off the walls. "Well, can you get her to be quiet?"

"What do you think I'm trying to do?" I try bouncing her, to no avail.

"Maybe she's hungry."

"Does it look like I have any food?"

His gaze drops to my chest.

"Oh my God, you're gross." I'd hit him if my hands weren't full.

"Jesus Christ, I'm kidding. You're so fucking uptight."

"Don't curse around the baby."

"Why? She can't understand us." He moves closer. "And even if she could, she's crying too loud to hear me." He sighs, then reaches out his hands. "Fine, give her to me."

I don't question his motivation, just wanting the crying to stop already.

He makes a shushing sound as he gathers the little girl in his arms, and whatever he's doing seems to surprisingly . . . work. The baby's screams lessen as she looks up at him, then she quiets completely, transfixed by his face.

Ugh. One more girl under his spell.

"Now, was that so hard?" he asks, that stupid smirk back on his face.

I roll my eyes. "You must be a baby whisperer or something. No normal person could do that."

"I think you're jealous that I'm better at something than you for a change."

What does he mean *for a change*? It took me four tries to get that dumb chainsaw started last week when he had no problem at all.

"I freely admit to having no experience with children."

His head tilts to the side. "You don't like kids?"

"I like them fine, but I don't know the first thing about them." I study him and the natural way he's holding the baby. "Do you like kids?"

He shrugs. "I've never thought about it much."

"You seem to be a natural."

He looks up at me, something soft in his gaze. It's the first time he's looked at me without disdain or distrust or some other kind of *dis* emotion. It makes me forget for a moment he's become my sworn enemy over the last week.

It doesn't last long, though, as his brows narrow. "Don't prank me with this baby around."

My mouth drops open. "Of course I wouldn't. You think I'm that bad?"

"You made me think someone had hit my car last week."

"And you made me think you'd blown up mine with whatever you did with those balloons."

"And then my coffee—"

"And then my sandwich—"

We both go quiet as there's movement from behind us, then Silas passes by, giving us a weird look, his gaze lingering on the baby before he moves on.

"What, he's never seen a baby in a fire station before?" I mutter.

Hunter chuckles, then stops, scowling. "We'll have a temporary truce," he says. "But all bets are off once she leaves."

That makes it sound like he's got something planned. Well, that's fine, because I do, too. "Agreed."

There's an awkward bit of silence until the baby's coo interrupts us.

"I, um, should put my lunch in the fridge," I say, holding up my lunchbox. I want him to get a good look at it.

I go to the break room and stow it away, then put my purse in my locker. When I return to the hallway, Hunter's profile is to me and he's gently murmuring something to the baby. He rocks her and she makes that cooing sound again.

He must not realize I'm here. There's no way he'd smile at her that tenderly if he knew someone was watching.

He straightens as Chief McClure rounds the corner, the warmth vanishing from his face.

"A social worker is coming to get the baby," Chief McClure says as he notices him. "She should be here in about ten minutes."

Hunter nods. "Should I keep holding her until then?"

Chief McClure claps him on the back. "Whatever keeps her quiet. Thanks for stepping up, son."

Pride fills Hunter's face as the chief walks away, and he smiles again at the baby.

I back away slowly into the break room, not wanting to interrupt this moment for some reason. It seems . . . private.

How am I supposed to hate him now when he so obviously has a soft spot for babies? Especially when it seems he didn't even realize it until today.

I glance at the fridge, questioning the prank in my lunchbox, then tell myself I'm being silly. He said himself our truce is over once the baby's gone.

Then it's back to war.

Chapter Six
MADELINE

"We've got ladder drills this morning," Chief McClure announces once we're all assembled outside.

The social worker already came and picked up the baby with little fanfare, her face weary as she'd taken it from Hunter. I hope they can find out who the mother was. Maybe a family member can take the baby in.

"No one's afraid of heights, right?" the chief asks, and I tune back in. "We'll start with the fourteen-foot ones solo, then you'll be partnered up for the twenty-four-foot ones." He motions to the two ladders leaning against the side of the brick building.

We have to climb all the way to the top of a twenty-four-foot ladder? Reading about it in the textbook and actually seeing it are two different things. It's really high up.

"Fourteens are thirty pounds, and the twenty-fours are about seventy, so be prepared." He doesn't look my way, but that comment had to be directed at me, right? "This exercise will test your endurance, speed, and ability to work with a partner. Grizz and I will show you what to do, but don't worry about being as fast as us. It takes hundreds of drills to get it down. Today is the first of many."

Chief McClure continues his instruction as Grizz models what to do, from showing us how the center of the ladder is marked with red to indicate where you should shoulder it, to where to place the ladder on a window ledge or sill. I reconcile everything he's saying with what I remember from the textbook, noting to myself any slight differences. Practical application from a seasoned veteran should trump what the text says.

We practice lifting the fourteen-foot ladders by ourselves, balancing them on our right shoulders, and bringing them over to the wall to place correctly. It's awkward at first, but I get the hang of it after a few tries. I don't look at anyone else, not wanting to compare myself. That's already too much of a slippery slope.

"All right, good," Chief McClure calls out. "Two-shoulder carry is next. Woodward, you're with O'Connor."

He assigns the rest of the men, but I'm not paying attention. He's partnering me with Hunter? The guy who has it out for me?

Hunter gives me a cool look. "You going to ask for a different partner again?"

Again? What is he talking about?

But before I can ask, Chief McClure and Grizz are demonstrating how we should perform our next task. I turn my back to Hunter, not wanting to look at him.

"Both of you should be positioned on the same side of the ladder," Chief McClure instructs. "One of you in front, one in back. Knees bent in a squatting position, back straight. This puts the load on the muscles in your thighs and not your back. Place an arm between two rungs, and on the leader's count, lift the ladder on your shoulders. If you don't lift at the same time, it could result in injury."

I glance at Hunter. He wouldn't purposely try to hurt me, would he?

"Now, we've marked here on the ground where the butt of the ladder should go to give it about a seventy-degree angle. Once it's in place, pull down on the halyard to extend the fly."

I watch closely and listen to the commands Chief McClure and Grizz call out as they work together to properly position the ladder and raise it to its full height. Grizz climbs to the top while Chief McClure keeps it secure at the base, and when Grizz is back down they dismantle it and return it to the starting position across the way.

They run through the scenario one more time, this time in opposite roles with the chief going to the top, then it's our turn. I wipe my sweaty palms on my pants, eyeing the ladder.

"You ready or what?" Hunter asks, arms crossed over his chest.

I nod, not at all ready, then shake my head. "How do I know you're not going to let me fall to my death?"

He scowls. "Don't be stupid. I wouldn't actually hurt you. Besides, if anyone gets hurt, it'll probably be me. How can I trust you're strong enough to brace the ladder?"

My teeth grind together. "I know what to do."

"Memorizing the textbook isn't the same as actually doing it."

Okay, he's got a point, but I'm not admitting that to him. "I guess we'll have to take a leap of faith and trust each other."

He rolls his eyes, but moves toward the ladder, implicitly agreeing. "So, you like it from the front or the back?"

I ignore his innuendo and move to the front of the ladder, not wanting to look at him anymore.

Wait, that means I climb first.

Chief McClure calls for us to get into position, so I do, banishing all the nervousness coursing through me. Nothing we've done so far has been as high stakes as this. As if we could seriously mess up if we don't get it right.

The chief calls out the commands for us, and there's no time to think about it anymore as we squat and lift the ladder onto our shoulders. Shit, that's heavy.

Everything goes according to plan as we get the ladder in place and follow the directions on how to raise it. I don't hesitate when it's time to climb, knowing I'll never do it otherwise, and I'm the first one to the top. I guess that's one advantage to being smaller than everyone else. I'm quicker and lighter on my feet.

Unfortunately, I make the mistake of looking down, my stomach leaping into my throat. "Oh, shit," I murmur, the distance to the ground much greater than I was anticipating. I clutch at the ladder rungs and take a deep breath.

"Okay, Woodward. You can come down now," Chief McClure calls out.

Right. I have to get down. No problem.

My feet won't obey my order to move, though. It's not until I imagine Hunter having to come up here and rescue me that I finally climb down. I'd never hear the end of it if he had to do that.

About six or seven feet from the bottom, my foot slips, panic zipping through me until a hand on my lower back steadies me.

"I've got you," Hunter says in a low voice, looking up at me.

I blink, confusion and disbelief and a weird kind of thrill mixing in my belly.

He removes his hand and I make it down, feeling better once my feet are on the ground.

"Thanks," I mumble, avoiding his eye.

What was that? Sure, he said he wouldn't hurt me, but that's different than . . . saving me. Not that I needed saving. I would have recovered. Probably.

Warmth burns on my lower back where he touched me, like the impression of his palm is still there. Like I can still feel him and the deep timbre of his voice.

Oh my God, I'm mental. What is wrong with me?

We gather the ladder together in silence and bring it back to its original spot, then switch places so he's at the front of the ladder and I'm behind. He faces forward, giving me an unobstructed view of his broad back. The shirt he's wearing clings to him, emphasizing the width of his shoulders and the way his torso tapers down to a narrower waist. My gaze travels next to the backs of his upper arms and the defined muscles of his biceps and triceps. He must work a physical job at the mill.

Would he have steadied any of the other guys on the ladder in the same way? Or was it only because I'm a girl? There'd been a gentleness about it, a confident surety that he wouldn't let anything happen to me. The same kind of gentleness he'd shown to that baby earlier.

I squeeze my eyes shut, pushing the thoughts aside. Just because he was nice a couple of times doesn't cancel out the other stuff he's done.

Even so, after we're finished with the morning session and I pull my lunchbox out of the fridge, I'm still not sure what to do. I carefully unpack the "brownie" I made last night, the chocolate frosting on top making it appear delicious. It's what's inside that'll get him.

I shouldn't give it to him, though. Maybe today was a turning point. Maybe our truce can be extended. I should be the bigger person and not retaliate anymore.

With that decided on, I search in my purse for my Kindle to read during the lunch break, but can't find it. Maybe it slipped out of my bag and into the passenger seat of my car. As I get up, I tell Harry in the seat opposite me to not let anyone touch my food.

Hunter's car is out in the parking lot, but he's not inside it. Huh. Where is he?

I shake my head, not letting him take up any more of my mental real estate, and search through my car, finding my Kindle hidden under my sweater in the passenger seat, right where I suspected it'd be. When I return to the break room, I pause in the doorway, my mouth dropping open.

Hunter is spitting into the sink, disgust all over his face. In his hand is my fake brownie.

Crap.

He looks up, accusation in his gaze. "What the fuck is this?"

Really? He's going to get mad at me? "Why are you eating my food?" I counter, ignoring his question.

"This isn't food." He clears some of the frosting away, but it's hard to tell it's a sponge in the middle since the frosting has filled in the holes. "What's this yellow stuff?"

"It's none of your business is what it is. It's my food. Just throw it away."

"You tell me first what it is."

Harry gets up from his seat and goes over to investigate. "Looks like a sponge," he says, leaning in close.

Hunter's brows punch down. "You made me eat a sponge?"

I throw my hands up. "I didn't make you do anything. I wasn't even in the room."

"You baited me and you know it."

"I actually didn't. I thought you'd left for lunch. But I'm also not stupid enough to eat food that isn't mine, especially two days in a row."

Heavy footfalls sound out in the hallway, and I glance behind me to find Chief McClure barreling toward the break room. I get out of the way, heading toward the lockers.

"What the hell is going on in here?" he says when he enters, gaze shifting between the three of us. "Why can I hear you arguing from my office?"

Hunter and I are silent. Me because I don't want to admit to the prank I unwittingly pulled. Hunter maybe because he doesn't want to admit he fell for it.

Chief McClure points to Harry. "You. What happened?"

Harry glances first at Hunter, then me, biting at his lip. He's caught right in the crossfire. "Oh, I don't want—"

"Tell me." His tone brooks no arguments.

Harry makes a helpless noise. "Hunter ate something from Madeline's lunch. But it wasn't food."

"What was it?"

"A sponge, I think."

Chief McClure gives a heavy sigh, then mutters something under his breath about *fucking millennials, gen z, whatever they are,* and stalks off. Out in the hallway, there's a heavy boom of laughter. Grizz must have been listening, too.

Harry moves back to his side of the table and picks up his stuff. "I'm finishing this in my car."

He leaves the two of us alone, but Hunter continues his silence and turns on the faucet to wash the frosting off of his fingers.

I guess our truce wasn't extended, then. If the pissed-off aura surrounding him is any indication, he's going to retaliate. I wish I hadn't made the sponge at all, or at least hadn't left it on the table before going to my car. He's right that it did seem like bait.

But before I can tell him about my change of heart, he leaves without a word. I just pray we're not paired up again in the afternoon.

Our next lesson is thankfully a solo activity as we learn and practice tying different knots we'll need to know. Hunter doesn't pay the least bit of attention to me, but that still doesn't help my anxiety. What is he planning? He has to be planning something.

I'm the first one done with our mini test at the end, but I don't meet anyone's eye as Chief McClure checks my work and declares me the winner. I don't want Hunter to accuse me of gloating or something else stupid.

When it's time to leave, we head to our lockers to retrieve our things, Hunter close behind me. His presence is like a live wire up my spine. Why do I let him get in my head like this?

He gets his wallet, keys, and phone, then whispers to me, "See you next week, Maddy."

I bite my tongue at the urge to tell him I hate being called Maddy. My dad called me that. After he died, I didn't want anyone else to call me that ever again.

But knowing Hunter, he'd probably call me Maddy all the time.

He leaves and I stare after him, thinking about his words. Coming from anyone else, they'd be perfectly pleasant. But from him, they're more like a threat.

What does he have in store for me next week?

Chapter Seven

HUNTER

Sitting at the break room table, I force my knee to stop bouncing, not wanting to come across as nervous to the other guy in the room, Jed. He's one of the full-time firefighters here, and I wish he'd leave already. So far, Harry's the only one who's wise to this feud Madeline and I have going on.

And I guess McClure, although he didn't say anything else to us last Sunday afternoon about the sponge prank.

Damn Madeline. Why does she get under my skin so badly? It's been a whole week and I still can't stop thinking about her pranks. I have no idea how she pulled off that coffee trick. And a sponge disguised as a brownie? How did she come up with that?

Not that I'd ever tell her the pranks were good. The girl's got a big enough ego already.

My prank this morning is definitely more crass, but it's sure to get a reaction.

Jed's bagel pops up from the toaster and Silas enters the room to put his stuff in his locker, giving me a head nod. I return it, then have a moment of panic. What if I got the wrong locker? He moves to the end of the row and I relax, then stiffen again as Madeline enters. Shit. I'm supposed to act natural.

I ignore her as she heads to her locker, but look up again as she turns away from me. My gaze zeroes in on the sliver of exposed skin between the bottom of her shirt and top of her pants that shows as she lifts her arm. I'd touched that same spot on her lower back last week when she'd nearly fallen off the ladder. It had been completely instinctual to catch her, for her weight to briefly rest against me as she'd righted herself, and my fingertips tingle in remembrance until I shake off the feeling. That's not what I should be focusing on right now.

Somehow, I manage to contain my glee as the avalanche of condoms falls out of her locker and onto her.

She makes a sputtering noise as the other two men in the room stare in shock at her. Bending to pick one up, her face is bright red as she spins around to face me. Even better is her murderous expression, the one I was anticipating.

But then her face unexpectedly clears, a smile replacing it. What's she doing?

"Hunter, I think you confused your locker with mine," she says. "These are your extra small condoms, right?"

Damn, that was a good comeback.

Silas lets out a choked laugh, glancing at me, then hurries out of the room.

Jed eyes us both carefully. "You two are part of the volunteer program?"

We nod, neither of us saying anything.

"I'd clean this up before McClure sees it. He lets a lot slide, but I wouldn't push it too far."

He grabs his bagel and exits the break room, leaving me and Madeline staring at each other.

She crosses her arms over her chest. "I'm not cleaning this up."

I shrug. "It's your locker."

"And your condoms."

"You don't have any proof of that."

I get up and head to the doorway.

"Hunter," she calls out, but I leave her there, grinning to myself.

She's late to our first lesson, but since Jed is the one instructing us today, he doesn't make note of it. It took her a while to clean those up. A part of me actually thought that might have been the last straw for her and she up and quit. The idea leaves me strangely unsettled.

It's a good thing she didn't, though. I've got another great prank planned for tomorrow.

"All right, we're talking about forcible entry today," Jed tells us. "It's best to work on these skills as a two-person team first to get the basics down before trying it solo. One of you will use a flat head axe or sledgehammer, and the other will have a Halligan bar. You'll be using the gap, set, force method you should have read about in the text."

Shit. I didn't do the reading for this week. There was so much of it, the idea of even starting had been overwhelming.

I'm paired with Waylon Clewis for the exercise, who I know for a fact didn't do the reading either, and I pay careful attention to Jed and Chief McClure as they demonstrate what to do, not wanting to mess this up. This would've actually been a good time to partner with Madeline. She probably has every step of this memorized already.

Fucking egghead.

For the second exercise, I'm partnered with Waylon's brother, Rodney, who's even dumber. The guy's got brute force on his side, though, and we muddle through fine, successfully opening our door.

Jed talks some more about door components and construction until I nearly pass out from boredom, then we break for lunch. I head inside to get my stuff, half expecting to find all the condoms stuffed in my locker, but they're not. Madeline is mysteriously absent, too, even though she ate lunch here both days last week.

Whatever. She's probably tired of me messing with her food.

My phone is blinking with a text, and I turn on the display, discovering it's from . . . Who the hell is this from? It takes me a couple of tries to understand what it says.

The idiot who doesn't have a password on his phone

What?

I open the message thread, the letters seeming to shift on the screen for a second before I focus, and it's clear it's Mom. She's asking if I want to come over for hamburger macaroni tomorrow night, but I ignore her for now, going to my contacts. Every single contact is set to the same name: *The idiot who doesn't have a password on his phone.*

I suck in a quick breath, glancing around, but no one's here. It had to have been Madeline. She was in here forever earlier, presumably cleaning up condoms. But she was really pulling this stunt.

Fuck.

She knows I won't tattle, too. I'd have to admit what I did in the first place, then. This is going to take me forever figuring out who's who and changing everyone back.

Okay, time to move up my plan for tomorrow to today. It's a good thing we're changing into our PPE to practice chopping doors later.

Getting what I need from my car, I slip into the empty bay to do what I need to, then get out of there before anyone catches me in the act. It's nothing that'll hurt her, nothing harmful. Just a little something sure to get a rise out of her. I'll have to come up with something good for tomorrow, now.

After lunch, everyone files back into the bay and to the protective gear lined up neatly in a row. Madeline is on the end again, her gear set aside since it's smaller than everyone else's. It still dwarfs her, but it's all they had on hand. She puts her gloves on last but doesn't react, and I frown, trying not to let my disappointment show. Maybe she can't feel what's in them, yet.

I rush to finish getting my own gear on, the heaviness of the added clothes weighing me down. They said this stuff weighs forty-five pounds, but we have to get used to doing the exercises with our gear on, since that's what we'll be wearing in an actual situation.

As Jed tells us what we'll be doing, I focus on what he's saying and half forget about my prank. He leads us outside the bay to where a dummy door that's seen better days is set up in the grass. Waylon gets a turn first at prying it open, and I shift on my feet, wishing I could fan out my turnout coat. It's not even summer yet and I'm sweating like a pig in the afternoon heat. Grizz warned us the first day it'd be hot and we needed to get used to it, but goddamn. How's it going to feel in an actual fire in all this gear?

Silas is up next and I resist the urge to wipe at the back of my neck. I'm only going to keep sweating.

Over at the far end of the group, Madeline takes off one of her gloves and swipes her hand across her forehead. Her gaze is glued on Silas forcing open the door and she doesn't notice the pink glitter covering her hand. The sweat made it stick better than I anticipated.

She absent-mindedly puts her glove back on, unaware there's a streak of pink glitter on her forehead. Damn, this is playing out better than I imagined.

Harry glances at her and does a comical double take, his eyes widening. His gaze shoots immediately to me and I narrow my eyes in warning. He straightens and looks guiltily at Jed, then Madeline again, but keeps his mouth shut. Note to self—never tell him a secret. The guy broadcasts everything.

Madeline picks up on his strange behavior and whispers something to him, but he shakes his head in response, not meeting her eye. She looks at me next and I turn away, keeping my grin at bay. She looks so ridiculous.

When Silas is finished, Jed calls on Madeline to come up next, then stops halfway through his sentence, blinking at her.

"What?" she asks, clearly bewildered.

Jed motions to her forehead. "You have . . ."

Her forehead wrinkles in confusion. "What? What is it?"

Jed clears his throat. "You have glitter all over your forehead."

Her brows knit and she wipes at her forehead with her glove on, smearing the glitter everywhere. She looks at her glove, blinking, then shrieks when she removes it and discovers her hand looks like a glitter bomb exploded all over it.

Taking her other glove off reveals another hand made of pure pink glitter, then her gaze snaps up, meeting mine. That same murderous expression I've become familiar with is on her face as she strides over to me. The other guys step back to give her a wide berth, but I'm stupidly rooted in place, unable to look away from the fury that surrounds her like a storm cloud, something terrible and captivating about it.

My stomach dips low as she reaches me, curious to see what she'll do.

"You like glitter?" she asks, restrained rage in her voice. "Here, have some."

She wipes her hands over my face and hair, and it's only then my limbs unfreeze and I jump away, getting her off me.

"Damn, Maddy. If you wanted to put your hands on me, all you had to do was say so."

She screams, frustration echoing through the open air of the fire station's lawn, and then she's there again, trying to get glitter on me. I run and she chases, the other guys howling with laughter as she follows me like a Barbie zombie on speed, her pink glitter hands outstretched and reaching for me. I have no idea how she's keeping up with me with all this turnout gear weighing us down.

I'm panting as Jed calls out, "Enough." He moves between us, a hand on each of our shoulders. "How old are you two?"

We're both silent.

"No, seriously. How old are you?"

Oh, I thought he meant that rhetorically.

"Twenty-five," Madeline says.

"Twenty-six," I mutter.

"Funny. I assumed you were a good twenty years younger with the way you're acting. Madeline, that was unacceptable."

Her nostrils flare. "He was the one who put glitter in my gloves."

"Do you have proof?"

She throws her hands up, exasperation pouring off of her. "You know it was him. He pulled the stunt with the condoms, too. You saw."

Jed turns to me, no doubt in his eyes that he knows it was me.

Shit. I have to defend myself.

"I wouldn't have had to if she hadn't changed all the contacts in my phone to other names. And made me eat a sponge last week."

A sponge, Jed mouths to himself, then shakes his head. "Whatever. Just go inside and clean up. And Hunter." He pauses, waiting until I look at him. "Why don't you take a shower?"

I wince. Is the glitter that bad?

She stalks ahead of me back inside, and as we get to the hallway, I shoulder bump her, unable to help myself. I move past her toward the bunk room and private showers in an area we don't normally visit, but the next thing I know, she's shoving me from behind, and I nearly trip and fall.

I whip around, that blaze back in her eyes.

"Don't shoulder bump me," she whispers in a low voice, all defiance.

"Or what?" I ask, not thinking rationally as I crowd her against the wall, trapping her there with a hand on either side of her head.

Our bodies aren't touching, but it's close with how fast her breaths are, her chest nearly brushing mine. My gaze flicks down to her mouth, her lips parted. Her bottom lip is bigger than the top, her cheeks flushed, the hair around her temples slightly damp with sweat.

I have the sudden insane urge to kiss her. To find out if she gives back as good as she gets with her kiss, too. If she'd try to dominate me in this way. If she needs to be in control.

Or if she'd let me take over and show her how it's done for once.

I glance back up, expecting to find fire in her eyes. To find challenge. For her to dare me to go ahead and kiss her already.

But there's none of that.

There's confusion. Unsurety. Maybe her heavy breaths aren't from passion but from . . . fear.

I stumble back, giving her space to slip away, but she stays where she is, still looking at me like she's lost.

"Sorry," I mumble, and I get out of there, heading to the showers. My stomach churns with guilt and leftover arousal. I really am a sick fuck.

I need to let this go. Figure out a way to ignore her.

Because otherwise, she might literally drive me crazy.

Chapter Eight
MADELINE

My legs are somehow both ramrod stiff and like jelly, holding me against the wall as Hunter stalks away toward the showers.

What just happened? I swore it looked like he was about to . . . kiss me.

No, that can't be right. I'd obviously misread that. He was only mad I'd shoved him.

Which, looking back at it now, was an incredibly stupid thing to do. Why am I picking a fight with a guy who could easily bench-press me?

Still, my body tingles remembering how close he'd been. How he'd caged me in with his big frame. It should have been frightening. Instead, it'd been . . . exhilarating.

Why do I keep reacting like this to him? The guy is a jerk. I can't stand him. He glitter bombed me today, for Christ's sake. Looking at my hands again, it's like I'm wearing two shiny pink gloves.

I head into the single bathroom and use about half the bottle of hand soap as I scrub my hands raw getting everything off, then scrub the spot on my forehead. Fucking glitter. It's the herpes of craft supplies.

The only thing making this bearable is knowing Hunter's probably having just as bad of a time getting rid of the glitter I wiped on him. He must be going crazy shampooing his hair.

Serves him right. Especially after that comment he made in front of everyone about me wanting to put my hands on him. Why is he so hell-bent on embarrassing me? What did I ever do to him?

I continue washing my hands, occasionally cursing Hunter's existence under my breath, but ultimately, this is my fault, too. I've been right there with him pulling pranks in retaliation. Shame pulses hot in my stomach remembering the disappointment in Jed's voice as he said what I did was unacceptable. I've never been reprimanded for my behavior ever. I'm the girl you can count on. The one who never messes up.

What I should have done is told Chief McClure about the fake cockroaches as soon as it happened. But there was something in me that didn't want Hunter to know he got the better of me. That turnabout is fair play.

Look where that's landed me, though. Covered in glitter.

This whole thing has to stop. It's gotten way too out of hand. Which is a real shame because I found a great idea involving putting Saran Wrap over a toilet bowl, so when you pee it goes everywhere . . . No, not doing that. I'm turning over a new leaf.

My fingertips are pruney by the time I'm finished, and I put my turnout coat back on before I rejoin everyone out in the front yard.

Well, not everyone. Hunter's not here.

Jed gives me an uncomfortable look. "Chief wants to see you in his office."

My lips compress tightly as I nod in acknowledgment and turn back around. Harry gives me a sympathetic smile, but I don't meet his eye, afraid I might cry if I do. This is like getting sent to the principal's office.

Hunter is already seated in one of the two chairs in front of Chief McClure's desk, his hair wet. There are no visible signs of glitter, but that doesn't mean there isn't some still sprinkled among the strands.

I remove the bulky coat before sitting, and squeeze my hands together in my lap, waiting for our judgment. Going on the chief's expression, it's not good.

"I've heard about the pranks," he says bluntly. "And frankly, they've gotten out of hand."

I nod but Hunter simply sits there stoically, not acknowledging the comment.

"We have our share of fun and games here," he continues. "But at the end of the day, I know all my guys have each other's backs. That when shit hits the fan, they're there for one another in an emergency." He eyes us carefully. "I can't say I get the same assurance from you two."

Silence lays thick and heavy in the room with the weight of his disappointment. I swallow hard, hating the lump forming in my throat. *Whatever you do, don't cry*, I tell myself.

"If you pass this training program, you'll be on a team. In potentially life-or-death situations together. The people of Green Valley are depending on us, and I take that responsibility seriously. I need my crew to do the same."

"Yes, sir," I croak out as Hunter finally nods in agreement.

Chief McClure leans back in his chair, steepling his fingers over his midsection. "What I want to know is why you're here. What's your motivation for joining this program? I'm going to need some good reasons if I let you stay."

I glance at Hunter, but he's looking down at his lap, his mouth a grim slash across his face.

Okay, guess I'll go first, then.

I clear my throat, hoping my voice is stronger than I suspect it'll be. "My dad was a firefighter. Before he died. Before my mom and I moved to Green Valley."

"Did he die in the line of duty?" he asks softly.

I clear my throat again, wishing I had something to drink. "No, but I wanted to do this as a way to honor him."

Chief McClure's gaze pierces me, until I have to look away.

"Do you think acting like this is the best way to honor him?"

Tears prick the corners of my eyes, and I glance at the ceiling, rapidly blinking them away. Shame washes over me again, stronger than when Jed chastised me. "No. But I'll do better."

He seems to take my measure, then nods once before turning his attention to Hunter. "And you?"

Hunter shifts in his chair. "I have my reasons."

"I'm going to need something more than that," Chief McClure replies wryly. "I've given you the benefit of the doubt so far, but the O'Connors aren't exactly known for their good deeds around town."

Hunter lets out a quick snort of disgust. "So that's it? I'm kicked out because of my idiotic family?"

The older man eyes him speculatively. "That remains to be determined. First, I want to know why you're here."

Hunter leans forward so his elbows rest on his knees, but doesn't reply. A solid thirty seconds pass, each one ratcheting the tension in the room higher. Is Hunter going to respond? Should I leave? This is so incredibly awkward.

Maybe it's only me feeling that way, though.

"I want to do something meaningful," Hunter finally says into the silence, his gaze on the floor. "Something that makes me feel good about myself for a change." He pauses, seeming to struggle with his next words. "Something where I'm not Ralph O'Connor's son."

I stare at him, surprised at the plaintive note in his voice, almost like a . . . yearning.

His head turns, his gaze catching mine. There's defiance there, as if he's daring me to say something about his confession. As if I'd make fun of him.

I look away, uneasy with his assessment of me.

Chief McClure rubs at his jaw as he considers us. "You both have solid reasons for being here. But I also need you to learn to work together if you're going to be on my team. I don't need any liabilities. So whatever differences you have, hash them out now because you're going to be spending a lot of time in each other's company."

Hunter jerks up straighter in his seat. "What do you mean?"

Well, at least I didn't have to ask it.

"You two are partnered up for all future training exercises. And not only that, but either you both pass the final exams or neither of you does."

There's a beat of shocked silence and then I blurt out, "That's not fair."

At the same time, Hunter jumps to his feet and says, "You can't do that."

Chief McClure's lips purse briefly. "I can do whatever the hell I want. I'm the chief of this fire station. And I need to know that everyone here has complete trust in their partners in any kind of situation. Call it unconventional, but if you're serious about this, you'll have to help each other." He points to me. "You help him with the written test." He points to Hunter next. "And you help her with the physical one."

"I can't make him smarter," I point out.

"And I can't make her stronger," Hunter shoots back.

"Guess you two have got yourselves quite the dilemma. I suggest you come up with a plan to fix that." He gets up from his desk. "Feel free to use my office as long as you need. You're excused from the rest of today's instruction."

As Chief McClure exits, the tension in the room ramps up again. Is he serious about this? I don't pass if Hunter doesn't either?

"This is fucking bullshit," Hunter mutters as he sits back down, raking a hand through his damp hair.

I turn in my seat, tired of all of this. "Why don't you like me?"

His gaze flicks to me and away. "What are you talking about?"

"You've had it out for me since our first day here."

He rolls his eyes. "You're delusional."

And now he's gaslighting me. A wonderful way to start out this new partnership. "No, I'm not. None of the other guys care that I'm a girl. But you started in right away on how weak I was."

"And you did the same with how dumb I am."

We stare at each other, unwilling to concede the other's point.

"I wouldn't have said anything at all if you hadn't started it." I could have played nice if he would have.

He crosses his arms over his chest and slumps further in his seat. "Finger-pointing isn't going to help."

Damn it. He's right. But still, I'm not letting him off the hook. "No, but I want to know what I ever did to you to have you single me out like that. We've never even really spoken to each other before this."

We weren't in any of the same social circles in high school and we only had one class together senior year.

"Speaking wasn't required," he mumbles.

Now it's my turn to ask what he's talking about.

He doesn't answer my question right away, though. He shifts in his seat, staring at the floor, the silence extending.

But I'll be damned if I break it first.

Finally, he sighs. "You were a brainiac in high school, always showing everyone up. Now you want to come here and do the same thing?" He looks over, his brows two dark slashes over his eyes. "Can't I have one place where I'm sort of good at something without you trying to be better?"

Responses flit in and out of my mind, nearly too fast to grasp. He thinks I'm some kind of narcissist? "I've never tried to be better than anyone else."

He makes a sound of dismissal. "Bullshit."

I inhale and exhale slowly. I won't lose my cool. "I hold myself to high standards, but that doesn't mean I'm competing with other people. I'm competing with myself." He doesn't say anything, so I continue, "I admit I'm not on par with everyone else with the physical stuff here, so I make up for it with the academic stuff. It's what I'm best at."

Another eye roll is all I get in response.

"Hey, if your ego is threatened by that, that's on you to deal with. Not me. I'm not dumbing myself down so you can feel better about yourself."

He shakes his head, angling himself so that he's fully facing me. "No, so *you* can feel better about yourself. That's all that matters, right?"

What is he talking about?

His head tilts to the side, studying me. "What, you don't remember economics?"

The one class we shared senior year? Well, his repeat senior year.

"What about it?" I have no idea where he's going with this.

"We were partnered for that project where we had to make the fake business. And you begged Ms. Norwich for a different partner. If I remember right, you asked for *literally anyone else*."

My mouth opens and shuts, no words coming to defend myself as the vague memory resurfaces. How does he know about that?

"You said you didn't want to be stuck with me," he accuses. "That you knew how I was. That you knew you'd end up doing the whole project by yourself."

There's such contempt in his voice, it's hard to look at him, but I do. "That had been after class," I whisper through dry lips. "And privately to the teacher. No one else was around."

His gaze narrows. "If you'd bothered to look, you'd have seen me in the doorway. I'd come back to ask you when we could get started. I . . ."

He trails off, hesitation in his voice now.

"What?" I ask.

He's silent again.

"Really," I plead. "Tell me." I swallow hard. "I want to make this right."

He studies me again for a moment. "I was glad to be partnered with you," he says in a softer tone, the accusation gone from it. "I thought someone could finally show me how to do a project like that. I would have done the work."

Something in my chest twists, hot and sharp. Disappointment? Guilt? I'm not sure.

"I thought I might get a good grade for once," he continues. "That you might be willing to tutor me in the class, too. You were the smartest girl in school." His breath hitches for a moment. "But you laughed with Ms. Norwich about me and she reassigned you."

He drops his head and rubs at the back of his neck. "Shit. I don't know why I'm saying any of this to you. Forget I said it, okay?"

He gets up and I grab at his arm, not letting him leave. "I'm sorry," I blurt out. "That was shitty of me and I obviously didn't mean for anyone to overhear it. Least of all you."

The thought that this could be an elaborate prank crosses my mind briefly before I dismiss it. He wouldn't paint himself in such a pathetic light. Or maybe his acting skills are that good.

"I was really stressed out at home," I explain. "Stuff with my mom at the time. Not that it's an excuse, but I didn't want to add any more to my plate since that project was a big part of our grade. I'm . . . I'm sorry, okay? I sincerely apologize."

His gaze is on me again, and it's all I can do not to squirm under the weight of it. Finally, he shrugs. "Yeah, okay."

"Are we good? I don't want to get to the end of this training program and find out you still hate me."

He looks away, then down at his arm. Oh God, I'm still holding on to it, aren't I?

I release my grip and he tucks his hands into his pockets. "I don't hate you," he mutters.

For some reason, that moment out in the hallway returns to the forefront of my mind. Him dangerously close to me, our faces inches apart.

No, stop thinking about that.

"Dislike me, then. Or resent me."

"We're good," he says with finality. "God, you're tenacious, aren't you?"

I don't think he means it as a compliment, but that's fine. "I can help you study for the written test," I offer. I need to do something to relieve this gnawing, twisting guilt in my chest. "It's seven years too late, but I'll tutor you."

"Because if I don't pass, you don't pass?"

My lips thin. "Are you determined to think the worst of me?"

"Sorry," he mutters, not meeting my eye.

"Are you free sometime this week? We could go to the library."

"Is that your home away from home, Miss Brainiac?"

I bite back the sarcastic response that's sure to set off another war between us. He's on edge, his hands twitching in his pockets. I can't take the bait.

He rolls his shoulders back, stretching his neck from side to side. "Yeah, the library's fine," he says, not acknowledging his acerbic question. "How's Monday night?"

"That works for me."

"I'll be there at seven," he replies, and stalks off.

I sit in the empty office for another minute, collecting myself. Has he really been holding on to that grudge all this time? It was seven years ago. I had no idea I've taken up this much of his mental real estate.

And what about his other accusations? That I always showed everyone up? That I tried to be better than everyone? Was that true? Or were his opinions coloring how he viewed it?

Well, I could sit here and obsess over high school endlessly, going over every interaction I ever had with anyone, but I'll save that for tonight when I'm trying to sleep. For now, there's nothing I can do about the past. Instead, I need to figure out how to make amends.

Even if it kills me.

Chapter Nine
HUNTER

I rub my damp palms on my pants for the third time in less than a minute, gathering the mental strength to open my car door and go inside the library.

This is so fucking stupid. Why the hell can't I open the door? Do I think the librarians are going to take one look at me and laugh their asses off?

Well . . . they might.

Shaking my head, I force myself out of the car and into the building, keeping my head down, then pause as I realize I don't know where to go. Crap. I didn't check the parking lot to see if Madeline's car is even here. Where's my brain today?

It's still caught up in everything you confessed to Madeline on Saturday. At the pity on her face. How she knows how fucking pathetic you are.

I roll my shoulders and dismiss the nagging thought, then approach the librarian at the desk. Her long, silver hair is wild about her head, reminding me of a witch. At least she doesn't cackle as I ask if she's seen Madeline Woodward here.

"She's right over there," she says, pointing to a table in the corner.

Madeline is hunched over the firefighting textbook in front of her, her hair nearly obscuring her face, until she pushes it back impatiently and tucks it behind her ear as she flips to the next page.

She's so absorbed in her reading, I'm tempted to sneak up behind her and spook her, but that's sure to get me kicked out. Instead, I pull out the chair opposite her and sit, surprised when she doesn't acknowledge me at all. Is this a power play or something?

I clear my throat, and that's when she finally looks up, those deep brown eyes of hers widening.

"When did you get here?" she asks, seeming taken aback.

"Did you seriously not notice me?"

Her lips tip down at the corners. "I get absorbed in whatever I'm reading."

"Hmm." I cross my arms over my chest and lean back in the chair. "We probably should work on your reactive skills, then. Need those to be a firefighter."

She opens her mouth—probably to argue—then gives me a tight smile. "Right."

What, she won't take my bait? Lame.

She looks around me. "Where's your stuff?"

"What stuff?"

"Your textbook. A notebook. A pen. Something."

I shrug. "You didn't say I needed any of that."

The look she gives me screams *unimpressed*. "It was implied."

I wave off her statement. Does she actually think I've ever studied in my life before? "You can teach me what I need to know."

She inhales deeply, then exhales. "You're putting all the burden on me? This is supposed to be an equal exchange."

"You said you'd tutor me. And Chief McClure said I have to help you with passing the physical test."

She shifts in her seat. "I'm working on that. I don't need help."

I keep my laughter at bay. And I'm the King of England. "What are you doing to *work on it*?"

"Don't worry about it. Now, do you want me to tutor you or not?"

I finally relax at the annoyance in her tone. As absurd as it sounds, it feels more like we're on an even playing field when we're at odds. If she'd been pitying me today the way she was on Saturday, I don't think I could take it.

Holding up my hands in defeat, I drop the subject of the physical test for now because I really do need her to tutor me.

Not that I'm telling her that.

When I look back at her, she's studying me curiously. "What's your preferred learning style?"

What's she going on about now?

"Like, are you a visual learner? An auditory one? Kinesthetic?"

I stare at her blankly. That last one definitely wasn't a word. "What the hell are you talking about? Can't you teach me already?"

She lets out a sigh and rubs at her temple. "Hunter, I can't do this if you're going to be surly and defensive."

I groan and thump my head down on the table. Why does she have to make everything so difficult?

She nudges the side of my head. "I'm serious. I need you to work with me here. We're on the same team and I want us both to succeed. But we can't do that if we're at odds."

Damn it. Why does she have to make it sound so reasonable?

Sitting up, I roll my head from side to side. "We're on the same page."

Her brows rise dramatically. "Really? Because you showed up here completely unprepared today. And if what I suspect is right, you haven't done much of the assigned reading on your own."

My heel taps against the floor as I stare silently at her, unwilling to address her last statement.

The silence lingers until she finally says, "I'm sorry," surprising the hell out of me. "I'm not trying to judge you. Honestly. But my ass is on the line, too, and

I'm starting to get nervous. So I need to know you're serious about this or we might as well call it quits now."

I let the retort that bubbles to my lips die. She's being sincere and I . . . I need to get over myself. I'm never going to pass otherwise.

"I'm serious about this," I tell her. "And I'm sorry for showing up unprepared." The words taste bitter on my tongue but I forge ahead. "I'll do better."

"How much of the textbook have you read?"

I swallow hard. "The first two chapters."

I'm such an idiot. We're supposed to have read through chapter twelve by now. Sixteen really so we're prepared for next weekend. But those two chapters alone had been so painful, my stomach had twisted even thinking about opening the textbook again.

So I just . . . hadn't.

She nods once, matter-of-factly. "Okay. I'll make a plan then to catch up on past chapters next time we meet."

And that's it. Nothing more about it. No berating me. No disappointment. Just acceptance and moving on.

"You're not going to yell at me?"

Her head tilts slightly. "No sense in beating a dead horse." She pauses, then looks at me. "Do you want me to yell at you?"

My mind flashes back to the anger and defiance radiating off of her after my pranks and the way I'd unexpectedly liked it.

That's not happening again, though.

"No," I mumble.

"Then I won't. So, this week's chapters cover the principles of fire, water supply and fire protection systems, hose nozzles and fittings, and fireground hydraulics." She pauses and taps her pen on her notebook. "As a heads up, I skimmed through that last chapter and there was a surprising amount of math."

I blink stupidly. "There's math?"

"Yeah. You have to calculate pump pressure, flow conversions, pump discharge maximums, the available water flow at different hydrants . . ." She trails off, probably because of my slack-jawed stare. "Not that we'd likely be doing that stuff as volunteers. But it might be on the test."

I nod, panic setting in. I can't do that shit. Can she?

"What do you do for a living?" I blurt out instead of admitting I have no idea what pretty much everything she said meant.

"I'm a web developer."

That's something with coding, right? Makes sense she'd go into a field like that since she's a genius.

"And you work at Payton Mills?" she asks hesitantly when I don't say anything else.

I nod.

"Something with saws?"

"Sawmill operator."

"Do you like it?"

Is she trying to make small talk?

I shrug. "It pays better than anything else I could do in Green Valley. Probably nowhere near your level, though."

She fiddles with her pen, looking down at it. Is she . . . blushing? What, is she embarrassed by my compliment?

I test my theory by telling her, "It makes sense you'd have a job you need to be crazy smart for. You're probably the smartest person I've ever met."

Sure, I'd told her she was a brainiac the other day, but that was with contempt. Today, I let awe leak in. And if I'm right . . . Yep, her blush intensifies. Maybe she was being truthful when she said she wasn't trying to be better than anyone else.

"Well, I couldn't do what you do," she says to her notebook rather than my face. "And you probably have a lot of pressure to not make any mistakes with all that dangerous machinery. I spend hours sometimes debugging code and fixing mistakes."

"I mean, I guess." I rub at the back of my neck, never having thought of it like that before.

She finally looks up, the wash of pink on her cheeks fading, and gives me a shy smile. The action transforms her into something else entirely. Something . . .

I'm afraid to find the right word, to examine the thought too closely. Things were easier when I hated her. When she wasn't looking at me like I'm . . . nice. Because I said she was smart? It's not like it's a secret.

My gaze zeroes in on her mouth, on that full bottom lip I couldn't stop looking at the other day. Have I ever seen her smile? I can't remember now. I've seen her furious. Smug. Serious.

But never smiling.

When she smiles, she looks sort of . . . beautiful.

Her eyes widen as pink returns to her cheeks.

Oh, shit. Did I say that out loud?

Before I can backpedal, she says, "Why don't we get started studying?"

I nod a little too eagerly, glad she doesn't bring my mishap up as she opens her textbook to chapter thirteen. What the fuck am I doing saying that to her? The girl's not the least bit interested in me.

Not that I'm interested in her. Obviously. The idea is ludicrous.

Look at her. The girl can't even take a compliment without her cheeks turning red. How would a guy ever—

Okay. Not thinking about this anymore. It's a moot point.

"Well, since you don't have your textbook," she says, "I guess we can't both read the chapter to ourselves and then discuss the key points. Do you want to take turns reading it?"

If we do that, we'll be here all night waiting for me to stumble through it.

"Could you maybe read it all out loud?" I ask. "So we get through it faster."

I leave it at that, not wanting to admit anything else. If she heard me read, she'd laugh herself right out of this library.

She considers me for a moment, and I'm afraid she'll start in about how I'm not pulling my weight or how I'm putting more of the burden on her. I mean, I am. But it's not intentional. It's just . . . how it is.

"Okay," she says finally and begins reading.

After each section, she stops and talks about what she thinks are the most important points, then writes them in her notebook. I'm silent, content to listen to her and soak it all in while doing my best not to let my brain wander. When else will I get an opportunity like this?

I'm getting a crash course in everything concerning the principles of fire, and even though some of it is a little too scientific for my liking, especially the things about fire chemistry and combustion, studying this way is a million times faster than attempting to do it by myself. I don't know how she does it, but she seems to actually understand this stuff the first time reading it through based on the way she easily summarizes it afterward. Without struggling. Without having to reread it over and over again until it makes sense.

What's she doing that's so different from when I try it? What's her secret? Would she laugh if I asked her?

"Okay, that's everything for chapter thirteen," she says, setting her pen down on her notebook.

I glance at my phone. It's only been half an hour. Half a freaking hour. I could weep with joy. I'd have been here all night trying to do it by myself.

"We could move on to the next chapter," she continues, "but I think we should quiz each other first to make sure we remember this one."

Quiz each other? The previous elation running through me dries up as my muscles go tense. "We don't need to do all that."

"No, really. Quizzes are a great study tool for comprehension."

"I'm good."

"Well, can you quiz me? Recall works well for me to reinforce the information."

She thrusts her notebook at me and I have no choice but to accept it. Her handwriting is perfect, everything proper and in its place on the page, in neat paragraphs and bullet points. If she saw my messy scrawl, she might have an aneurysm. The girl is type-A to the max.

But that's what's going to help me pass this test. I need her brain.

And apparently need to quiz her, too.

I pick a random spot on the page and reread it until it makes sense. "What are the four heat types?"

"Chemical, mechanical, electrical, and nuclear."

That . . . sounds right.

I flip the page back and pick another random spot. "What characteristics of smoke should a firefighter look for?"

She taps her thumb on the table. "There's volume and velocity. Those are easy to remember because they're alliterative. And I think color is one. There's one more . . . Oh God, what is it?"

She purses her lips as she stares at the table. "Can you give me a hint?"

I read through her notes, probably taking way too long, until I find the one I'm looking for. When I look up, she's studying me.

"What?" I ask, probably too aggressively. What's she looking at me like that for? Like I'm something to figure out.

There's a beat of silence and then she shakes her head. "Clue?"

"It starts with a *d*," I mutter. "It's a scientific thing." At least, I'm pretty sure it is.

"Oh, density. Duh."

Yeah, duh. Like it was so obvious. How does she remember this stuff so easily?

We keep going through questions until I think I've covered everything in the notes and hand her notebook back to her.

"Did that help you, too?" she asks. "Going over the information again like that?"

Actually . . . it did. Damn her for being right.

I don't respond but she still smiles softly to herself, as if she knows. "You want a five-minute break before we start the next chapter?"

What I want is to power through this and not waste any of the time I have with her, but if she needs a break, fine. "Sure."

She gestures to the shelves of books near us. "I know you don't like textbooks, but do you ever read for fun?"

She's kidding, right? "No."

"Nothing? Graphic novels? Comics? Audiobooks?"

Is she trying to show off how smart she is? "No," I repeat.

She makes this *hmm* sound, her gaze assessing me. What's she going to do now?

"I'll be right back."

She leaves and I take the opportunity to stretch my legs, glancing around the library. Never thought I'd be spending any significant amount of time here. If the next chapter we go over turns out the way the first one did, though, I'm going to ask Madeline to meet here twice a week. Maybe even three times to get caught up on the earlier chapters. Would she be up for that? Is that taking too much of her time?

If she wants to pass this training program, though . . . that means I have to pass, too. I'm the weak link.

I scrub a hand down my face, ignoring the tug of shame and guilt mixing in the pit of my stomach. Did I bite off more than I can chew? Is all this worth it?

My eyes squeeze shut as I recall seeing that flyer about the volunteer fire-fighting program on our bulletin board at work. The way I'd initially dismissed it. And then how I'd kept returning to it every day during break. Reading it slowly. And then rereading it over and over until I'd pretty much memorized it. Imagining myself doing something like that. Something I'd be proud of. Being someone others looked up to.

But if I'm so proud of it, why haven't I told anyone about it? Because a part of me doesn't believe I'll pass the final? If my track record with finals in school is any indication, the chances are slim. But maybe with Madeline's help . . .

She returns, holding a thick book with what looks like a hot-air balloon on the cover.

"Doing some light reading?" I ask, eyeing the doorstop. That thing has to be over five hundred pages.

"It's for you," she says, sliding it across the table toward me.

I stare at the book, then her. "You're fucking with me."

She frowns. "You can't curse in here. It's a library."

Which is probably akin to a religious space for her. "Fine. You're messing with me. I thought we were done with that."

"I'm not. I think you'd like it. And it's not as big as it seems. I already checked it out for you."

I glance at the cover. *The Invention of Hugo Cabret*. The label on the spine indicates it's a children's book, too. What the fuck? What kind of Harry Potter nerd children are reading books this big?

"Yeah, okay." I take it, having no intention of doing anything with it when I get home other than using it as a paperweight.

We start in on the next chapter and after I quiz her again, we call it quits for the night. My brain is too full to cram much more in there.

"About your physical training—"

"I said I have it handled," she interrupts, packing her bag with all her study materials.

I don't want to push too much for fear she might not tutor me again. I'm realizing now I can't rely only on the instruction they give on the weekends. That's more for hands-on demonstrations, not actual learning.

"We can talk about it more later," I say, trying to be diplomatic. "Can we, um, meet again this week? For the next two chapters?"

I'll swallow my pride about asking for her help if it means I pass the written exam.

"How about Wednesday?"

"Sounds good. Same time here?"

She nods, then shoulders her bag and taps the book still on the table. "I think you'll be surprised. See you."

She leaves and an odd feeling of loneliness settles over me, especially as I look around the library. I don't belong here.

There's a blonde at the information desk who calls out a cheerful goodbye as I make my way out.

"Thanks," I mumble. Guess I'm going to be seeing a whole lot more of these people in the coming weeks.

Whether I like it or not.

Chapter Ten

MADELINE

Hunter gives me a head nod, sipping coffee at one of the tables as I enter the break room area of the fire station. I smile back, more relaxed in his presence. For the first time, I'm not worried about what kind of prank he'll pull on me.

We'd met three nights this week at the library, each time a little easier, a little less awkward. The last time he'd even let me quiz him for a few minutes, and I picked easy questions to boost his confidence. It's strange how insecure he is when it comes to studying, considering how confident he is with everything else.

Then again, I suspect there's something he's not telling me. Or maybe even something he's not fully aware of himself. I need more time observing him and doing some research before I bring it up, though. Also, I don't want to push him away right as he finally seems receptive to studying for the written exam seriously. His success is my success, too.

I still can't believe Chief McClure made that stipulation. He must be a secret evil genius.

Pausing in front of my locker, I joke to Hunter, "I'm not going to open this and silly snakes will pop out, right?"

Knowing him, it'd probably be more like a bunch of dildos, though.

He grins. "There's only one way to find out."

See, this is great. We're being friendly with one another. This is all going to work out.

Heavy footfalls sound down the hall and stop in the entrance to the break room. "I don't want any funny business today," Chief McClure says, his gaze switching between us.

Hunter's smile drops as he straightens in his chair. "Yes, sir."

There's no trace of sarcasm in his voice, only deference. He's humbled himself a lot over the last week, being polite and respectful for the entirety of our Wednesday and Friday studying sessions. It seemed too good to be true, to be honest. I keep waiting for the other shoe to drop.

Well, even if his family are Iron Wraiths, I guess his momma instilled some kind of manners in him.

For the morning session, the department's EMT, Sebastian, gives us a demonstration of the kind of work he does when called to a scene, and after lunch is our hands-on practical. Related tangentially to what our chapters in the textbook covered, Chief McClure first shows us how to hook a nozzle up to a hydrant and gives us each a turn to practice, then it's time for a timed practical. The hose drag is one of the things on the Candidate Physical Ability Test, or CPAT as actual firefighters call it. It's the first time we're practicing an event that will be directly on the final. Even the ladder extensions we practiced the other week weren't an exact replica of what we'll be tested on.

Chief McClure demonstrates running forward seventy-five feet with the hose draped over his shoulder, then turns around a large drum and runs another twenty-five feet to a marked-off area on the ground. He drops to one knee, then pulls the hose hand over hand toward himself until fifty feet of the hose has crossed the threshold.

Silas is up first, and Chief McClure stops him before he can go, putting a forty-pound weighted vest on him designed to simulate the additional weight of the gear we'll be wearing. Rodney's next, then Hunter. It's not until it's Harry's turn that I start to worry. Harry is probably the closest to me in terms of physical fitness, or lack thereof. Not that he's out of shape, but he's not as young and spry as the rest of the guys on the training team.

He does fine running to the spot, but struggles toward the end of the hose pull, his arms shaking as he finishes.

If his arms shake . . . what will it be like for me?

I'm up next, and as Chief McClure straps the weighted vest on me, I nearly slump down at the oppressiveness. At least it's not as hot as the full gear.

The hose is heavier than I expected, but I don't let it show on my face as I hold the nozzle tight to my chest and run forward, then around the drum that marks our turning point. Dropping into position at the designated spot, I pull at the hose, but not nearly as much comes forward as when Hunter pulled it. Not that I'm comparing myself to him. I can't do that. I'm bound to come up short.

I try again, hand over hand, pulling, but it's like pulling a mountain toward me. It's two hundred feet of hose, I remind myself. Of course it's going to be heavy. And it has to go around the curve of the drum, adding extra resistance. And this damn weighted vest is so freaking heavy . . . No, I can do this. I might not be as fast as everyone else, but I can do it. I only need to get fifty feet of the hose across.

I have to stop and shake my arms out at one point as the feeling goes out of them, but I grit my teeth and persevere, earning a head nod from Chief McClure as I take the vest off with numb fingers and hand it to him. Some of the guys give me commiserating looks as I pass them, and Harry even pats my shoulder.

My heart sinks. That was a pity pat. From the second-worst person on the team.

I join Hunter at the back of the group, who looks at me with a grave expression.

"Was it that bad?" I whisper, unable to help myself.

He sighs. "Well, it wasn't good."

Really? "I finished, though."

"We'll talk about it later."

That doesn't sound promising.

We run through the exercise again, and this time is even harder since my shoulders and upper arms are sore. By sheer force of will, I finish, and vow to myself that I'll become strong enough to do this by the final without my arms shaking. This is a ten-week course, with the written exam and CPAT on the eleventh week. We're already on week four, which means I have about a month and a half to get in shape. That's doable, right? Maybe? Hopefully?

When we're dismissed for the day, Hunter pulls me to the side, probably to chew me out for taking twice as long to finish as him.

Yes, I'd counted.

"You know what I'm going to say."

I cross my arms and stare at my sneakers. "Yeah, I know."

"So we need to get you on a strength training program. Probably something aerobic, too."

"I told you, I've got it covered."

I'll step up my workouts from twice a week to four times. And add some weights, I guess. I'm not really sure how that works but I'm sure there are a ton of tutorials online.

"Then I need to know what you're doing," he replies. "Remember, this affects me, too."

I open my mouth to argue, then pause. If he kept insisting he could handle studying on his own when all evidence suggested otherwise, I'd be livid.

"I'm not trying to put you down, but you weren't up to the level of everyone else today," he says, his tone softer than I thought it could be. He almost sounds like he . . . cares.

"I don't need a reminder," I mutter, annoyed with him for stating the obvious. And because I almost wish he was surly about this. Defensive Hunter I can deal with. Compassionate Hunter . . . No, thank you.

"You need to get in shape."

My lips purse with irritation. Again, he's stating the obvious.

"I'm not calling you fat," he amends. "You're not fat."

His gaze rakes over me, not lasciviously, more like he's assessing me. But there's also something in his eyes, like he's . . . aware of me. Or maybe it's me that's aware of him.

Oh my God, I'm mental. What is wrong with me?

I look back down at my shoes so he can't see how ridiculous my brain is being.

"Shit, I'm messing this up," he mumbles. "I just . . . I want to help you. To return the favor." He blows out a breath. "When the chief was going over that fire hydrant stuff earlier, I actually understood what he was talking about because we had gone over it at the library. So . . . yeah. I guess what I'm saying is . . . thanks."

I glance up at him, but he's looking away, an uncomfortable expression on his face. Like it was painful for him to admit that.

Fine. I should give him something.

"I'm doing a workout video at home twice a week."

He blinks and looks back at me. "What is it?"

"That's not important."

"Madeline . . ."

There's a jump in my belly at the way he growls my name. No, no. Wrong thing to focus on.

I mumble something unintelligible, hoping he leaves it alone, but of course he doesn't, asking me to repeat myself.

I throw my hands up. What do I have to lose at this point? "It's 'Buns of Steel.'"

His brows knit together, but before he can say anything, I shove a finger in his face to cut him off. "Don't go dismissing it before you try it. It's challenging."

At least for me. He's probably already got buns of steel.

Not that I was watching him run today.

He considers me for a moment, then nods. "Okay."

That's all? "Okay, what?"

"Okay, I'll do the 'Buns of Steel' video with you."

I tug at my ear, sure I didn't hear him right. "That wasn't an invitation."

"Well, I'm making it one."

Now this is the Hunter I'm more familiar with. Barging his way into whatever he wants without a care for anyone else.

"You're not doing the video with me."

"I am."

Oh, wait. Duh. I'm so stupid. "You're messing with me, aren't you?" I laugh, but stop fairly quickly when I realize he's not laughing or grinning or giving his signature Hunter smirk. "Wait, are you serious?"

"Yes."

"But I'm sore from today."

"At the rate you should be training, you should be working out every day. You've got a lot of work to do."

Shame washes over me for a second before I push it away. "Hey, I've been trying. It's not my fault I'm not naturally as strong as the rest of you."

"Then you need to train that much harder."

Damn it. He's right. Wasn't I so resolved to get better after the practical earlier?

"Fine. We'll go to my house."

I give him my address and stalk inside to grab my purse, muttering under my breath the whole time about how insane this is. Is he really going to do the workout with me? Or just make fun of it the whole time? I'm the first to admit it's pure eighties cheesiness. But when I'd found the VHS tape and a somehow still-working VCR player in a box of junk in the attic the other week, it had seemed serendipitous.

Hunter pulls in behind me in the driveway, and I curse myself for not calling Mom on the ride home to prepare her.

I stick my key in the front door lock, then pause and turn to face him. "Don't get caught up in conversation with my mom," I warn him. "She'll talk your ear off all night."

"You live with your mom?"

Glaring at him, a mixture of something like embarrassment and resentment bubbles in my stomach. It's not what he thinks, though. I'm helping her out by living here, not the other way around.

I'm not getting into all that with him right now on the porch, though.

Especially within earshot of Mom.

"Yeah, so?"

He doesn't take the bait I'm dangling in front of him for a fight, though. He just gives me a nonplussed look. "Don't talk to your mom. Got it."

"I'm not saying don't talk to her. But don't let her monopolize your time."

"How about you put a paper bag over my head so she doesn't even see me?"

I ignore his sarcasm and open the door.

Mom looks up from her spot on the couch and tilts her head in confusion. "Hi, honey. Who's this?"

I'm antsy, wanting to go to my room already. "This is Hunter. He's training with me at the firefighting program."

She rises and joins us in the front entryway. "Well, it's nice to meet you. Madeline never brings anyone over. Can I get you anything to drink? To eat?"

"No, thank you, ma'am."

Ugh, he actually sounds polite. How come he couldn't have acted like that from the beginning?

"I'm sorry," Mom says, "but I can't place you. Do I know your folks? Did you go to school with Madeline?"

"We're kind of on a tight schedule," I interrupt, knowing we'll be here all night otherwise. "We'll be in my room. Please don't bother us."

I tug at Hunter's arm, pausing at his amused look. Oh, shit. That probably sounded bad, didn't it?

"Not that we're doing anything weird," I amend. Now that sounded suspicious. "We're training together."

Mom smiles warmly. "Okay, honey. I understand."

I get out of there before I can stick my foot in my mouth any more and guide him to my room, restlessness coursing through me as I shut the door behind us. With him in here, the area seems smaller, like he's sucking up all the square footage with his big frame. He looks around, studying my room, and I bite at my bottom lip, viewing it through his eyes.

Plain white walls. A purple comforter on the full-sized bed. The same basic white furniture I've had since my childhood. I've never had a reason to update it. It's still functional. But looking at it now, it seems so . . . childish.

No one ever comes in here, though. And definitely not a guy. It's only me and Mom in the house. Even when I was dating my ex, he never visited here over school breaks with me in college.

I clear my throat, getting Hunter's attention. "Should we get started?"

We're still both in athletic gear from the training, so there's no reason to delay the inevitable. The sooner we're finished, the sooner he stops judging my room.

"Do we need to warm up first?" he asks. "Or do we get straight to steeling our buns?"

"There's a warm-up in the video," I mumble, turning on the ancient VCR.

"Wow, super eighties." He nods toward the grainy image on the screen. "Sorry I left my leg warmers at home."

I pause the video. "I'm not doing this if you're going to make fun of it the whole time."

He holds his hands up and away from himself. "Sorry. I'm on my best behavior now."

I mumble under my breath about what I think of his behavior, but don't unpause it yet. "Are we actually doing this?"

"If it gets you to pass the fitness test, then yeah."

"I can do it myself. You don't have to be here."

He moves closer, but I don't retreat the way my instincts scream for me to.

"You scared?" he murmurs in a low voice, that stupid grin on his face.

Ugh. I thought we were past this. "No." I jam my thumb on the play button, then realize he reverse-psychologized me. Damn it.

The way the TV is positioned means we can't exercise side by side, so I slip behind him as the warm-up starts, but he quickly switches positions.

"Uh-uh," he says, shaking his head. "The whole point of this is so I can see what kind of workout you're doing."

I'm conscious of him behind me as the warm-up takes us through squats, my neck prickling with awareness. I can't believe I agreed to this. What choice do I have, though? It's obvious I'm in desperate need of training. The hose pull is supposed to be one of the easier tests, and I clearly sucked at it.

I glance behind me, expecting to see Hunter squatting, too, but instead, he's staring at my ass.

"What the hell?" I blurt out. "You're supposed to be exercising, not ogling me."

His gaze flicks up to meet mine, and he seems flustered for a moment before he composes himself. "I'm studying your form."

Embarrassment washes over me. Duh. That was the whole point of this.

"Right. Sorry."

How freaking stupid of me. Of course he wasn't staring at my ass. Even if things are . . . friendlier between us the past week. He's not interested in me like that.

My mind conjures up that moment last Saturday when he'd cornered me at the fire station and stared at my mouth. No, stop thinking about that. Besides, I wouldn't even want him to be interested.

I blow out a breath of annoyance. Who am I trying to convince here? Myself?

At least he can't see the redness in my cheeks from this angle. I need to get these stupid thoughts under control.

Before I make a complete idiot of myself.

Chapter Eleven

HUNTER

Madeline has a great ass.

There's no other way to say it. Every time she squats, the fabric of her leggings stretches tight over her perfectly shaped ass. If I didn't already know I'm a sick fuck, I'd be aware of it now.

The girl can't stand me and here I am undressing her with my eyes, imagining reaching out and cupping her. Would she make a soft moan as she melts into my touch? Or slap my hands away with that fire of hers, challenging me to do it again?

Fuck. No. It's not happening.

Sure, she's a girl, but she's off-limits. She's my partner for this training program, not someone to scratch that itch.

The thought crosses my mind to give Lydia a call. She's always down for a quick fuck. But as soon as the idea occurs, I dismiss it almost as quickly. For some reason, it doesn't seem as appealing as it usually does.

The rest of the video is near torturous as I watch Madeline thrust and squeeze and do all sorts of nonsense the instructor has the participants do. Half of my mind appreciates the view, but the other half really is assessing how good the workout is for what she needs to accomplish. The video is actually semi-challenging, especially for her, so it won't hurt her to continue doing it.

It's the other stuff I'm worried about, though. She'd had to stop during the hose pull today to shake out her arms. She'd been breathing heavily, too, as she'd joined me afterward. Building upper body strength and some kind of aerobic activity are on the list, then.

Well, there's one aerobic activity I could help her with . . .

Damn it. I have to stop that. That's not what this is.

I pause the video, unable to take anymore, and Madeline looks at me in confusion, placing a hand on her chest to catch her breath.

"I've seen enough," I tell her.

"And?"

"It's fine, but what we really need is an 'Arms of Steel' video. You have one of those around here?"

She shakes her head. "There is one, but I don't have it. It's probably out of print, or whatever the equivalent is for videos. Maybe I could search on eBay—"

"No, don't do that," I interrupt before she runs too far with it. "We'll figure something out. But you do need more upper body strength. You were struggling with the hose today." I keep my voice as neutral as possible, not wanting to set her off again. "That's not a criticism, just an observation."

She nods warily.

"How about you show me how many pushups you can do?" That'll give me some kind of baseline.

She gets into position on her hands and knees, but I don't let her begin.

"Whoa, whoa. No knees."

She looks up at me, aghast. "I have to use my knees."

I sigh heavily. "Fine."

An image flashes in my mind of her on her hands and knees in a different way, me pumping into her from behind, our bodies slick with sweat, her throaty cries echoing in the air.

Fucking Christ, what is wrong with me? Why does stuff like that keep popping in my head? Because her ass was just in my face?

That doesn't explain all the other times, though . . .

She gets off the floor and I realize I completely missed how many pushups she did, so I nod like I have a clue what I'm doing.

"I have a weight bench in my garage," I tell her. "Why don't you come over tomorrow and I'll get you started with a training plan?"

Her nose scrunches. "Like the kind you . . ." She mimes pushing a bar from her chest.

"Yeah."

Her expression turns to alarm. "I can't do that."

"Well, you're gonna have to learn. You need to step up, Maddy."

"Madeline," she says harshly, her tone brooking no room for argument. "Not Maddy. Madeline."

It startles me, so much that I take a step back, running into the edge of her bed. In a previous week, I would have teased her, or even only called her Maddy from now on, but the idea doesn't sit right with me now.

She clears her throat and looks at the floor. "I don't like being called Maddy. That was my dad's nickname for me. And I don't . . . I just don't want anyone else to call me that."

"Okay," I say after a few seconds of silence, an awkward tension settling in the air. More than anything, it reminds me I don't know all that much about her. We've only now breached the barrier from enemies to . . . not enemies.

A loud noise from somewhere else in the house breaks the silence.

"Let me go check on her," Madeline mumbles, presumably talking about her mom.

As she opens the door, a heavenly smell wafts in, and my mouth waters. What is her mom cooking? Something a hell of a lot better than anything my mom makes, for sure. Me, too, for that matter.

She leaves me alone in her room and I stick my hands in my pockets, looking around again. The furniture doesn't seem to match her, everything done up in white and purple. I'd imagined her personal space to be something more neutral, with maybe grays or blues. One thing that's as expected, though, is how neat everything is. There are no food wrappers or dishes, no clothes on the floor, nothing out of place. Her bed could probably pass some kind of military-grade inspection with how tightly it's made up.

Everything is squared away on her desk, with one of those fancy mechanical keyboards in front of dual monitors, and an expensive brand of headphones placed off to the side. The computer looks custom-built, and it's the only area of the room that seems to have any kind of real personality. She said she did something with computers for her job, so I guess it makes sense.

Wandering over to her nightstand, I uncap the candle on top and take a whiff, surprised it's a sweet scent. I thought she'd be one of those clean linen candle owners. I peek behind me, but she's still nowhere to be seen, and I open her nightstand drawer, hoping to find something naughty, but no such luck. She really is a goody-two-shoes.

There's a small container filled with ChapStick, nail clippers, hand lotion, and a floss pick. God, she's boring. Other than that, the only other item in here is a journal. Oh, maybe we're getting somewhere now. A diary, perhaps? If I read it, will I discover a rant about me?

I flip it open to a random page, but can't make sense of the indecipherable scribblings. And this isn't my normal issue with reading. This is something on a whole other level.

<?php

$users = array("Basic","Premium","Admin");

var_dump($users);

?>

What the hell does that mean?

Oh, duh. She does coding. This must be computer code. So, she actually understands this stuff? And not only that, but writes it herself? I knew she was a brainiac, but damn.

I place the notebook back in the nightstand drawer and linger for another moment, then leave when it gets weird being in here by myself.

"I'm fine, really," Madeline's mom is saying to her in the kitchen.

"You almost broke your neck trying to get this from the top shelf." Madeline motions to a platter on the table.

"Well, we have a guest tonight. We should use the fancy china."

"He's not staying for dinner."

"Oh, he has to. I made extra." Her mom looks up, catching sight of me in the entryway. "You're more than welcome to join us for dinner. I'll take it personally if you don't at least try a bite before leaving."

Next to her, Madeline rolls her eyes. I can't tell if it's good-natured annoyance or serious, though. "He probably has plans. It's Saturday night."

"I don't," I say, enjoying the stink eye she gives me. "And I'd love to stay for dinner."

At the very least, the kitchen smells amazing, so the food must be good, too. And there's something about riling Madeline up that gives me such satisfaction. If I can't do it in ways that'll seriously piss her off anymore, I'll have to get my fill another way.

She shrugs, and as she passes by me on her way out of the kitchen, she murmurs, "It's your funeral."

What the fuck? Is she trying to psych me out? Staying for dinner can't be that bad, right?

Fifteen minutes later, I understand what Madeline meant when we first arrived about talking to her mom. I don't think the woman's taken a breath the entire time, other than to ask me rapid-fire questions about everything under the sun, from my work to my favorite meal. Why would she care about any of that?

"And do you have a girlfriend?" her mom asks, slipping another piece of Swiss steak on my plate. She takes a heaping spoonful of mashed potatoes and plops that down next to it, not even asking me if I want more. I mean, I do. But that's beside the point. "Boyfriend? Partner? I can't keep up with what everyone's into nowadays."

"Mom," Madeline says on a tired sigh.

"What? I'm making conversation with your colleague." She tries to load seconds onto Madeline's plate next, but Madeline doesn't let her.

Colleague. That sounds so formal.

"No, ma'am," I tell her, taking a bite of my second helpings. Everything really is delicious. "I'm not seeing anyone."

She reaches over and pats my hand in a motherly way. "Well, not to worry. You're still young. You'll find someone."

I keep my smile to myself. Does she think I'm worried about that?

I glance at Madeline. Is she worried about that? Actually, I've never asked, but I assumed she was single. Someone who spends all their free time reading textbooks and writing computer code must be single. Plus, she's met up with me so many nights recently at the library. What guy would want his girl hanging out with another guy so much? If she was my girl, I wouldn't want her—

Whoa. Weird train of thought. Let's pump the brakes on that one.

"That's what I always tell Madeline," she continues. "Plenty of time to find someone. Just because you have one failed relationship doesn't mean—"

"Mom," Madeline hisses. "Hunter doesn't need to hear about that."

Oh, but I really do. Especially if she *doesn't* want me to hear.

"What's the big deal?" her mom asks no one in particular, waving her forkful of mashed potatoes around. "We're all friends here."

Madeline's lips thin. "I didn't say he was my friend."

Ouch. But also . . . completely deserved.

"Well, don't be rude, honey. You know, you catch more flies with honey than vinegar."

Unfortunately, the subject of whatever this failed relationship is gets dropped, but during the rest of dinner, I discover such hidden gems as Madeline being unable to swim without water wings until she was ten years old and that she still harbors an intense fear of E.T.

"E.T.? Really?" I ask her. "He's supposed to be a friendly alien."

She shakes her head before I'm finished speaking. "No, he's terrifying, as any rational person will tell you. That scene with him by the river is nightmare fuel."

She's got a point—not that I'm telling her that.

"What's strange is Madeline's never been afraid of death," her mom says. "She was so rock solid after her father's death, and such a comfort to me." She squeezes her daughter's hand. "So I don't understand why E.T. affected you like that."

Madeline stares at her plate, seeming to withdraw after her mother's mention of her father. She got weird earlier, too, after saying she didn't want anyone calling her Maddy because her dad did.

Thinking about it, she also said he's the reason she's involved in this fire-fighting training to begin with.

Guess the girl's got some unresolved daddy issues.

"Now, you haven't mentioned your folks at all," Madeline's mom says, nearly flinging mashed potatoes at me with her fork. "You're local, right?"

"Yes, ma'am." Hardly anyone here isn't.

"And who's your momma?"

"Bonnie O'Connor." I doubt she knows her. Doesn't seem like they'd run in the same circles.

Her lips purse. "Bonnie . . . Only Bonnie I know is Bonnie Walker."

I pause before taking another bite. "That's her maiden name." I glance questioningly at Madeline. "I thought you moved here in high school." How would her mom know mine from that long ago?

"Mom grew up in Green Valley," she replies steadily. "She moved away when she married my dad."

Guess that's why they moved back, then. And that explains the slight Southern twang in her voice.

"Oh, Bonnie was such a pretty girl," her mom reminisces. "She was a few years older than me, so we didn't talk much. Smoked like a chimney stack, that one." She laughs to herself. "She ever kick the habit?"

I shake my head. Growing up, my clothes always reeked of cigarette smoke, but what do you expect from a Wraith kid?

"She doing good? There are so many people I used to know way back when that I haven't seen since we've been back." The laugh she gives this time is more forced. "Guess I've been a bit of a shut-in."

For the last decade? Not going to touch that topic with a ten-foot pole. "Uh, she's fine." If by fine you mean married to my cesspool of a father for nearly thirty years and working as a gas station attendant for about the same length of time.

"Her and your daddy still married? And who's he again?"

Wow, does she ever stop with the questions? She must drive Madeline insane. "Yeah. Ralph O'Connor."

"Hmm. That name doesn't ring any bells. He must have graduated before my time."

He didn't graduate at all. But no need to go into that.

"Well, this has been lovely," Madeline interrupts, standing and bringing her plate to the kitchen sink. "But it's late and I'm sure Hunter has places to be." The look she gives me practically lifts me from my seat and escorts me out the door.

I shovel the last of my food into my mouth and bring my plate to the sink, too.

"Oh, you don't have to take care of your plate," her mom says, making a fuss at me. "Madeline will do it for you."

I grin around the mashed potatoes still in my mouth and hand an unamused Madeline my plate for her to wash.

"Thanks," she mutters. "I'll walk you out."

"Now, you stop by anytime you'd like," her mom calls out to me as I take my leave. "You're always welcome to dinner."

"Thanks, Mrs. Woodward. The meal was great."

"Oh, you call me Vera, honey. It was lovely to meet you. Madeline never has anyone over."

She'd mentioned that when I first got here, too.

"And you're definitely leaving now," Madeline murmurs as she ushers me out.

When we're in the safety of the driveway, I ask her, "Why do you live with her if you're so annoyed?"

She rubs at her temple. "Because I pay pretty much all the bills. She's terrible with money."

Shit. I didn't know that. And here I was ready to give her crap for still living at home the way Nate does. Green Valley's not like other parts of the country where it's impossible to move out. Real estate has stayed pretty stable around here the last few years.

Thinking about it, though, she's not a moocher at all. And she probably makes beaucoup bucks at her job.

"You know she actually fell for one of those email scams?" she continues. "The one where a foreign dignitary needs access to your bank account info to keep their millions safe temporarily."

My brows raise. "Seriously?"

"Yeah. And I can't afford to pay for two households . . . So here we are. Also, can you forget pretty much everything she said in there? You don't need any more ammunition against me."

I can't help the smirk that crosses my lips. "What? That you can't swim?"

She plants her hands on her hips. "I can swim now. It just took me a little longer than other kids."

I rub at my jaw, the stubble there rasping. I should throw her a bone. "You know that spot out at Bandit Lake everyone swims at?"

She nods, confused by my sudden change of topic.

"My brother threw me in there when I was three thinking I could swim, and I nearly drowned."

Her eyes widen.

"I didn't go back in the water until I was eight, and that was only because other kids were making fun of me. So you're not the only one who learned to swim late."

She squints skeptically at me. "Are you making that up to make me feel better?"

My smirk grows wider. "So distrusting."

"Hmm, I wonder why."

"Hey, we made a truce. I'm on the straight and narrow now."

The laugh she lets out is infectious, and I find myself chuckling, too, even though it's probably at my expense.

The air of irritation surrounding her throughout dinner finally lifts. "You couldn't be on the straight and narrow if you tried."

Though the words are a little harsh, she says them with an almost . . . affection.

I rub at the back of my neck. "Listen, how about we start you on arms tomorrow?"

Her mouth twists to the side. "We have training all day."

"Afterward."

"But—"

"Are you going to use that excuse every day?"

Her lips compress, eyes flashing fire for a moment. There she is.

"Fine."

I nod. "See you tomorrow, then."

As I drive home, it startles me for a moment to realize how much I'm looking forward to tomorrow. And now that I think about it, when was the last time I looked forward to anything?

The only thing is, is it because of the training program?

Or because of Madeline?

Chapter Twelve

HUNTER

The morning's session isn't at the fire station, but rather the elementary school. I swear we're in the same classroom I suffered through second grade, faint echoes of Mrs. Campbell berating me still ringing in my ears.

Dog is d-o-g, not g-o-d. If I have to tell you one more time, Hunter, I swear. You should be past this by now.

I cross my arms over my chest, unable to recline in the too-small chair at the too-small table. My knees are practically in my armpits.

Next to me, Madeline has her notebook open, ready to capture everything Chief McClure says during his lecture about fire hydraulics. And just as she warned, it seems there's a fuckton of math.

Chief McClure stands at the front of the classroom, gesturing with a dry-erase marker as he talks. "So, the basic equation the pump operator needs to calculate when operating the fire pump is EP equals NP plus FL plus APP plus ELEV."

He writes the formula on the whiteboard behind him, my eyes glazing over. It had been hard enough when Madeline had explained it to me at the library.

"Now, who remembers what those acronyms mean?"

For a change, Madeline's hand doesn't shoot up to immediately answer. Instead, she nudges my arm.

"You know this," she whispers.

I shake her off. There's no way in hell I'm answering. I learned my lesson in classrooms. Keep your mouth shut at all costs.

"Woodward? O'Connor? You have an answer for me?"

Shit. Why'd she have to get us in trouble like that?

Both Madeline and Chief McClure look at me expectantly. Seriously? She's not going to answer?

"Uh, EP is engine pressure and NP is nozzle pressure," I say haltingly. I remember those two for sure. Does FL mean fluid? No, it's something else. Something . . . loss. What had Madeline said at the library? Oh, right. "FL is friction loss, APP is appliance friction loss, and ELEV is elevation loss or gain."

"Good job," the chief says as he returns to his lesson.

Madeline smiles, and I find myself returning it for a second before I shut it down, my cheeks heating. I look like an idiot, about to pump my arms in the air for getting one stupid question right. It shouldn't be a big deal, but that still doesn't stop the center of my chest from warming with pleasure.

I answered a question right in class. For probably the first time ever.

Chief doesn't call on me again for the rest of the lecture, but I make sure to pay attention, ready for it. And, honestly, it's not so bad listening to him now that I know what the hell he's talking about.

Thanks to Madeline.

After our lunch break, we return to the firehouse, where a firefighter we haven't met yet, Huey, has set up a search maze for us, designed to simulate searching for a fire victim in an unpredictable area. We have to army crawl through an enclosed tunnel around obstacles, although it's possible Madeline's small enough to do it on her hands and knees. Each person is timed during their turn, and out of the six of us trainees, I come in second and Madeline comes in fourth.

Thank God. That's one less thing we have to train for.

We run through it again and after listening to some pointers on ways we can improve our time, we're dismissed for the day.

"You ready for arms?" I ask Madeline as we make our way to the parking lot, then nearly laugh at the look of reluctance she gives me.

"I guess."

"If I had said that, you'd say I have a bad attitude."

She groans. "Fine." She brightens, putting on a toothpaste-commercial smile. "I can't wait for my arms to fall off," she says in an overbright, bubblegum-sweet voice.

I resist the urge to roll my eyes. "I'm supposed to be the smartass, not you."

She shrugs, her smile more normal now. "Thought I'd give it a try."

It continually surprises me that she actually has a sense of humor underneath all that seriousness.

She follows me back to my place and I open the garage door to let in some fresh air. With summer fast approaching, it gets too stuffy in here otherwise.

She joins me, her gaze scanning over the weight bench, then behind her to the street. "Will people see us?"

Does she mean see us exercising? Or see us . . . together? Does she not want to be seen with me?

No, that's stupid. We've met up at the library three times now.

That's different than getting spotted at my house, though.

I clear my throat, pushing aside the thought. "I promise no one cares what we're doing in here. The lady across the street has cataracts and can barely see, anyway."

She nods, then holds up her nearly empty water bottle. "Could I refill this inside?"

"Come on." I motion for her to follow me inside, and silently thank my past self for cleaning up last night. Not that it was a pigsty or anything, but based on the immaculate neatness of her room last night and knowing she was coming over today . . . Well, I didn't want to come across as a total slob.

I don't have people over all that often, preferring my private space to stay, well, private. Occasionally a few guys from work come over to play something on the PS5, maybe a girl every once in a while—though I prefer to go to her place if possible. Growing up in a house where I not only had to share a room with my brother, but was reminded at every turn that nothing was mine and could be taken away whenever my dad felt like it . . . It makes you hold something you finally get for yourself sacred.

Taking her water bottle from her, I fill it up from the dispenser in the fridge door while she tries not to be obvious about inspecting my home.

Her gaze meets mine and she looks away quickly, knowing I caught her.

"Your place is nice."

"Thanks." I'd scrimped and saved, putting away every dollar I made for the down payment on this house. Not that it's a mansion by any means. It's an average ranch-style home, built in the sixties, with brick siding on the front. But it's mine.

"I didn't imagine it like this."

"What'd you imagine?"

She shrugs, a smirk hovering around her lips. "A dungeon where you concoct your evil pranks."

"Evil? You're the one that was evil, making me eat a sponge."

She points her finger at me. "I didn't make you do anything. And anything involving glitter is definitely evil."

Yeah, it kind of is.

"And maybe some kind of crazy sex swing or something," she says, motioning to the living room. "You have a reputation, you know."

"Well, you haven't seen the bedroom."

She blushes and looks away. God, she's so easy to provoke.

"Is this a delay tactic?" I ask her. "So you don't have to work out?"

She half chuckles, half sighs. "Let's go."

Taking her water bottle, she heads back out to the garage and sits on the weight bench, then scoots back to lie flat.

"So I'm supposed to lift this?" she asks, wrapping her hands around the barbell.

I wasn't going to start her on that, but if she wants to try, she can. "Sure."

I move behind her to spot her.

Her fingers flex on the bar. "You won't let this fall on me?"

She'd asked something similar when we'd done the ladder exercise at the station, too. If I'd let her fall. How bad does she think I am?

"No. My hands are right here. The bar's not going anywhere unless you or I tell it to."

She nods and releases the bar to wipe her palms on her shirt, then grips it again. "What do I do?"

"Lift it off the rack and toward your chest, then straight up. Do it as many times as you feel comfortable doing."

My hands hover under the bar as she follows my instructions, but as she goes to lift it from her chest, she whimpers.

"Holy fuck."

I'm momentarily startled by her curse. I've never heard her say anything like that.

She manages to lift the bar enough to get it back on the rack, then her arms collapse on the bench. "Oh my God, you didn't tell me it would weigh that much."

"It's forty-five pounds. That's common knowledge."

"For you, maybe. I need a lower weight. That was way too hard."

Well, this is starting out great.

"Besides," she continues, "it's not like bench presses will be on the test."

"So look up what is on the test."

She grabs her phone from its spot next to her water bottle and fiddles around on it, then reads aloud the eight events we'll have to complete in less than ten minutes and twenty seconds while wearing a fifty-pound vest to simulate the weight of normal gear. By the end, she's chewing on her thumbnail, her face worried.

"I'm surprised you haven't looked this up before," I tell her, not sure what else to say. It's obvious from what she read she can't do everything on there. Or, at least, not within the time limit. The rescue event alone has us dragging a heavy mannequin around. If she had trouble with the hose pull, that one will be worse.

"I was afraid to," she mumbles.

"Looks like we'll need to start running, too. We'll need stamina."

She looks up at me. "Do you run now?"

"No. But I used to, back in high school. For football in the fall and baseball in the spring." Sports were a great excuse to be out of the house and away from Dad.

"Right. I forgot you did those. Well, um, Green Valley doesn't have a gym, does it?"

Hmm. "All I know of is the MMA place. You want to try that?"

She gives me a deadpan look. "No."

That's what I thought. "What time do you start work?"

"Around eight-thirty, usually."

"What do you mean usually?"

She shrugs. "I can start my day whenever. No one's looking over my shoulder. As long as everything gets done, it doesn't matter when I do it."

The idea is completely foreign to me. "Well, I have to be at work at seven. So we can either go running before six or after I get out at three-thirty."

"Wait. We're running together?"

"Will you actually run every day if you're not held accountable?"

Her mouth tightens. "To spite you, I would," she mutters under her breath.

I laugh, unable to help myself. "It'll keep me accountable, too."

"Okay," she says grudgingly. "But I'm not waking up that early, so how about we do it in the early evening when it's not so hot? Maybe five-thirty?"

So we go from hating each other to spending every day together now? Life's funny that way.

"Did you really hate me?" I blurt out before I can think the question through.

She blinks at me, her brows knitting. "What?"

Shit. Why did I bring this up? "Back a few weeks ago," I mumble. "Before we had to work together."

She studies me carefully. "I hated the pranks you pulled," she says finally.

Is that a nice way of saying yes?

I nod, looking at my shoes. "I'm . . . sorry. I don't think I ever said that properly, back in the chief's office." And the crazy thing is, I mean it. Have I ever sincerely apologized for anything in my life? "I . . . I don't know what got into me," I end with lamely.

Sure, I'd held a grudge against her for that day in high school, but that wasn't really the why behind it, at least not past that first prank.

Maybe it was because she gave back as good as I gave her. Because I liked riling her up, seeing how she'd react. She always surprised me.

There's something so . . . intriguing about her. Maybe because she's different from anyone else I know. So different from me.

"Apology accepted," she says, a soft smile on her face. "Even if you still drive me crazy."

She's teasing me. I think. It's hard to tell with her. "Right back at you."

I pull out the lightest set of dumbbells I own and lead her through a set of exercises I think will help her best, then take her on a twenty-minute run around my neighborhood and back.

When we return, she guzzles an ungodly amount of water in my kitchen, then collapses on the living room floor.

"I'm dead," she moans. "And my ghost will haunt you forever for making me do that."

If she's this sore now, she'll be in hell tomorrow. No sense in bringing up that fun tidbit now, though.

"You'll survive," I tell her. "How about I make you a protein shake? You need to build muscle." I should have some vanilla-flavored protein powder in the cabinet.

"I won't be able to drink it because I can't sit up."

"It's that bad?"

She nods pitifully.

"What do you want me to do?"

Groaning, she says, "I don't know. Get me a new body?"

"You need a massage?"

Whoa. Where did that thought come from? And why can't I keep control over my mouth today?

She opens one eye and squints at me from her spot on the floor. "Is this a prank?"

"What?" I laugh. "How could it be a prank?"

"Because it sounds too good to be true. And it doesn't sound like something the Hunter I know would offer."

The Hunter she knows. Who is that exactly? Even I'm not sure at this point.

"I'm turning over a new leaf," I tell her.

"Okay," she says warily. "I'm not in any kind of position to turn down a free massage right now."

I kneel next to her on the carpet and the reality of what I offered hits me. I'll have my hands on Madeline. It shouldn't matter, but there's a jump in my lower belly all the same. If anything, I should be grossed out. The girl's a sweaty mess, lying boneless on the ground.

My gaze moves to her ass, the same one I watched yesterday doing that stupid "Buns of Steel" workout. The same one I watched today while jogging behind her. I can't massage her ass. Even in her half-dead state, she'd take issue with that.

The back it is.

Her shirt is cool to the touch, still damp with drying sweat, and I'm reminded that my own shirt isn't much better. The standards are low at the moment, though.

"Oh, sorry. I'm gross, aren't I?" she says, reaching back and touching her sweat-soaked shirt.

"Maybe you could, um, take off your shirt?" I find myself asking. "So I can massage you better."

What am I saying? If she wasn't so tired, she'd probably slap me.

She groans, lifting up on her forearms. "Okay, but don't be a perv."

It's a Herculean effort for her to heave herself up enough to strip her shirt off, leaving her in a black sports bra and athletic shorts. She collapses back again, her arms at her sides.

What she's wearing is the kind of thing you'd see at a gym all the time. Perfectly normal.

But that doesn't stop my mouth from watering at all the creamy, porcelain skin on display. Only a few freckles mar the otherwise perfect expanse. She must not go out in the sun often. Or she's one of those people who's diligent about wearing sunscreen. Yeah, she seems like the type.

She's normally all covered up in oversized shirts that don't give any hint to her shape. And there's no way in hell I would have ever guessed she has two dimples on her lower back, right above her shorts.

I reach out and sweep a thumb over the area, goosebumps flaring on her skin. Does my touch affect her? Or is she cold?

The sweat on her has dried, leaving only soft, smooth skin. What must she think of my work-roughened, calloused fingertips? The sawmill hasn't been kind to my hands. Countless scrapes, cuts, and splinters over the years, even wearing work gloves most of the time, have taken their toll.

I'm reminded that I'm a sick fuck again as I trail my fingers up her back, taking an inordinate amount of pleasure in the act. What the fuck is wrong with me? I've seen plenty of girls in a whole lot less. I can't even see her front. Only her back.

But this is Madeline. And, for some reason, that makes it different.

As I dig my thumbs into her trapezius muscles, she lets out a low groan.

"Oh my God, that feels good."

There's that jump in my lower belly again, even knowing she didn't mean that as a sexual thing. She said it because she's in pain and I'm supposed to be helping her.

What I'm not supposed to be doing is getting excited.

I continue what I'm doing, moving around to different areas of her back, silently reveling in her softness, in the way she's pliant under my hands. She's rarely this easygoing, this agreeable. And she's making these quiet noises of satisfaction under her breath that are driving me insane. I'm not sure she's even aware she's doing it, but all I can think of is if she'd make those same sounds if I was touching her in a different way. If my hands traveled just a little further south . . .

My fingers flex, pausing, and I swallow hard, getting myself under control. I'm not actually attracted to Madeline. I can't be. She's a know-it-all goody-two-shoes. She's nothing like my type.

But tell that to my dick.

I block out the noises as much as I can, focusing on massaging her back, trying to get this over with as quickly as possible. This was a terrible idea. The longer my hands are on her, the more I'm afraid they might . . . roam. Especially as I get to her lower back. Her ass is right there. That wonderful, perfect ass I've spent the last two days watching intensely with her completely unaware. It would be nothing to massage that, too. She'd probably like it. I could even slip my hand around and—

"You're all done," I tell her, snatching my hands away, my voice unsteady. "I'll make that protein shake now."

I get up before she can respond, and head to the kitchen, gripping the counter.

Get yourself under fucking control. She's your partner for this firefighting training program. You need her help to pass. You train her physically, she trains you mentally. That's all this is.

There's nothing more between us.

Chapter Thirteen
MADELINE

"Look at you, Miss Muscles."

I laugh at Adelaide over the screen and flex my biceps. "You like that?"

I'm pretty sure my arms don't look any different. It's only been three weeks since I've started seriously training with Hunter. But they do feel different. And I'm only mildly sore now compared to being on my deathbed when we first started exercising together.

She flutters her hand in front of her face, as if she's impressed. "It may be an unintended consequence, but you're going to have an amazing beach bod this summer if you keep up this training."

I snort. "What beach? Tennessee is a land-locked state."

She waves her hand in dismissal. "You know what I mean. And if *I* was working out every day, I'd look amazing for beach season."

She lives in New England. Isn't it too cold to swim in the ocean up there? Admittedly, I know nothing about that area, having lived in Tennessee my whole life.

"You don't seem like the beach type to me."

Adelaide's not an outdoorsy kind of girl. And though I've only known her for about a year and we've never met in person, I can say that with a pretty high level of confidence. Thinking about it, she's actually become my closest friend. As an introvert who rarely leaves the house, the bar is pretty low, admittedly.

As the only other woman on our web development team, she'd suggested when she joined that we share a virtual celebratory drink at the end of every work week, as a way to get to know each other better, vent about our week, and support one another. We've made it a standard Friday afternoon thing over the last year, and lately I've been telling her all about my firefighting training.

"Well, I don't go in the ocean," she says, taking a sip of her martini. Her drinks are always of the alcoholic variety. "Beaches are for showing off bikinis, not swimming."

That sounds more like her.

"But they have lake-beach things in Tennessee, right?"

"Around here, people go to Bandit Lake. But I'm not really a strut around in a bikini kind of girl."

Adelaide bats her eyelashes. "Maybe you would for Hunter." She draws out his name in a singsong way.

I shake my head, willing myself not to smile at her antics. "I never should have told you he was cute."

"No, you shouldn't have," she agrees.

It had been a slip of the tongue, I swear. She should have been focused on the parts where I ranted about what an ass he was. Although, he hasn't been like that lately. Now that we've set aside our previous rivalry, he's almost like a different person. Not that he's a saint, by any means. The teasing and smirks are still in full force, but it's good-natured now. Like we're on the same team. And out of the two of us, he might actually be the one taking the training more seriously now. He's really starting to understand the material we go over at the library, now that I've made a few adjustments to how I present it.

Speaking of, I still need to talk to him about that. I think I finally figured out what his problem is.

"I'm just saying," Adelaide continues, interrupting my train of thought. "In the year I've known you, I've never heard you talk about a guy. And now, in the last month and a half, he's all you've talked about."

"Yeah, because he was annoying me. And you're a good listener. And you always bully me into giving you every last detail about everything."

"So sue me for being interested in your life. And, to be fair, you usually have nothing going on. No offense."

None taken. She's right. This volunteer firefighter training program has been the most exciting thing I've done in probably . . . ever.

"Why don't we talk about you?" I ask. "How's your sister's crazy wedding drama going?"

"Don't try to change the subject. I'll get to her and how she ruined my grandma's veil soon enough. I want to know what's going on with you and Hunter. You're seeing him tonight, right?"

I shrug, not sure what she's getting at. "I see him every night. We either go running together or to the library to study. And there's nothing going on."

That'd be . . . crazy. Even if he's been nicer lately. And we both apologized for past misdeeds. But that doesn't mean I've forgotten everything that's happened.

Her lips purse. "Okay, fine. But you tell me the minute anything does happen. I have this feeling . . . Like psychic intuition or something."

I roll my eyes, chuckling. "You are not psychic."

"I could be. My grandma was psychic, you know."

"The one with the ruined veil?"

"Girl, let me tell you."

I get lost in her family drama for the next twenty minutes, then have to excuse myself to get ready to go running.

"Say hi to lover boy for me," Adelaide says, blowing a kiss to me.

I ignore her comment and wave goodbye, not taking her bait.

After getting dressed in workout clothes, I drive over to Hunter's house, surprised when he answers the door without his customary smirky smile. Hmm. I didn't realize that had even become the norm until he didn't do it.

"Everything okay?" I ask, setting my purse on the entryway table like I always do.

He rolls his shoulders back, tenseness still lingering. "Just a shit day. My boss was up my ass about one thing or another. His wife is leaving him, so he's taking it out on everyone else."

"Oh. Well, we don't have to go running today if you're not up to it."

He squints at me. "You trying to weasel your way out of it?"

"Me? Never." I infuse as much levity into the words as I can, hoping to cheer him up.

It seems to work as he finally smirks back. "Come on. We'll kick it up a notch tonight."

Though he usually runs behind me, today he takes the lead, setting a faster pace than I'm used to. I don't say anything, trying to keep up, but less than ten minutes in, there's a stitch in my side I can't ignore.

"Hold up," I call out, slowing until I can rest my hands on my knees, bent over and breathing heavily. "I can't do anymore. You're too fast."

He rubs at the back of his neck. "Shit. I wasn't thinking. Sorry."

I nod, still catching my breath. At least I didn't get shin splints. It happened once during that first week, and I nearly asked Hunter to carry me home it hurt so bad.

"How about we walk back?" he asks.

"Okay." It'd be embarrassing if I was with anyone other than Hunter, but the man's seen me at my worst in the last few weeks—a red-faced, sweaty mess who stinks to high heaven after our workouts. A little side stitch as I limp home is nothing. "That way's a shortcut."

His gaze follows where I'm pointing, and his brows punch down. "Not that way."

"Why? It's faster."

"Because I don't want to."

I roll my eyes and head that way, anyway. "You have to give me a better reason than that." Sure, the neighborhood's not that nice, but who cares?

"Madeline." He tugs at my arm, and not gently, either.

"Hey, what are you—"

"I don't want to go that way, okay?"

I stare at him, his face somehow both begging me to understand and not giving anything away.

"Okay," I whisper, and follow him, holding my hand to my side until the stitch fully disappears.

What was that all about? What's down that street? It looked like residential homes. Does he know someone who lives there? Does he not want to be seen with me?

The silence stretches between us as we backtrack our steps to the street we just turned from. I'm normally comfortable with silence, but this feels different. Like there's something itchy under my skin. Like I did something wrong by even making the suggestion in the first place. Well, how was I supposed to know it would set him off? I made a perfectly reasonable suggestion—

"I can hear your brain working from here."

I glance over at Hunter, his expression one of bemusement.

"Are you done being mad, then?"

He sighs and laces his hands behind his neck, causing his biceps to pop in his sleeveless muscle tee.

No, don't look at that.

"My parents live that way."

Oh. "I didn't know."

Nodding, he explains, "I didn't want them to see me out running."

I swallow, the question I was thinking earlier coming out whether I want it to or not. "With me?"

He looks over at me sharply. "It has nothing to do with you."

Jesus, Madeline. Self-centered much?

"Well, maybe a little to do with you." He sighs again, releasing his hands from behind his neck to rest them on his hips. "I don't want them to ask what I'm doing."

That day, nearly a month ago at this point, when we'd been in Chief McClure's office, he'd said he didn't want to be like his family. We've had countless conversations since then, but anytime the topic of his family even remotely veers close, he changes the subject.

"They don't know you're part of the training program?"

He shakes his head. "Somehow—I don't know how—they haven't got wind of it."

"And you don't want them to?"

"No."

There's a finality in his tone, but I can't help but push a little.

"You think they won't like it?"

"I know they won't," he mutters darkly.

What's not to like? Firefighters are community heroes. And this is something we're volunteering to do, pro bono. They should be proud.

Then again, his family are Iron Wraiths. And I get the sense his family dynamics are very different from my own.

He scrubs a hand down his face. "I need a drink. You want to go get one?"

He's asking me out for a drink? No, not asking me out. That's ridiculous. We're . . . friends now. Sort of. This is a friendly invite. Because he's had a shitty day and needs alcohol to make it better, apparently.

"Um, sure. Where?"

A ghost of his normal smirk returns. "How about the Pink Pony?"

"Hunter." I shove at his arm. "Be serious."

"What? They serve drinks there."

His too-innocent act doesn't fool me. "I'm not going to a . . ." I glance around us, but there's no one within earshot, only an elderly man sweeping his driveway across the street. "A strip club," I whisper, just to be safe.

"Have you ever been?"

"No. Have you?" Wait. I don't want to know the answer to that.

He shrugs, like it's no big deal. "Yeah. A few times."

Right. Of course. Why wouldn't he? He's a guy. That's what single guys do . . . I guess. But that doesn't stop a growing ball of disappointment from bouncing around in my stomach.

God, I'm stupid. Why should I care at all if he pays to go see naked girls? Actually, I don't know anything about the Pink Pony. Is it full strip? Topless? Bikinis? The only thing I do know is that it's better than the G-Spot, that place over by the Iron Wraiths' biker bar. I've heard the girls there are all strung out.

I give Hunter a fake sympathetic smile. "Can't see girls any other way than by paying them?"

He barks out a laugh, no trace now of the crappy mood he was in before. Well, this convo accomplished something, at least.

"I'm not some sad man going there by myself and paying for lap dances. I went there once for a bachelor party and twice for coworkers' birthdays."

Are strip clubs the venue of choice for adult get-togethers now? What happened to places like the bowling alleys or skating rinks we went to as kids?

"You know, maybe you could get some lessons from the girls there," he says, unsuccessfully keeping his grin at bay.

Where is he going with this? "On what? Pole dancing?"

"Yeah, for sliding down the fireman's pole at the station."

I shove at his arm again, but he's too quick, dancing away as he laughs.

"What? It's a solid idea."

I point my finger at him. "No Pink Pony."

Mirth lingers in his gaze. "Fine. How about Genie's?"

"I'll do Genie's," I agree. "I just need to go home and shower first."

"How about I pick you up in an hour?"

He wants to ride together? "Um, okay." I guess that makes sense, since we're going to the same place and all.

Adelaide's voice rings in my mind. *Tell me the minute anything happens.*

No, this isn't anything. It's going out for drinks. The only reason I had any other kind of thoughts in my head was because she put them there to begin with.

Hunter and I are training partners.

End of story.

Chapter Fourteen

HUNTER

Some country song blasts over the loudspeakers, a guy crooning about how someone left him, as I hold the door to Genie's Country Western Bar open for Madeline. I can't tell from the lyrics if he's talking about a dog or a woman, though. Maybe even his truck.

Madeline swishes past me in a black top and jeans I've never seen her in. Then again, we're usually in athletic clothes, but even at the library she doesn't dress in shirts that show the slightest peek of her cleavage, or jeans that highlight that fantastic ass of hers.

Not that I was looking.

I'm not exactly sure what I'm doing inviting her out like this, but I really do need a drink after my shitty day. What had made it bearable, though, was knowing I'd see her later. The thought had cheered me up, strangely enough. And as we'd been walking back to my house, all I knew was that I didn't want my night with her to end yet.

So here we are.

I snag us an empty table, and almost as soon as we sit down, Patty Lee is there, asking us what we want.

"Um, I'll take a sangria," Madeline says, looking over the laminated menu.

"Oh, and some wings and mozzarella sticks." She glances over at me. "What? I haven't had dinner."

Was I giving her a look? It's just, I've never gone out with a girl who ordered that stuff on a first—

Whoa, whoa. This isn't a date. Obviously.

"And for you?" Patty asks me when I continue to sit there like a bump on a log, caught up in my thoughts.

"Oh. Fried chicken and a Yuengling on tap."

She nods and returns to the bar to put our orders in, bringing us the drinks fairly quickly. I take a long swallow of my beer, enjoying the crisp, malty flavor. Madeline sips at her drink, her gaze darting around the room.

"You ever been here?" I ask, my foot tapping to some new song on now.

"Only to pick up takeout. I've never stayed to hang out."

"You don't seem like a bar scene girl."

Even in the dimmer lighting, the slight flush on her cheeks is obvious.

"No, I'm not." She gives a self-deprecating laugh. "My scene is more staying at home with a book."

And that's exactly why we'd never be friends in real life. Without the training program, I'd probably never even have realized she moved back to town three years ago.

And what a shame that would have been. She's actually pretty fun—when she's not feeding me sponges, that is.

"Oh, yeah. That's definitely my scene, too."

She laughs, more genuinely this time. "Right. What's the last book you read, then?"

"You know, the one with the people, and the stuff . . ."

She smiles and takes a longer sip of her sangria. "I love that one."

I scratch at the back of my neck, not sure if I should say this, but it comes out, anyhow. "I started that book you gave me."

Her brows raise. "I was wondering about that. I had to renew it on my account, you know."

Shit. I didn't even think about it possibly being overdue.

She tucks her hands under her chin and leans in. "How far in are you? What do you think?"

"Well, it totally weirded me out when it started with those black-and-white pencil drawings. I didn't think there were going to be any words for a while."

She nods, excitement on her face. "I love the opening. It's so unique."

Yeah, it is. "I'm maybe a third of the way through. He just found out the guy at the toy shop didn't actually burn his journal."

"And do you like it?"

I shrug. "Yeah, it's cool. I thought you were fucking with me when you first gave it to me, but it's not so bad once you take into account the pictures, too."

"I really love that book. You know, they made a movie out of it, too."

"Yeah? Maybe you could come over one night so we can watch it together."

She gives me a strange look for a second before her face clears. "Sure."

I can't explain why, but her agreement causes my stomach to make this funny floating sensation, like I'm buoyant.

I clear my throat and take another swallow of beer. "Have you seen the movie?"

"A while ago. It's not new, maybe a decade old by now. So enough of the finer details have escaped me that I can watch it again and be surprised."

"Well, I'll have to finish up the book soon, then."

She circles her index finger around the rim of her glass. "Have you, um, had any issues reading it?"

Something about her question puts me on edge. "What do you mean? I can read."

Her hand reaches out, briefly touching my forearm. "I know you can." She presses her lips together, then smiles. "Forget I said anything."

Our food arrives then, and I order us another round of drinks, too, since both our glasses are nearly empty. We end up sharing all the food, and by the time we're finished, Madeline is noticeably more relaxed. It could be my stellar company . . . or the additional two full glasses of sangria she drank throughout dinner. She's not drunk, though, just a little looser than normal. It's about time she unwinds some.

"Did you ever think back in high school you'd be out here with me at Genie's one day?" I ask her, polishing off my second beer. I won't order another since I'm driving us home later.

She laughs, freer than she usually does, but that's only because I know the difference in her laughs now. Huh. When did that happen?

"Uh, no," she says. "Especially not when I first got there."

"Why not then?" Was there some kind of difference?

She leans in conspiratorially. "Well, we moved to Green Valley when I was fourteen, during the summer before freshman year, and I didn't know anyone. So that first day of high school was a real shocker."

Brand-new town and brand-new school? Yeah, I can see that being rough.

"I was trying to find my first class—I think it was gym—and somehow got turned around and ended up outside over by the bleachers. And guess who I saw under there making out with Lydia Marino?"

"That was your first impression of me?" Well, shit. Hope I gave her a good show.

She nods, smiling. "I'd never seen anything like it before in real life."

In real life? "What do you mean?"

"You know, like . . . sexy."

I sit up straighter in my seat. "Yeah?"

"Guess I led a sheltered life." She looks at me, then reaches out tentatively, brushing soft fingers through my hair. "Your hair was longer then."

Tingles race over my scalp and down my neck and arms. Holy fuck. Is she flirting with me?

She sticks her hand back in her lap and lets out a nervous laugh, looking over toward the dance floor. "Sorry. I don't know why I did that."

I'd probably embarrass her if I said she could do that whenever she wanted. "It's not a big deal," I murmur. I don't want her to be uncomfortable the rest of the night.

She nods, still not looking at me.

"So, did you have a big crush on me after you saw me under the bleachers?" I wait until she's looking to waggle my eyebrows for comedic effect, making sure to slap on a lascivious grin.

It does what I wanted, her stiff shoulders loosening as she rolls her eyes. "Why would watching you make out with your girlfriend make me crush on you?"

I frown. "Lydia was never my girlfriend."

"Oh. I just thought since . . ."

"No. I mean, we've hooked up. But I've never been serious enough about a girl to make her my girlfriend."

Her brows raise skeptically. "You love 'em and leave 'em?"

I shift in my seat, not liking the turn of this conversation. "That makes me sound like a player."

"Well, that's what I've heard. Remember, I did say you have a reputation."

Wiping my palms on my jeans, I stare down at my empty mug. "Right." So that's how she sees me.

"But what other people say or first impressions aren't a full reflection of a person," she continues after a beat of silence. "Some people surprise you once you get to know them."

I look up, finding her gaze steady on me. "How?" I ask, my throat suddenly dry.

She drops her gaze and plays with an abandoned straw wrapper on the corner of the table. "Sometimes the bad boy has a different side to him. He can actually be nice when he wants to be."

She's talking about me, right? I can't assume anything with her.

"And sometimes the know-it-all has a wild streak in them," I tell her.

Her brows lift in surprise. "Wild?"

"You messed with my car, my phone, my coffee, the food I ate. That's pretty wild in my book."

She holds her hands to her cheeks, her eyes going wide. "Oh my God, I just remembered I signed you up for a bunch of spam sites."

I blink at her. "What?"

"The email you put on the emergency notification sheet at the fire station. I used it to subscribe to a ton of spam."

"Oh. I never check that email. No harm done."

She gives me an exasperated glare. "But what if they need to reach you?"

"Then they can call me. But look at you. Pulling badass pranks left and right."

She bites at her bottom lip, trying to hide a smile. "It's not very like me. But I guess I can be kind of stubborn."

"You? Stubborn?" I wave my hand exaggeratedly. "Never."

She holds her hands up in surrender, the smile turning into a laugh. "Okay, okay. I get it." She stands and pushes in her chair. "I'll be right back."

She walks away, disappearing into the bathrooms on the far side of the room.

Not two seconds later, there's a scrape as her just-emptied chair is filled by Josie, a girl we went to school with. I wouldn't call us friends, more like acquaintances, but from the way she smiles at me, it seems she has more than acquainting on her mind.

"Hey, Hunter." She twirls a finger around a long strand of blonde hair. When did her hair get that long? Or blonde? Maybe they're extensions. "Are you on a date with Madeline?"

Wow. Guess she's jumping right to it. "No. Why?"

"We were wondering." She motions behind her to a group of five girls in a booth across the way, two of whom I've slept with. I wonder if they know that about each other.

"We're . . . friends," I tell her, knowing she's waiting for some kind of explanation.

Not that it seems believable, even if it is the truth. What reason would Madeline and I ever have for being friends? We're complete opposites.

Josie doesn't seem to need any further explanation, though, as her smile grows wider and she leans in. "Oh, okay." Her finger slides down my right pec. "You want to dance?"

I look down at her finger, then back at her. Coming on strong, isn't she? "I'm hanging out with Madeline tonight."

My rejection doesn't seem to faze her. "And if she weren't here? I've heard you can give a girl a good night on the dance floor."

Her finger trails down further, over my abs, straight toward . . .

I catch her wrist and set her hand away from me. It's obvious she doesn't mean just dancing. *That* dancing would end up with the two of us in her bed tonight.

Josie's a pretty girl. She could easily bag most guys here. So, why me? Why tonight? Actually, I thought she was seeing someone. What's his name? Jimmy? James? I don't remember.

"Don't you have a boyfriend?" I ask her. Not that it's been a deterrent before.

She shrugs one shoulder, her confidence finally waning. "We broke up."

Ah, so that's why she wants me. Rebound sex. Madeline really was right about my reputation.

Any other time, this would be a no-brainer. But now . . . I don't know. Something about it feels cheap. Josie doesn't know me, other than the most superficial things. And I don't know her. There's no connection other than a surface-level attraction.

She doesn't make me smile. Or surprise me. Or make me want . . . more.

"Sorry, Josie. I'm not into rebound sex anymore."

Her hand flutters toward her chest. "I was only asking to dance." She gets up and scowls at me. "You don't have to be a dick."

If there were any beer left in my mug, she'd probably fling that in my face, but she settles for flouncing off back to her friends.

If she wants to pretend she wasn't propositioning me, fine. But we both know the truth.

At least Madeline wasn't here to witness that.

When she returns from the bathroom, I don't mention anything about Josie, instead asking her if she wants to dance.

"Oh my God, no," she says, taking her seat again. "Trust me, you don't want to dance with me."

Actually, I do. I didn't want to with Josie, but with Madeline . . .

"Why?"

She chuckles. "Because I have two left feet. Besides, I thought we were here to drink."

"I already had two beers. I shouldn't have any more if I'm driving you home."

"Wow, look at you, Mr. Responsible." She nudges my shoulder. "You're a changed man."

In a way, I kind of am. With her, at least. She makes me want to be . . . better.

"Did you want to go, then?" she asks, reaching for her purse. "Since we're done?"

"No." Again, I don't want this night to be over yet. "How about we do something else?" I rack my brain for something to do. "How about truth or dare?"

Her brows knit together. "Are we twelve?"

"Come on. It'll be fun. Pick one."

She rolls her eyes. "Fine. Truth."

"Of course you'd pick that."

She shrugs, not caring.

All right. Truth. "Did you really think I was sexy in high school?" I grin and point a finger at her. "And no lying. You're under an official truth-or-dare oath."

Her gaze narrows. "I said what you were doing was sexy. Not that you were. There's a difference."

Hmm, interesting. I stroke my jaw, thinking about her response. "You didn't actually answer the question."

She huffs and twists her lips. "Okay then, yeah. Of course. Every girl thought you were."

A smirk spreads over my lips. "So you were attracted to me."

"I didn't say that."

My smirk drops. "You just said I was sexy."

"Physical attraction isn't the same as being attracted to someone. There's the mental aspect of it, as well. The emotional one. That's just as important. For me, at least."

I think back to a few minutes ago with Josie. How despite thinking that she was pretty, I wasn't interested in sleeping with her. "Okay, I get it. So what attracts you to a guy, then?"

She purses her lips, seeming to give my question thought. "Well, there's the physical attraction, obviously. But I would also want him to be kind and considerate. Someone who listens to me, who makes me laugh. Someone who makes time for me, who makes me feel like I matter."

Her mom had said she'd had a failed relationship. Did that guy do those things? Or is that why they're not together anymore?

"And that's two questions," she says. "You were only supposed to get one."

I force a smile on my face, still caught up in her answer. "Guilty. Your turn, then."

"Truth or dare?"

"Dare."

She makes a *tsking* sound. "Of course you'd pick that," she repeats. "Fine. I dare you to tell me—"

"No, no. That's the same as truth."

She grins, knowing exactly what she was doing. "Your whole life is a dare, you know that? You'd do whatever I say and have no shame about it."

I shrug. She knows me better than I thought. "Only one way to find out."

"And if I dared you to strip to your boxers and sing 'The Star-Spangled Banner' on the bar counter?"

I lean in closer. "How do you know I'm wearing boxers? I could be going commando."

She pushes me away, muttering under her breath about how ridiculous I am, and I laugh.

Tapping at her chin, she says, "No, a dare should be something that doesn't come naturally. That has some personal difficulty tied to it."

Hmm. "What diabolical scheme do you have hatching in there?" I tap the side of her head. "What have I unleashed?"

"Who me?" she asks in a faux-innocent voice, then sits straighter in her chair. "I dare you . . . to get an A on the final written exam."

My stomach drops. "That's not fair. You're setting me up to fail."

She blinks rapidly. "No, I'm not. It's a challenge, but not impossible."

I thought we were having fun, teasing each other. But this isn't fun anymore. "That isn't a dare. That's making sure you get to be a volunteer firefighter. If I pass, you pass."

"No, I'm asking you to push yourself. To go beyond what you think your limits are. You're already leaps and bounds ahead of where you were when we first started."

"Pick another dare."

She throws her hands up in exasperation. "What do you want me to dare you to do? To pants the chief?"

My lips quirk unwillingly with amusement. "Then we'd both get kicked out of the program."

"Exactly. So I stand by my original dare."

"It's not even something I can do right now. Our exam isn't for another month."

She shrugs. "I'm willing to wait."

I let out a sigh of exasperation. This is so stupid. "Fine. But you have to do an actual dare. No hiding behind truths."

Her head tilts to the side, considering me. "Okay. But you also have to answer a truth. No hiding behind dares."

I hold my hand out and she shakes it. I guess our rivalry isn't fully at rest.

"What's my truth?" I ask her.

"I have to think about it. You have a dare in mind for me?"

I study her the same way she did me. "It should be something you don't want to do. Something you'll find difficult."

"Stop using my words against me."

"Okay. I dare you to kiss me."

Chapter Fifteen
MADELINE

I stare at Hunter, not sure I heard him right.

Actually, I'm almost positive I heard him right, but I'm having trouble interpreting the words.

"Be serious," I mumble, heat stealing over my cheeks.

"I am," he says, challenge in his gaze.

He wants me to tell him it's unfair, just like he said his dare was. He wants me to demand a different dare. He wants me to be a hypocrite.

That bastard.

"And no quick peck on the lips," he says, looking now like he's having fun with the idea. "It has to be an actual kiss."

"And if I forfeit?"

Something flashes over his face, so quick I almost miss it. Disappointment? No, wouldn't he be happy if I forfeited?

His signature smirk is back. "Then I'll lord my win over you for the rest of the training program."

"Well, we can't have that." There's something about him that makes a competitive streak within me rise to the surface. I swear, no one else affects me like that. "But not in the bar."

Wait, am I actually considering this?

He pulls his car keys out of his pocket and jingles them. "Let's get you home, then."

Wait, right now? I need more time to prepare. More time to wrap my head around this.

I gape with my mouth open like a fish and he grins wider, then gets up and walks to the bar.

I sit there, not sure what he's doing, until I realize he's paying for our drinks and food. Snatching my purse, I join him, but it's too late. He's already signing the credit card slip.

"You didn't have to do that," I tell him. "I meant to pay for my own."

"No, I invited you out," he says, like it's no big deal. Like friends pay for each other's meals all the time. Do they? I never go out with anyone.

He slides the receipt and pen back over to the bartender, then guides us out of the bar and into the parking lot. He holds the passenger door of his Mustang open for me and I slide in, the cool leather soft under my fingertips. I buckle myself in and stare out the windshield at the clear, cloudless night, my stomach in knots.

What am I doing? Why did I agree to this?

The heavy rumble of the engine underneath me startles me for a second, and I glance over at Hunter as he reverses out of the space, his palm resting on the back of my headrest. This close, I can smell his cologne or aftershave or soap or whatever it is. Something fresh and masculine that I've already come to associate with him. Will it smell even better when I'm closer? When I'm kissing him?

His movements are sure and steady as he switches gears and navigates us back to my house. How is he so calm? Is it because he's kissed half the girls in town already?

Okay, not half. That'd be impossible. But . . . a lot. I'd even noticed a few girls checking him out while we were at Genie's.

And why wouldn't they? Like I told him, every girl thought he was hot stuff back in high school. And time has only been kind to him, as he's grown more handsome in that way men do.

But he didn't go home with any of them. He's going home with *me*. To kiss *me*.

My cheeks flare with heat and I look out the passenger window, hoping he doesn't see. What the hell is wrong with me? He's not *coming home with me*. That's not what this is. Jesus, Madeline. Get your head on straight.

All too soon, we're pulling into my driveway, my belly doing somersaults.

I tell my stomach to stop it. This doesn't have to be a big deal. It's a teasing dare. He's trying to get a rise out of me, the same way he did all those weeks ago when we first started the training program. But I'm onto his tricks now.

"Hunter," I say into the silence as the engine dies. "I don't want this to change things. We've finally got a good rapport going."

He's quiet for a moment. "No, it won't."

He opens his car door and I follow suit, wishing the porch light wasn't on. That we had some kind of ten-foot-tall privacy fence around the yard. That my mom wasn't inside the house, potentially peeking at us from the front window.

Damn Hunter and his stupid dare.

I could forfeit, but I couldn't bear for him to be insufferable about it for the next month.

I tug at his sleeve before he can reach the front door, directing him toward the closed garage door instead. It's in the semi-shadows and slightly more private, at least.

"So, was Genie's okay or do you think you would have liked the Pink Pony better?"

It takes me a second to get out of my head and process his question.

"It's not too late to still go, you know," he says, smiling.

His smile eases the rising tension within me enough to reply, "Genie's was perfectly fine."

I fiddle with the strap of my purse, knowing I need to get this over with. If I don't do this tonight, I'll obsess over it all weekend. "Guess I should do my dare now."

He nods, stepping closer.

If he was a gentleman, he'd notice how nervous I am and call the whole thing off. Actually, he wouldn't have dared me to begin with.

But he's not one. I knew that from the beginning.

Reaching for his shoulders, I angle my face up, taking in the dark stubble on his jaw, the way his body seems to sway toward mine, how he really does smell better even closer.

Just do it already.

Our lips touch, his warmer and softer than I was expecting, and there's a jump in my lower belly, this time not from nerves, but excitement. His lips move over mine, establishing a slow rhythm, that excitement in the pit of my stomach turning into an ache as it continues on, neither of us backing away. It's soft and drugging, lulling me under his spell, and while I may have initiated the kiss, it's soon apparent he's in charge. He changes the angle, deepening it, and a lick of heat washes over me, surprising me with its intensity.

My hands curl upward, from his shoulders to behind his neck, and I step into his hard body, pressing against him. That ache strengthens, wanting him to touch me, too. To feel those rough hands on my overheated skin. I've only felt them once before, when he gave me a massage after our first run weeks ago, but I was too out of it to appreciate them then. I didn't know I'd want him to touch me for real.

I arch into him, signaling my interest, but he doesn't touch me back. He doesn't wrap his hands around my waist and tug me even closer, until all I feel is him. He doesn't cup the back of my head and slide his hands through my hair, leaving tingles over my body.

He doesn't slip his hands under my shirt to squeeze my breasts, the way he did with Lydia that first day I saw him, over a decade ago.

Because this isn't a real kiss. This is a dare.

I break away, breathing heavily, my body betraying me by showing him exactly how much that kiss affected me.

But it looks like maybe I'm not the only one affected.

He's staring at my lips, his gaze unwavering. And he looks . . . hungry.

"Hunter," I whisper, unsure what I'm saying. What I want to happen.

His gaze flicks up to meet mine, then back at my lips before he shuts his eyes and steps further back, that earlier pull in me toward him now fading.

"See," he says. "Nothing's changed. We're good."

"We're good," I repeat, knowing nothing about this is good. How am I supposed to act normal around him tomorrow during training? Knowing what he tastes like? What it feels like to press against him?

I may not be as experienced as him, but I know he kissed me back. He didn't have to do all that. To let it go on as long as it did.

And I didn't, either.

"Do you have your question for me yet?"

I blink, taking a second to register his question. "The truth?"

He nods.

Right. The game. That's how this all started.

I look up at him, his eyes appearing darker than usual in the shadows. His lips are the slightest bit fuller, and it makes me want to touch my own lips, to see if they're swollen from his kiss.

"Why did you dare me to kiss you?" I ask, nothing else on my mind but that question.

He's silent for the longest time, his gaze roaming over me, almost as if he can see through me, see how he made me go temporarily weak with lust.

"Because you wouldn't have done it otherwise."

My brow wrinkles. "What does that mean?"

The seriousness surrounding him breaks as he wags a finger at me and tsks. "Only one question. Besides, I like seeing you squirm."

So it was to unsettle me. Well, mission accomplished.

And also my cue to leave.

"Good night," I say, turning away and fumbling for my keys in my purse. I need to get out of here before I'm tempted to reach for him again, to make an absolute fool of myself.

That wasn't an actual kiss. It wasn't anything.

Even if, for a second, it seemed like maybe it was.

* * *

"You sure you're okay?"

Hunter hands me the part I dropped for the second time, and I let out a slow breath, willing my nerves to calm. "I'm fine. Thanks."

I'm over last night. Really. I am.

And maybe if I keep repeating that, it will come true.

Hunter's been acting like his usual snarky, smirky self all morning, nothing out of the ordinary. He's right that the dare didn't mean anything.

So why am I so off-kilter?

"How about I read the directions and you do the cleaning?" I ask, handing him the regulator I keep dropping. Our fingers brush as he takes it from me, and I nearly drop it again.

Get a freaking hold of yourself, Madeline.

We're supposed to be working in pairs to learn how to maintain and clean the self-contained breathing apparatus that's part of a firefighter's standard gear. This is the stuff we'll be using when there's an actual fire. This is important and I should be paying attention, not off in la-la land.

Picking up the sheet of instructions, I read aloud, "Rotate the regulator a quarter turn clockwise to remove it from the facepiece, then take off the low-pressure hose and separate it from the Air-Pak."

I watch as he does what I say, then instruct him to take a sponge and the cleaning solution to remove debris from the outside. Normally, there wouldn't be any, but there definitely is after I dropped it.

"Didn't know I'd be cleaning today," he mutters.

"Firefighters probably have to do a lot of cleaning. All that smoke and soot that gets over everything has to be taken care of by someone."

"And because we're volunteers, we get the grunt work?"

I shrug. "We're learning the basics. Okay, now we're going to disinfect the inside. Depress the manual shutoff and close the purge knob by turning it fully clockwise, then spray four pumps of the disinfecting solution into the regulator opening."

When we finish, we clean the Air-Pak and facepiece, then switch places to do another one, this time with me cleaning it. Hunter stares at the paper, his lips moving silently, but I tell him I remember the directions so he doesn't have to read them aloud.

A look of relief crosses his face, and it reminds me I need to talk to him about that.

"Do the letters ever seem to move on the page?" I ask him casually, concentrating on scrubbing the outside of the regulator.

In my peripheral vision, I catch him frowning. "Yeah, I guess."

"Do *b*'s and *d*'s especially seem to switch on you?"

"Why?" His voice is laced with suspicion.

"Just curious." I say it as breezily as possible, not wanting him to shut down. Maybe if I have this to focus on, I'll stop thinking about last night.

"Sometimes they do," he admits.

Well, that strengthens my suspicions. "Did you have an IEP in school?"

"What the hell is that?"

Must be a no, then. Besides, from what I know of his family, they don't seem like the type to fight for an individualized education plan for their son to accommodate his needs. I don't think anyone was even aware he had special needs.

"Do you ever have trouble confusing left and right?"

"What the fuck are you getting at?" he whispers so no one else can hear. The firefighter acting as our instructor today, Dan, seems like the no-nonsense type who would call us out if he heard us cursing at one another. "You sound like you're diagnosing me with something."

I kind of am. "What, I can't make casual conversation? It's just a question. So, are you going to answer it or not?"

I almost laugh at his look of confusion, but restrain myself.

"As a kid, yeah, but who doesn't?"

"Until what age?"

"I don't know, through elementary school?"

Oh yeah, that's way later than normal.

"You going to tell me what's going on?" he demands, taking the regulator from me after I disinfect it.

I debate my options, then tell him, "I think it should wait until we're alone. Maybe next time we study."

His irritation melts away as he looks at me, probably picking up on my seriousness. "Yeah, okay."

After our self-contained breathing apparatus maintenance instruction, we're given a ten-minute break, and I head from the open engine bay over to the break room to check my phone. Three text messages and a call, all from Mom.

Mom: *Mr. Garrison came over again to remind us about our tree needing to be cut back.*

Mom: *What should we do?*

Mom: *Also, the knob to the cabinet under the sink came off.*

I sigh. Why am I the one always in charge of getting these things fixed? It would take her just as long to call a handyman or tree service as it would to tell me about it. I get that she relied on Dad to take care of that stuff, but it's been eleven years. Besides, she only works part-time. She has way more time to do this kind of stuff than me.

I mentally add the two things to my running list of household needs. The water spigot outside is leaking. The grass is overgrown and needs to be mowed. And don't get me started on the garbage disposal.

Sometimes it sucks being a homeowner. And the worst thing is, it technically isn't even my home.

"Something wrong?" Hunter asks from his spot at the break room table.

Oh, I didn't realize he was here. Guess I found something to finally take my mind off of other things.

"Just some house issues."

He cracks open an energy drink—one of those ones that'll probably give him cancer in thirty years—and takes a big swig. "What's the problem?"

I wave off his concern. "Our tree needs to be cut back and it's suddenly *a big problem*." I roll my eyes. "Guess I need to find a tree trimmer."

He sets his drink down. "I could do it for you."

"Oh no, I wasn't trying to get you to—"

"I know. Let me know when I should come over."

"Um, okay." I guess that settles that. "How much should I pay you?"

His offended look surprises me. "I'm not taking your money."

"But you already paid for last night."

"Madeline, it's not a big deal."

Harry walks in, effectively putting an end to the conversation as he asks Hunter what he thought of some recent hockey game I don't have the first clue about.

Two minutes before our break is over, a red light flashes overhead as a loud tone echoes throughout the building, and the three of us freeze, staring at the ceiling.

Dan's voice calls out in the distance, "Come on, boys. Let's get moving." He appears in the doorway of the break room a moment later. "The rest of today's instruction is canceled."

He's gone before we can ask what's going on, not that it needs much explanation.

There's an emergency.

I catch Hunter's eye and he seems to understand what I want to do without me saying anything. He follows me to the edge of the open bay, away from the action, as the firefighters on duty don their gear and prepare to leave. They work as a team, each person pulling their weight, knowing exactly what to do.

"That could be us one day," I whisper.

Beside me, Hunter swallows and nods.

"Puts it into perspective a little, huh?"

"Yeah."

By the time the fire engine leaves the station, siren screaming, both Silas and Harry have joined us. I'm not sure where the Clewis brothers are, or if they already left.

"Well, free day, I guess," Harry says, and wanders off to the parking lot. Silas follows him, leaving me and Hunter alone.

"Should we stay and keep practicing?"

He shakes my shoulder. "Come on, you heard Harry. It's a free day."

Yeah, he's right. When's the last time we even had a free weekend day?

"I could do the tree for you."

I look over at him, confused. He'd spend his one day off doing something for me? "Are you sure?"

He shrugs. "Yeah. I've got nothing else going on."

It's strange how before getting to know him, I thought his free time would have been spent with endless parties and whatnot. Maybe even an orgy or two.

But he's been diligent about training with me pretty much every night the past few weeks, either jogging or working on my upper body strength, or both. Not to mention the three nights a week we still go to the library to study. I haven't seen any evidence he leads any kind of wild lifestyle.

"Okay, that'd be great." It'll get my mom and Mr. Garrison off my back and let me check another thing off my never-ending household to-do list. "You can come over whenever."

He nods. "Will a pole saw work or do I need my chainsaw?"

He actually owns one of those? Then again, he works with lumber all day. I guess it makes sense. Also, I have no idea what a pole saw is.

"Um . . ."

"I'll bring both," he says when I can't answer. "Do you have a ladder at your place? I have one, but I'll have to figure out another way to get it to your house than my car."

Right. Mustangs aren't exactly equipped for hauling around stuff like that. "We have one." I'm pretty sure.

"All right. See you soon."

He taps the back of my hand in a friendly goodbye gesture and leaves, his footsteps loud in the now-empty bay.

I can't believe he offered to help like that, especially when I didn't even ask. Not that I think he's unhelpful. Now that I consider it, he's actually done an incredible amount. All the time and effort he's put into helping me train is ridiculous. Everything we do is tailor-made specifically for me and my goals, and we've trained together enough by now that he knows how to strike that balance between pushing me when I need it and backing off when I'm at my limit. I'd be paying out the nose to get that kind of personalized attention at a gym.

And not only that, but now he's paying for my meals and drinks when we go out and then kissing me . . . What does it mean? Does it mean anything? Or is it a separate set of coincidences I'm making into a thing?

Curse my overanalytical mind.

It's probably nothing. I'm being ridiculous. Overthinking things as usual. I mentioned I had a problem and he offered to fix it. I should accept it at face value and move on. Nothing to it.

Then why don't I fully believe myself?

Chapter Sixteen
HUNTER

Cleaning up the tree in Madeline's yard is easy enough work, though she told me herself she wouldn't have the first clue how to get started. Funny how she can be so smart about other things and not know how to do something like this.

She watches me work for the first five minutes or so, but when I ask her if she likes ogling my muscles, she scowls and heads inside. Laughing to myself, I continue working, my thoughts turning—yet again—to last night and that hot kiss in her driveway as I'd dropped her off. Who knew she had it in her to be that seductive?

It'd been obvious she was teasing me, cleverly turning my dare against me. And damn her if it didn't work. It had been all I could do to keep my hands to myself as she'd wrapped her arms around my shoulders and pressed herself against me, her body soft and yielding. Pretending to be that into the kiss had been a low blow on her part, but she had no idea how much it had meant to me. How much I had wanted to kiss her. How pathetic I've become to resort to begging for a kiss from her, when girls normally beg me.

But those other girls aren't Madeline.

If I had called her bluff and really kissed her, gripping her ass and pulling her into me, making good on all she was promising, she would have freaked out. Would have told me I took it too far. And she would have been right.

Lusting after Madeline Woodward hadn't been on my radar that first day of firefighter training, but here we are. She's just . . . so much more than I expected.

When I'm nearly finished, she brings a cold water bottle out for me, and I gratefully accept it, downing half of it in one go.

"Mom's making lunch and insists you stay," she says, a hint of exasperation in her tone.

So, her mom wants me to stay, but does she? The last time I was over, I stayed at her mom's invitation to spite her. But things are different now.

"Do you want me to stay?" I ask her.

Her head tilts to the side. "Why wouldn't I?"

I shrug, feeling dumb now. "I don't know. The way you phrased it . . . Never mind. Yeah, I'll stay for lunch."

She steps closer, laying a hand on the back of my arm for a brief second, her touch imprinted there even after her hand returns to her side. "I'm sorry if I didn't make you feel welcome. You are, you know. And I really do appreciate you working on this today. I, um . . ." She presses her lips together. "I actually made you something inside as a thank you."

She made me something? "What is it?"

"Come in when you're finished."

She walks away, leaving me staring after her. She's going to leave me in suspense like that?

I finish as quickly as I can and cram the cut branches into the yard recycling bin, then join her indoors, the air conditioning blessedly cool.

Madeline is in the kitchen, pulling a pan of heavenly smelling brownies out of the oven.

"There better not be sponges in there," I tell her.

She laughs and my heart beats a little harder, loving the sound of it. It's only in the last few weeks she's opened herself up enough around me to do that.

"They're brownies, I promise. I'll even take the first bite myself."

"What are you two laughing about in here?" her mom asks, bustling in and pulling deli cold cuts out of the fridge.

"Nothing," Madeline says, her eyes still dancing with mirth.

I'm glad we can laugh about it now. That it feels like our own private joke.

For lunch, we have sub sandwiches with all the fixings and a homemade baked potato soup that has me wanting to lick the bowl it's so good. In my opinion, it's a perfectly fine trade-off to have to listen to Madeline's mom talk all throughout the meal if it means I get to eat her food.

This time, Madeline doesn't seem as annoyed or embarrassed by her mom, that is until the topic turns to more things that need to be fixed around the house.

"Now while you're here," Vera says, "it would mean the world to us if you could take a look at the outside hose that's been leaking. Oh, and do you know anything about fixing cabinet knobs? The one in the kitchen fell off the other day."

"Mom," Madeline grits out. "Hunter isn't our personal on-call handyman. It was already so generous of him to help us out with the tree."

"Oh, I know it was." She gives me a warm smile filled with Southern charm. "But it's not every day we get a big, strong man over here. We have to take advantage while we can."

Madeline's hand slides along her temple, as if she's trying to hide, and mutters something unintelligible under her breath. The only words I can make out are *his ego*.

"I could take a look at it, Mrs. Woodward."

"You call me Vera, honey." She wags a finger at me good-naturedly and pushes her chair back from the table. "I'll get my list."

"Don't get your list," Madeline calls after her mom, who's already left the kitchen. She turns to me next. "You're not actually doing anything on that list."

I lean back in my chair, crossing my arms over my chest. "Why are you so resistant to me helping?"

"I'm not. But I'm also not going to take advantage of you. She's ridiculous for thinking you're going to come over here and do all this stuff for free."

"Why is it ridiculous?"

A line forms between her brows. "Because it is."

My lips curl at the corners, unable to help my smile. "I've never met anyone with a stronger sense of fairness than you."

That line between her brows deepens. "What?"

I shrug. "Fairness. Justice. Quid pro quo. Whatever you want to call it. Not everything has to be a completely equal exchange, you know."

She looks down at the table, circling a figure eight in the wood grain. "I guess I do like things to be fair."

"Of course you do. That's why you couldn't let my pranks slide."

She blinks up at me, seeming to consider my words. "I never thought about it like that. When did you get so insightful?"

I lean forward, resting my elbows on the table. "You think I haven't noticed anything about you?"

Her eyes widen the slightest bit. "I didn't know you were looking."

"Yeah," I murmur. "I've been looking."

She ducks her head again as her mom returns, but she can't fully hide the faint flush that steals over her cheeks.

Her reaction has something hot settling in the pit of my stomach. Something I don't want to examine too closely at the moment, especially with her mom in the room.

Vera hands her a page that appears to be ripped out of a notebook. "Why don't you show Hunter the hose outside? Oh, and that wasp nest out there, too."

Instead of arguing, Madeline silently gets up and leads the way out of the house through the garage. She hits the button for the garage door and stops in front of an ancient-looking toolbox on a shelf off to the side.

"I tried tightening the thing around the hose last week, but I didn't know what I was doing."

I sift through the random assortment of tools, none of them matching. "Is it leaking from the spigot or is there a hole in the hose itself?"

"The spigot. Listen, you don't really have to—"

"Madeline. I like being able to do this for you. I like feeling . . . useful." It's weird saying that out loud, even putting it into words to begin with. But it's the truth.

She looks up at me, studying my face. "That's why you joined the training program?"

I lift a shoulder in a shrug. "I guess."

"Okay. But I still feel like I should do something for you, too."

I shake my head. "There's no keeping score anymore. We're a team. And I wouldn't do this for anyone else. Just you."

I'm not sure what I'm trying to tell her, but she picks up on it all the same, seeming to shift closer without moving as she nods in agreement.

The urge to kiss her again is overwhelming, filling me up, screaming at me to close the distance and fit my mouth to hers. With any other girl, it'd be a no-brainer. But I don't want to mess this up. Everything is so different with her. More . . . important.

I take too long, though, and the moment slips by. She steps away, her face angled away from me, and she grabs a can of wasp spray off another shelf.

"I've been meaning to use this stuff for a while," she says, something in her voice off. "I never seem to have time to do everything I need to do."

"Yeah," I agree dumbly, staring at the back of her head, cursing myself for not taking the chance when I had it.

What if she wasn't feeling the same way, though? What if this attraction is entirely one-sided? Because I can't deny it to myself any longer.

I want Madeline.

"Let me show you the hose," she says, walking toward the open garage door.

I grab the toolbox and follow her, finding it's a simple fix with the right wrench. We power through most of the list in the next hour, though there are a few things I can't do without making a trip to the hardware store. Madeline forbids me from doing that, though. She says she's taken up enough of my weekend already.

I want to tell her she could take up all of it and it wouldn't be enough.

Jesus, where is this coming from? It's like that kiss last night unlocked a need for her I hadn't admitted to myself. Hadn't known could be this strong.

I soak up the praise her mom heaps on me as I leave, and Madeline promises to be over at my house at the normal time for our workout later. Today is chest and back, then a twenty-minute run. Pretty soon, I want to start her on interval training, but I don't think she's ready quite yet.

I linger for a second, wanting to kiss her goodbye, but that's not what this is. That's not who we are. I need to remember that. Just because I dared her to kiss me, because she actually did it, doesn't mean anything's changed for her.

Only me.

When I return home, I slump on the couch, glancing at the clock. Three hours until Madeline gets here. I'm fucking pathetic. I can't remember the last time I even pursued a girl. Girls come to me, as evidenced by Josie at the bar last night. I have a feeling my normal tactics wouldn't work with Madeline, though. She doesn't care about shallow things like sex appeal. That hadn't been anywhere on her list of things that attracts her to a guy.

And, to be honest, that's pretty much all I have going for me.

My reputation is a point against me in her book, not a benefit. And even if it was, I'm not looking for one night with her. Not that I know exactly what it is I'm looking for, but it's more than that. One night would only be the beginning. I want to discover everything about her. What makes her gasp. Makes her moan. Makes her call out my name.

But also the other things I've never thought all that much about with another person. What makes her happy or laugh or cry. I'm already well versed in what pisses her off. It makes me realize there's really no one in my life I know all that about. That I only know the most superficial things about the people I sometimes hang out with on the weekends, about my coworkers, even about my goddamn family that I actively avoid.

For the first time, I want someone to know all those things about me, too. I've held others at arm's length, not letting them get close. Not letting them see the real me. Why?

Because then they'd know for sure how stupid you are.

The little voice pops up out of nowhere, and as awful as it is, I can't dismiss it. Maybe it's right.

Madeline has to know by now, though. Right? She's with me all the time at the library. She knows how slow I read. How it takes me a couple of passes through to understand it. How it's easier for her to tell me everything I need to know rather than read it myself.

After we started working together, she hasn't brought it up. Only asked me those weird questions earlier today. I forgot to ask her about it at her house, but she said she'd tell me the next time we study. Guess it can wait, then.

On the side of the coffee table, the book Madeline gave me from the library sits, and I pick it up, opening to the spot I'd stopped at last night. I'd been motivated to read more after talking with her about it yesterday, and I'd made more progress than I expected. I've got time to kill this afternoon, too. Maybe I could even finish it.

I chuckle to myself. And maybe pigs will fly.

Chapter Seventeen
MADELINE

Looking up at the sky for approximately the millionth time since we started our run, I eye the dark clouds rolling in toward us that seemingly popped up out of nowhere. The weather was fine all afternoon. Is it Murphy's Law that it would only turn bad as soon as I need it to be nice?

"You worried about that?" Hunter asks, pointing above. Though he usually runs behind me, today he's beside me. Not like we could have a conversation, though. I'm always breathing too hard to talk.

I nod and he asks, "You want to cut it short?"

A clap of thunder overhead has a yelp escaping from me, and he laughs. I push at the immovable wall of his shoulder and tell him I want to head back, though we're probably still almost ten minutes away from his house.

Thunder rumbles again, and a few minutes later, the downpour comes, soaking us to the bone. It's one of those summer showers that goes from zero to sixty with little warning, but there's nothing to do other than keep running the last five minutes, even when I accidentally step in a puddle that submerges my foot up to the ankle.

Lovely.

The sight of Hunter's home in the distance is the best thing I've seen in a long while, though I'm a cold, shivery mess as we finally reach it and he opens the garage door for us. I shove my hair out of my face, sure I look like a drowned rat, but I can't care about that as I pant, catching my breath after that last sprint.

"Let me get towels for us," Hunter says, toeing off his shoes by the door that leads inside.

I nod, a puddle forming around me as water drips from my clothes onto the concrete floor.

My eyes widen as he strips off his shirt and drops it on the floor, raindrops running in rivulets over his impressive chest and down the length of his flat abs. He's never taken his shirt off around me before, even when working out. Sure, I've seen his clothes cling to him, but that's nothing compared to the sight of him like this, so close I could reach out and brush my fingers over the dusting of hair on his pecs. Over the hard ridges of his abdomen. Over the dark trail of hair that leads into his gym shorts.

The dripping shorts in question come off next, followed by his socks. That leaves him in only a pair of tight boxer briefs, molded over him in a way that leaves little to the imagination.

He turns and I school my expression to remove the shock from it, not wanting to appear like a prude.

"Be right back," he says, leaving me alone in the garage.

My hand cups the back of my neck, feeling the heat there, despite the chill surrounding me. He was undressing so he wouldn't drip water all over the house. It was a practical thing, not a sexual one.

If I'd seen his body like that before he kissed me, though, I might have been more insistent as I pressed against him.

Oh God, I'm awful. Hunter does not think of me like that. He's called me a know-it-all. A teacher's pet. He didn't even touch me when I kissed him.

This is only a biological reaction to seeing a mostly naked man. That's it. Hunter's body is Greek sculpture–worthy. It only makes sense I'd drool a little.

Yeah, that's it.

When he returns, he has an oversized towel looped over his shoulders, hiding that amazing body, but I don't focus on that as he spreads an identical towel over me, enveloping me in soft, fluffy terry cloth.

"Oh my God, that's amazing," I murmur, wrapping myself into a towel cocoon.

"You're welcome to use my shower," he says, eyeing me with amusement. "To get actually warm."

A hot shower sounds heavenly, but it wouldn't solve the problem. "I'd only be changing into wet clothes again afterward."

He shrugs. "I'll stick them in the dryer and you can borrow a shirt and boxers until they're done. But I can't help you with the . . ." His gaze flicks to my chest and back up. "The bra."

Tingles spread over my chest at his attention, and I mentally scold myself. Stop being ridiculous.

I should suck it up and drive home. It's not like it's a far distance.

But it is still raining . . . and I'm pretty cold, even with the towel . . .

"Okay," I say, agreeing before consciously deciding to. "Thank you."

"Yeah, no problem."

I take my shoes and socks off before going in the house, but don't strip off my clothes the way he did, instead holding the towel tighter around me. He leads me past the guest bathroom I've used a few times, and further into the house where I've never been.

We enter his bedroom and I pause in the doorway, taking in the king-sized bed covered in a soft-looking gray comforter. Matching nightstands flank either side of the bed, along with a dresser on the opposite wall. Again, I'm surprised at how nicely it's decorated in here, with brushed silver lamps and a beautiful map art print hung above the headboard. I'd love a place like this. Too bad I'm stuck with Mom for the foreseeable future.

I didn't take Hunter as the kind of guy who would care that much about his surroundings, but it was obvious from the first day I came over he didn't have some gross, half-furnished bachelor pad. Maybe an ex of his helped decorate when he moved in? No, he said he doesn't have any exes.

Just conquests.

I shake off the thought and follow him to the en suite bathroom, where he's waiting for me.

"I could use the shower in the guest bathroom, you know," I tell him.

"Nah, this one's a lot nicer. It's a walk-in."

I peek around him at the luxuriously big shower. There's no way that came standard with this house. It even has one of those overhead rainfall showerheads.

I almost make a joke about getting out of the rain, only to shower in the rain again, but I don't. My tongue feels too big for my mouth, something about being in his personal space messing with my head.

"Your home is so nice," I say instead. "I really love it."

A shy smile creeps over his face, transfixing me. It's the first time I've seen him smile without any trace of mischief or amusement or any of the other things he normally infuses into it.

"Thanks," he says softly. "This place is important to me." He shifts the towel on his shoulders, looking down. "I kind of think of it as my sacred space."

"I can see why."

His lips part, as if he's going to say something, then he shakes his head. "Let me get you some clothes to change into."

Right. The shower. That's why I'm here.

A moment later, he hands me a faded Green Valley High Athletics T-shirt and a pair of blue plaid boxers. "You might have to roll down the waist a few times to get them to fit."

I nod as I accept them, sudden nerves coursing through me. Why am I nervous? All I'm doing is taking a shower.

"Do you want me to put your clothes in the dryer before or after your shower?"

"Um, before, I guess. So they finish quicker."

He steps out of the doorway to the bathroom, and I shut the door, dropping the towel to the floor. The sodden fabric of my clothes clings to me, and I have to practically peel everything off, then wring it out over the sink. I situate the towel around me and open the door, handing him the wet pile.

His gaze rakes over me as he takes it, not that there's anything to see. The towel fully covers me. His gaze meets mine again, something in the depths I can't define. Like he's holding something back.

I don't understand what it means, and when he doesn't say anything, I slowly close the bathroom door again, saying, "I'm going to shower now."

He nods but doesn't move as I shut the door practically in his face. Okay, that was weird.

Turning, I catch sight of myself in the mirror and nearly laugh at the way the rain plastered my hair to my head. No wonder he was staring. I really do look like a drowned rat.

I set the water to hot and get in, indulging in the steam it produces and the rainfall showerhead that I make a mental note to add to my Amazon list for my own shower. This is divine.

The shampoo he uses smells pretty standard, but as I crack open the bodywash, I discover that elusive scent of his. I inhale deeply from the bottle, sighing. I'm probably a weirdo, but I've always loved the smell of men's products. While other girls complained back in high school about swimming through clouds of Axe body spray, I secretly reveled in it.

Lathering up, I study the picture on the front of the bottle, where a kraken fights a bear. I don't get the branding at all, but at least it smells good. After a few more minutes, I finally shut the water off and find a fresh towel in the small linen closet in the corner to dry off with.

I have no shame in poking around the closet, but there's nothing of interest in there. Up next is the medicine cabinet, where the only semi-embarrassing thing I can find is an open container of gas relief pills. Come on, I thought he'd have something better than that in there.

He doesn't have any hair-detangling spray, unfortunately, so I brush out the snarls in my hair with his hairbrush, sans product. It doesn't look like he even owns a hair dryer.

How many other girls have discovered the lack of a hair dryer the morning after sleeping over here? My gaze lands on the shower, thinking about all the girls that have showered there, too. Hunter was probably in there with them, fucking them against the tile wall.

My stomach drops, and I push the sour sensation away. Hunter can do whatever he wants, especially in his own home.

I dress quickly, but linger before I leave his bedroom, staring at the bed. Even more than the shower, how many girls have slept there? How many have rolled around on that mattress with him, screaming his name?

My gaze flicks to the nightstands next. He probably has crazy sex toys and condoms and lube and God knows what else in there. My fingers itch with the sudden urge to rip open the drawers and discover what's in there, to paw through his personal belongings like a madwoman, enraged about something that has absolutely nothing to do with me.

I squeeze my eyes shut and force myself out of the room before I do something I regret, and stop short outside of the kitchen. Hunter's dressed in casual clothes, his profile to me. His lips are moving, brows narrowed in concentration as he reads the back of a frozen pizza box.

As he notices me, his head jerks up and he nearly drops the box, like I caught him doing something he shouldn't. He hates when I watch him read. I usually pretend to look at the textbook when he reviews my notes to quiz me at the library.

"Hey, you feel better?"

I stare at him blankly. How'd he know what I was thinking in his room?

"After your shower?" he prompts when I'm silent. "Now that you're warm and dry?"

Right. Duh. "Yeah," I tell him. "Thanks."

"You want to split this with me?" he asks, holding up the pizza. "It's still raining and your clothes aren't dry yet. I was thinking we could watch a movie. Maybe that one based on the Hugo book?"

He stumbles over the last couple of words, his pitch higher than usual, then bites at his bottom lip. Is he . . . nervous?

"I thought we were going to wait until you finished reading it," I say, not sure what to make of this.

He runs a hand through his hair and ducks his head. "I actually finished it today, after I got back from your house." His voice is more normal now, modestly pleased with himself. "It's probably the first book I ever read all the way through."

Guilt swamps me at my thoughts from earlier. Here he is offering me dinner and the use of his home. Reading a book that *I* asked him to. And I'm irrationally angry at him for having an active sex life? Just because I don't have one doesn't mean he can't. It's none of my business, anyway.

"Pizza sounds great," I tell him. "And I'd love to watch the movie with you."

His answering smile is tinged with relief. "Great. I was hoping you'd say yes."

"Why?"

One of his shoulders lifts in a shrug. "I like hanging out with you."

He does? Funny, but I feel the same way. What a strange path we've been on, that what started as a punishment is something we both like now.

He sets the pizza on the counter and preheats the oven, then rips open the box.

"Would it be corny if I said I was proud of you for finishing the book?" I ask, watching him get out a pizza pan from a lower cabinet.

He glances at me, then back at the pizza.

"It would."

"Well, I'm going to say it anyway." I lean against the counter, swirling my finger around a pattern in the faux-granite surface. "I'm proud of you for trying something new and succeeding."

Even from across the kitchen, the sudden warmth in his cheeks is apparent.

"I finished a book. Big deal."

"You said yourself it was your first one. That deserves some fanfare."

He gives me a sardonic look. "You got some confetti hidden in a back pocket I don't know about?"

I look down at myself. "Well, they're your boxers. You tell me."

When I glance back up, there's unexpected heat in his eyes. "They look good on you, by the way."

Now it's my turn to blush. "Um, thanks." The back of my neck burns, but I resist the urge to touch it. Time to get back on track. "So, how are we going to watch this movie?"

Chapter Eighteen
MADELINE

We end up renting the movie online, pausing it partway through to get our pizza, the top smothered with pepperoni and cheese, just how I like it. I make note of the brand because I've never had it before. He offers me a beer but I decline, wanting to keep my wits about me. The last time I drank around him, I agreed to his crazy dare.

Somehow, by the end of the movie, we're sitting side by side underneath one throw blanket, which I swear I don't remember happening. Maybe I was too caught up in the movie.

His whole right side is warm against my left, but I scoot away, putting space between us. On the screen, the credits roll, the rest of the room dark, the rain outside long gone. I should see about getting my clothes and heading home. There's no reason to be here any longer.

And yet, I don't.

I look over at him, finding him already looking at me, his expression unreadable.

"Did you like the movie?" I ask.

He grabs the remote and pauses the credits, down at the production assistants no one pays attention to at this point in the listing. "Yeah. You?"

I nod, finding a loose string on my borrowed shirt and looping it around my index finger. "What did you like best?"

He reaches out and places his hand on mine briefly, stopping my nervous action. "That I got to watch it with you."

Then, holding eye contact with me, he tucks a loose strand of hair that's fallen forward behind my ear. Carefully. Slowly. Giving me time to stop him. To pull away. To let him know that's beyond the bounds of this tentative friendship we've forged.

But I don't. Instead, my breathing picks up as his thumb sweeps over my jaw and down my neck, tingles racing in its wake.

He leans forward and presses his lips to mine, so gently I'm not sure it's really happening. Not sure I'm dreaming all of this. Maybe I'll wake at any moment to discover it's time to head to the fire station for the day.

He cups my face and deepens the kiss, his mouth warm and encouraging, and I let myself drift away, not wanting to face all the reasons we shouldn't be doing this. I only want to feel him as he makes good on all those things I wanted last night but he didn't give.

His other hand slides through my hair, his nails scraping softly against my scalp, and a whole-body shudder runs through me, a moan escaping me. He does it again, his hand on my face sliding down my body to my lower back, pulling me closer. I comply, wanting his warmth, his touch.

His hand moves even lower, gripping my ass, and I arch into his touch, wanting more. There's this deep rumble in his chest, then he shifts, picking me up and adjusting me so I'm on his lap, straddling him. I'm momentarily shocked out of my stupor, but then he's kissing me again, both his hands on my ass now, pressing me against his hardening length. Oh my God, that feels good.

A mixture of desire and lust and wanting swirls in my gut as I go along with it, my hands greedy as they run over his broad shoulders, then into his hair, tugging at the thick strands. His lips break from mine and travel over my jaw to my neck, sucking gently on the tender skin. It's as if there's a line directly from that spot to the core of me, pressure building, and I shift against him, needing relief.

"That's it, baby. Ride me," he whispers against my neck, and I bite my lip to contain the moan that wants out. He sounds so sexy, his voice full of rough promise.

One of his hands stays on my ass, guiding me in the rhythm, the other slipping under my shirt to press hot against my back. I'm suddenly aware I'm not wearing a bra, that it's still in the dryer. My breasts ache with a heavy fullness, anticipating his touch, and as his hand moves to my front, trailing up my stomach, I hold my breath, desperately wanting more.

He strokes the underside of my breast with light passes, until I'm practically straining against him, and as he finally fully cups me, I bear down harder on him, riding him like he said, seeking a pleasure I haven't experienced in what feels like forever.

"You like that?" he murmurs, squeezing me gently, then switching breasts to do the same to the other.

I nod frantically, and as his thumb rubs my nipple, teasing it into a hard peak, the edge I've been hurtling toward is suddenly there. I cry out as the orgasm overtakes me, swift and sure, my nails digging into his shoulders as I ride him for all I'm worth.

I'm panting as he releases my breast, his hand resting on my hip, and I lean back, a fluid, boneless, tingly sensation spreading all through me.

Hunter's gaze is hazy with lust as he watches me. "Did you come?"

That boneless feeling fades, a rigid panic taking its place. Oh my God, I did. I came on top of Hunter, dry humping him like there's no tomorrow, our clothes still fully on. And in an embarrassingly short amount of time, too. What is wrong with me?

"I, um . . ." I scramble off of him, tripping over my feet, and land hard on my ass on the floor.

He leans forward to help me up and I scoot back, not wanting his hands on me. I can't think right when his hands are on me.

My face is an inferno as I get to my feet, not knowing how to explain myself, how to explain that I didn't mean to do what we just did, how all of this is happening too fast.

So, I do what any crazy girl would do. I bolt.

"Thank you for letting me borrow your clothes," I mumble, already halfway to the door. "And dinner. And the movie." Wait, was this a date? No, of course not. What am I thinking? "I have to go," I say, as if that wasn't obvious.

He stands and my lips part as my gaze zeroes in on his hard-on, straining at the thin fabric of his gym shorts. I'm awful to leave him like this, high and dry while I already got mine. But I can't . . . I don't know how to undo what I've already done.

I grab my purse and search the front door area for my shoes, then remember they're in the garage. Shit. They're probably still soaking wet, anyway. I'll get them another time. Or, better yet, I'll buy new ones. Same with my clothes in the dryer. Because I'm going home to bury myself in a hole so deep, I'll never have to face Hunter again. How can I?

He calls my name as I open the door, but I don't stick around. The sidewalk is wet, everything outside misted in a fine dew from the rain earlier, but I ignore all that as I fumble in my purse for my keys, needing to find the unlock button on the fob.

"Madeline."

I make the mistake of glancing behind me, Hunter barefoot and jogging toward me. No, no, no. I'm not ready for this. I have no idea what any of this was. If he's actually attracted to me or maybe he was just horny. Maybe he was looking for a quick hookup.

But that's not me. I don't do things like this.

I finally find the right button, but then his hand is on the driver's side door, preventing me from opening it. Why can't he let me escape with a scrap of dignity left?

"I'm sorry," he says, and I pause, an apology the last thing I expected from him. "I didn't mean to go too fast or push you into anything you weren't ready for. I thought you were on board with it."

I stare up at him, at the sincerity on his face. And underneath that, the vulnerability. The worry. As if he's afraid he messed this up.

No, I messed it up.

"Do you want to talk about it?" he asks when I stay silent.

I squeeze my eyes shut, knowing what he's suggesting is the right thing to do. The responsible thing. He deserves it.

"Tomorrow," I whisper through dry lips, taking the coward's way out. I need time to think this through, to figure out how to explain myself. To figure out what I want out of all this.

Because I don't have the first clue at the moment.

"You'll be at training?"

I nod, owing him that at least.

"I'll see you then."

He steps back. Doesn't reach for me. Doesn't try to kiss me. He's giving me space. The space I implicitly asked for when I ran from him like a crazy person.

I get in my car, the pedals feeling weird under my bare feet, but I ignore that as I back out of his driveway and speed away, until I can't see him in the rearview mirror anymore. The tears come then, hot and urgent, until my vision is so blurry, I have to pull over.

What the hell is wrong with me? Am I mad at myself for screwing everything up? For risking everything we've built so far for a quick release? Out of the two of us, I'm supposed to be the responsible one. Hunter and I have to work together for another month until the exams, and adding sex to the mix is a terrible idea. What if it all goes wrong?

And what if it goes right? What if he's everything you never knew you wanted in a man?

I shove that thought aside, not willing to entertain it. I'll figure this out. I will.

There are no other options.

* * *

THE NEXT DAY at the fire station seems to both simultaneously drag on forever and zip by. Hunter asks me in the morning if I'm okay, but otherwise doesn't mention last night. The ball is in my court, and though I stayed up way too late thinking about it, I don't have an answer for him other than I don't want to potentially mess things up between us. That's what it boils down to.

I leave for lunch so I don't have to talk to him, just like the coward I am, but I can't escape him when we're dismissed in the late afternoon. He walks me to my car, waiting for the others to leave, and asks if I'm ready to talk.

I nod, even as I think to myself, what man wants to talk about something like this? Don't men actively avoid talking about their relationship status?

Not that this is a relationship.

"I don't really understand what happened last night," I say, looking down at my backup pair of sneakers, the ones that are older and worn down. I still have to get my stuff from his house. "How all of a sudden we were making out when a month ago we were at each other's throats."

He tucks his hands in his pockets and leans against the hood of my car, sighing. "What's that saying? There's a fine line between love and hate."

I look up at him sharply. Love?

He pales, as if he realizes what he said. "Not that we were at either of those extremes. I don't love you. Or hate you." He runs a hand through his hair, tugging at the ends, then mutters, "Shit."

His unease actually sets me more at ease. "I get what you mean. We've had strong reactions to each other since the beginning."

"Right," he says, nodding.

My hands twist together in front of me, tugging at the hem of my shirt. "But I wasn't expecting that at all. I thought that kiss Friday night was a joke. Something you did as part of the game. I didn't know it would turn into anything more."

Something like shame crosses his face for a second. "Sorry I tricked you."

Tricked me? "What?"

He toes a line in the gravel between us, then wipes it away with his foot. "Because I wanted to kiss you and you didn't feel the same."

My breath catches in my throat. He what? "But you stopped the kiss. I wanted to take it farther and you didn't."

He pauses, looking up at me. "I thought you were teasing me."

"No, I . . . I was into it."

"I was, too. I've wanted to kiss you for a while."

He has? "Since when?"

He runs a hand through his hair again, thinking. "Since that day you rubbed glitter all over me and threatened me not to shoulder bump you."

So I'm not crazy. He really did want to kiss me that day.

"But I didn't let myself think about it again until the other night," he continues. "I wasn't sure I had a chance with you. I'm still not."

A chance with me? Like he wants to date me? No, that's ridiculous. That's not what he means. He must mean a night together. The way he does with all those other girls.

"I . . . I don't know what to say," I mumble.

One side of his mouth lifts in a half smile. "Can't believe I made you speechless."

I nudge his shoulder, glad we're still on good enough terms for him to tease me. "Be serious."

"I am. You always have something to say."

Nodding, I look down at my shoes again. I don't want to look at him for this next part. "We have a month left of training. A month left to be partners. And I don't want anything to ruin that. For other feelings and emotions to possibly undo everything we've worked so hard to build."

He's silent for a few moments, but I don't glance up at him. "You think it would?"

"I don't know," I admit. "But I'm afraid to jeopardize it. I could continue the physical training by myself if I had to, since you showed me everything I need to do. But the studying . . . I think you really need me for that."

He doesn't respond, and as the silence stretches out, a breeze picks up, blowing loose tendrils of my hair in my face. I think back to last night as Hunter had tucked my hair behind my ear. How gentle he was. How he'd kissed me with such passion afterward.

No, no. Don't think of that.

"You can tell me you're not interested," he says, his tone harder than expected. "I'm a big boy. I can take it."

I finally look up at him again, at his carefully neutral expression. "It's not that. I'm just trying to be practical. We're so close to getting what we both want."

"And if what I want has changed?"

A shiver runs over me at the look in his eye. Does he mean he wants me? It certainly seemed like he did last night.

But that's temporary. Fleeting. I can't risk it all for a night with him. That's crazy.

I laugh nervously, the sound escaping me unwillingly. "We agreed to be training partners. Not anything more."

He moves closer, his hand settling on my hip. "I want more. I want you."

I swallow past the sudden thickness in my throat, reeling for a moment before I get myself under control. He can't be serious. He probably has residual horniness from last night. Did he take care of himself after I left? Did he think of me when he did it?

Oh my God, what is wrong with me? It's not the time to be thinking of that. "You . . . you're probably just excited by the thrill of the chase. Because I'm not the kind of girl you're usually with."

He releases his hold on my hip and steps back, out of reach. "Yeah, you're probably right." His voice is expressionless, jaw set tight.

Oh, no. I hurt his feelings. Playing back the words in my head, they're practically one big insult. "Hunter, I—"

"I can't go running tonight," he says, backing away toward his car. "I have stuff I need to do."

Pressure builds behind my eyes. He won't even look at me now. "Okay." I swallow again, willing myself not to cry. "Text me if you're available tomorrow to study." We always go to the library on Mondays.

He nods curtly and gets in his car, the engine of his Mustang rumbling to life a moment later. He peels out of the parking lot, and I sniff loudly in the following silence, running my hand under my nose. I will not cry two days in a row.

Even if I have a feeling I just lost a whole lot more than I bargained for.

Chapter Nineteen

HUNTER

I drive aimlessly for I'm not sure how long, not wanting to go back to my house. Not wanting to remember Madeline on my sofa, kissing me with abandon, my hands all over her. The way she'd cried out as she came, totally uninhibited. I've never seen her like that before.

And I desperately want to again.

But she's not interested in that, apparently. She thinks I only want her because she's a novelty. That I'll tire of her as soon as I have her. As if I'm some animal.

How can I fault her for thinking that, though? My track record with girls isn't doing me any favors. Maybe who I'm really mad at is . . . myself.

How can I convince her I'm not that guy? That things are different with her? Especially when she made perfectly reasonable points about us still working together for the next month.

Can't she ever be unreasonable? Can't she ever do something simply because she wants to without considering every angle?

And how sad is it that I'm basically admitting I'm a mistake? That to be with me, it means she'd be making the wrong decision.

Fucking hell.

I eventually end up out at Bandit Lake. A guy I work with said he was having a party out here tonight at a friend's house. I don't even know whose house it is, but I know enough people here to not stick out. Grabbing a beer, I nod at others but don't let myself get sucked into conversation. I thought this would be better than being alone, but it doesn't seem I'm in the right headspace for company, either.

A guy passes by with a joint, offering me a hit, and I shake my head.

"You sure?" he asks, eyes glazed over.

"I don't smoke," I tell him. It'd be hypocritical of me to use the same stuff I get on Dad and Nate's case about selling.

"You still won't smoke weed?" a new voice asks. I don't have to look to know it's Lydia.

She takes a drag from the stranger's joint and hands it back to him, smiling. He gives her a sloppy smile back and continues on his way.

"No," I say, taking a small sip of my beer. This will probably be my only one of the night, so I don't want to finish it too quickly.

"You in a mood?" she asks, circling around me, her fingertips trailing over my chest, my biceps, my back, then repeating again.

It's not like I can tell her not to touch me. The girl's touched a hell of a lot more on me in the past. "No," I repeat, taking another swig of my beer.

She grins. "Liar."

I shrug, not telling her she's right. "What makes you think so?"

She stops behind me and whispers in my ear, "Because you're all broody. It's kind of a turn-on, actually."

That's the thing about Lydia. She has no filter and you always know exactly where you stand with her. She's also too narcissistic to ever fall in love with anyone else. That's why she's the only girl I've ever hooked up with regularly over the years. Everyone else has pretty much been a one and done. No chance of Lydia catching feelings or wanting more than what I was willing to offer.

"How about it?" she asks, moving in front of me. "You down to fuck?"

Oh yeah, did I mention she's crass, too? I've never cared in the past, but her casual question feels . . . wrong now.

I shake my head and she frowns. "You've never said no before."

Looking away, I mumble, "I'm seeing someone."

Even though I'm not. I only wish I was.

She laughs, then stops when she realizes I'm serious. "You? Mr. Anti-Commitment?"

I roll my eyes. "I'm not that bad."

"Hmm. You kind of are." She eyes me speculatively. "So, is it serious?"

How the hell am I supposed to know that? But considering I can't stop thinking about Madeline, that all I want to do is spend time with her, learn everything about her . . . "Yeah, it is."

It's freeing in a way to say that out loud, to admit it to someone else. It makes it more real.

"Who's the lucky lady?"

There's no jealousy in her voice, nothing other than simple curiosity. Still, I shouldn't say anything. Shouldn't spread rumors when Madeline and I are nothing. She made that clear.

But she also didn't say she wasn't interested. She said she was trying to be practical. There's a difference.

So, of course I blurt out, "Madeline Woodward."

She blinks, her brows drawing together. "Who?"

Wow. I knew she wasn't popular, but damn. "She went to high school with us, a year behind."

Recognition dawns, then it's back to confusion. "Really? But she's so . . . And you're . . ." She waves her arm in no particular direction.

"We're what?" I grit out. What is she going to say? Some brainiac and jock bullshit? I don't need to hear it from her, too. I already know I'm not smart enough for Madeline. That I come from a piece of shit family. That I don't deserve her.

Lydia smirks, giving me a once-over. "She was more straitlaced than I thought you'd be into."

I thought that, too. Until I got to know her.

She pats my arm. "Well, best of luck to you both."

She turns, but I stick out my arm, stopping her as a strange kind of desperation takes hold of me. "How can I . . ." I swallow hard, knowing I should let it rest, but it seems I can't. "How can I let her know I'm serious about her? She doesn't believe me."

Her eyes widen. "Hunter, wow." She steps closer, studying me. "You really are serious."

I nod shakily under her scrutiny. What the hell am I doing exposing myself to Lydia of all people? If she wanted, she could have the word around town about me and Madeline with a snap of her fingers.

Which would be even more embarrassing when Madeline sets everyone straight that we are definitely not a couple.

Lydia taps a manicured finger to her chin. "From what I remember about her, she's not the kind of girl you can buy off. Flowers and jewelry aren't going to mean much to her."

I hang on her every word. I've never seen Madeline wear jewelry. And I have a feeling I'd freak her out if I bought her flowers.

"I think she's more of an actions speak louder than words kind of girl. You have to be there for her. Show her you're not going anywhere."

"That's . . . good advice." Is Lydia actually smart? "Thanks."

She beams. "You're welcome. Now, I've got to find someone else to fuck tonight."

And that's my cue to leave.

I say a brief goodbye to my coworker on my way out, then sit in my Mustang, not turning it on yet. I need to show Madeline I'm there for her. I've been doing that, right? So, what else can I do?

There's the rest of that list of things to do around the house. Yeah, she'd said I didn't have to do them, but this would be helping her. I could do other things she's not good at, too. Like . . . change the oil in her car?

Fuck. Why is this so hard?

My head falls against the headrest, my eyes closing. Does she really think I'm only after the chase with her? What do we even have in common?

All the little things we've discovered about each other come to mind, but I dismiss each one. Liking the same bands or hating onions in our food or both wanting to travel outside the country one day. Those things aren't important. I need something concrete.

I think what it comes down to is I like the person she is. What she stands for. Her tenacity, her fire, her commitment. The spark between us.

She can't deny the spark. I know she feels it, too.

But she has a point, we'll be working closely together for the next month. If we slept together and things went sour, she wouldn't want to see me anymore. She's right that I'd fail the exam if she didn't tutor me. And not only that, but . . . I would miss her. It hasn't been that long, but she's already become a part of my daily life.

I can't imagine sleeping together would make things worse, though. It'd only get better. I'd finally know what it's like to sink inside her. How warm and wet she'd be. Those gasps of satisfaction in my ear as I make her come. Holding her close afterward. Hearing her steady heartbeat, her soft breaths. Having her tucked into my side all night, where I can keep her safe.

I've never cared about the aftermath of sex before. Never felt that kind of wanting. Maybe the difference is we were friends first. That we've gotten to know each other so well.

All I know is . . . I don't want to lose her.

* * *

THROUGHOUT OUR STUDY session the next night, it's all I can do to focus on what she's saying, too interested instead in studying the shape of her lips. The graceful curve of her jaw. The way her hair frames her face when she leaves it down. How could I have not noticed how beautiful she is when first seeing her again at the fire station after all those years?

"Do I have something on my face?" she asks, and my gaze flicks up to find her brows knit in concern as she touches her chin.

Shit. Was I staring? "Oh, um, no."

She nods and picks up her notebook again, then sets it back down. "I can't concentrate," she mutters, rubbing at her temple.

Yeah, that's obvious. She's been stumbling over her words the last half hour. I have no room to judge, though. It'd be even worse if I was trying to read it.

"I think we should clear the air," she says, looking at the table rather than me.

I lean back in my seat and cross my arms over my chest, finally sufficiently distracted from staring at her like a stalker. "What about?"

Her head tilts to the side as she gives me an exasperated look, seeming to forget she was avoiding looking at me. "About yesterday. I . . . I don't want you mad at me."

Has she been worried about that? "I'm not mad at you."

Her brows knit again. "How could you not be? The way I said . . . I didn't mean to say it that way. And I never meant to hurt your feelings."

My fingers flex against my arms. So she picked up on that? I thought I'd done an all right job of hiding it.

"I'm sorry, okay?" There's this . . . longing in her voice. Like she needs me to believe her. "I'm very out of my element."

"Hey, hey." I reach across the study table, enveloping her hands in mine. She looks up at me in surprise, but I don't let go. "There is no element, okay?" Lydia said actions speak louder than words, but she needs some reassurance here. "I don't want you to feel that way. It's just me. And you can always talk to me."

She stares back at me, her gaze searching mine. I don't know what she sees, or what she's looking for, but she finally nods.

"Once I had time to think about it," I tell her, "I understand where you're coming from, even if I don't completely agree with it. And yeah, I got upset. But I'm over it."

"You're over it?" she repeats in a whisper.

"Yeah." No, wait. "Over being upset, I mean. Not over you."

She slips her hands out from under mine, looking away. "Hunter . . ."

Shit. I shouldn't have said that. I wanted her more at ease, not less. "Listen, uh . . ." I scratch at the back of my neck, trying to think of some other topic. "What was that thing you said you were going to tell me the next time we studied? After all those questions you asked."

She finally looks back at me. "Oh, that." She blows out a long breath. "Do you mind if I ask you a few more questions first?"

I make a *be my guest* gesture, confused when she asks about my spelling, handwriting, and even time management issues. I sweat, though, when she specifically asks if I have to read something multiple times to understand it.

"I'm not stupid," I say instead of answering the question. If I tell her yes, then I'm basically admitting that.

"I know you're not. But I think you might have dyslexia."

I stare at her blankly, unsure what to say. I wasn't expecting that.

"It's a neurological condition," she explains when I stay silent. "And it could be the reason you struggle with some things that come easier to others."

My jaw clenches as my pulse rushes in my ears. It was one thing for me to suspect she might know about my difficulties. It's another for her to throw it in my face.

This wasn't how tonight was supposed to go.

"Hunter, I can work with you—"

"I don't need your help," I tell her, standing and grabbing my stuff. "And I don't have whatever this is. I'm not fucking stupid."

I stalk out of the library, avoiding the librarian's eye as I pass her at the service desk, the one with all the wild, silver hair. Turns out, she's actually a nice lady.

It's not until I'm almost to my car that there's a tug on my arm from behind. Madeline's breathing heavily, all her study materials haphazardly gathered in her arms. But the thing that catches my eye the most is that fire in her eyes, so similar to those first days of the training program.

"You *know* I'm not calling you stupid. I'm sorry if I worded it wrong, but I wasn't saying that. I would never say that. Not . . . not now. Not after everything we've been through."

I step away from her, not wanting her hand on my arm, but she follows me. I guess her tenacity shouldn't surprise me. It's been there in spades since the beginning.

"Please don't shut me out." Her voice is pleading.

Still, I can't help saying, "Like the way you shut me out Saturday night?"

Her nostrils flare, even as guilt crosses her face. "I needed some time to process it first."

"And maybe I need some time, too."

Her lips press tightly together. "Okay." She steps back. "I just want what's best for you. And not because of the firefighting exams or the training program, but because of you. Because I . . ." She swallows hard. "Because I care about you."

My gaze darts over her, half of me still wanting to flee, half wanting to kiss the hell out of her. She cares about me?

It's not like it's a confession. It's probably actually the bare minimum. But it's something. A step in the right direction. Toward what, I'm not sure, but it's there all the same.

"Come here," I say, my anger deflating, and take the assortment of things she's still holding in her arms, then guide her over to my car, where I set the stuff on the hood.

Leaning against the side, I cross my arms over my chest. "What is it you want me to do?"

"You don't have to do anything," she insists. "Nothing has to change. But there are some strategies we could employ that might help. Things like text-to-speech software or trying out different fonts."

She says more stuff about using highlighters and making diagrams, but I'm not paying attention. Instead, all I can think of is the amount of research she must have put into this. For me. To help me out. Because she cares about me.

How sad is it that I'm riding high on that scrap of a compliment?

When she seems to be finished, I ask her, "So, is there a medication or something I could take?"

She shakes her head. "It's not that kind of disorder. And it's not curable. It's more about finding ways to adapt. And it has nothing to do with intelligence or vision or anything like that."

I nod, processing everything she's said. In a way, I'm glad she told me. I'm not just an idiot. There's an actual reason why it's hard to read.

"You won't tell anyone?" I ask her.

"Not if you don't want me to."

I shake my head. "I don't."

"It's nothing to be ashamed of."

If she says so. But I'm going to need some time to wrap my head around this.

"Sorry for springing it on you," she says.

I shrug. "Guess there's no easy way to tell someone that."

She bites at her bottom lip. "Anything I can do to make it up to you?"

I can think of a whole lot of things I'd like her to do, but none of them are appropriate for a library parking lot.

"Truth or dare?" I ask.

Her lips part in disbelief. "Really?"

I nod in mock seriousness. "It's the only thing you can do to make it up to me."

She rolls her eyes, finally seeming like herself again. "Okay, but I'm picking truth. I can only imagine what you'd make me do if I picked dare again."

There's a jump in my belly at the reminder of our kiss from last time, but I push it aside. There's something I've been curious about. "Have you ever dated anyone seriously before?"

I know she has. Her mom mentioned a failed relationship.

She frowns, her brows knitting together in confusion. "Um, yeah. I have. Why?"

No, she doesn't ask the questions. I do. "When?" I ask, ignoring her question.

"My junior and senior years in college."

I nod, wanting to know what I'm up against. On the ride home from that party last night, it had gotten stuck in my mind that if I knew about the kind of guys she's into, I could . . . I don't know. Not change. But be aware. To know if I even have a chance.

"Did you love him?"

She wraps her arms around her middle. "Yeah, I think."

"You think?" Wouldn't she know for sure?

She studies the pavement in front of her. "I thought I did. But then we graduated and Paul got a job in Seattle. We didn't even discuss me going with him. We just kind of . . . broke up."

I can't tell from her tone if she's sad about it. "Did you miss him?"

Her lips quirk to the side. "It sounds awful, but . . . not really. I realized so much of our relationship was about convenience. We lived in the same dorm and had the same major and classes."

"So, he was smart like you?"

"He was brilliant."

My stomach sinks. Back when I'd asked her what she looks for in a guy, she hadn't mentioned brains—not that I was hanging on every word.

"But he could also be callous," she continues. "If something wasn't important to him, he didn't understand how it could be important to anyone else."

"And that bothered you?"

She hugs her arms tighter around herself and lifts one shoulder. "Of course. He'd dismiss or mock stuff I liked all the time. And then had the nerve to get seriously offended if I did the same to him."

I want to reach for her, to unwrap the tight control she has around herself and let her borrow some of my strength. Instead, I simply run a hand down her upper arm in comfort.

"Does it bother you when I tease you about things?"

Her head tilts to the side. "I'm going to assume you mean now and not a month and a half ago."

A breath of laughter escapes me. "Yeah, now."

She gives a small shake of her head. "Teasing is different than mocking. I know you're only trying to get under my skin, or to make me laugh." She looks up at me, her face questioning. "Why are you asking all this, anyway?"

"I just . . . wanted to know." Wow, that sounded lame. Maybe it's time to leave. "I should get going."

"Wait. I still get a turn. I told you my truth."

I nod in concession. Fair's fair. "I pick dare, then."

"Of course you do." She taps her finger to her lips. "I dare you to do a cartwheel."

"What?" I laugh, not expecting her to say that.

She grins in response. "It'll be fun."

God, I haven't done a cartwheel in close to two decades. "Right here?"

She nods, her earlier mood when talking about her ex gone, replaced with something lighter. Whatever makes her happy.

Taking my phone, wallet, and keys out of my pockets, I set them on the ground, then do the world's worst excuse for a cartwheel.

She doubles over with laughter, wheezing out, "That was awful."

"Hey, now. I did what you asked." I gather my things off the ground, stuffing them back in my pockets.

She straightens and wipes at her eyes. "Sorry." Then, she laughs again.

"You think that's funny?"

I crowd her against my Mustang, loving the way she smiles up at me. The last time I'd had her in this position at the firehouse, she hadn't been receptive. Today's a different story.

Also, don't think about having her in different positions.

Unable to help myself, I bend down, giving her a quick kiss on the lips.

"Hunter," she admonishes. Even so, her smile doesn't fully leave her. "I thought we agreed not to do that."

"I thought you said you didn't want to sleep with me."

"No." She looks at my chest, then smooths down the fabric of my shirt. I love when she touches me. "I said we shouldn't let feelings and emotions get in the way."

"Well, it's too late for that. For me, at least."

Her hand tightens on my shirt, twisting the fabric. "You can't say stuff like that."

"Why?"

"Because."

She leaves it at that, not elaborating further.

Fine. She can have it her way. For now.

"All right. But for the record . . ." I wait until she looks up at me. "It's not about the thrill of the chase with you. It's about you. Period."

I kiss her again, briefly, not wanting to push my luck, and leave her there, wide-eyed.

We won't be training partners forever. And when that day comes, she better watch out.

Because she's all mine then.

Chapter Twenty
MADELINE

Hunter doesn't kiss me again all week. Not on Tuesday after our evening workout where we started interval training. Not on Wednesday when we studied at the library and I showed him more research I did on dyslexia. Not on Thursday when he came over to my house after work and insisted on mowing my lawn and helping with more household fixes on that god-awful list my mom made. Not on Friday after Adelaide screeched at me for not telling her sooner about everything that happened with Hunter the weekend prior. And not on Saturday when after our training at the fire station he said he had to go to his parents' house for dinner because his mom won't stop hassling him.

He's been an attentive study partner. A diligent trainer. An actual gentleman.

And I can't stop thinking about him. About the playful light in his eyes as he'd kissed me after I laughed at his cartwheel. At the way his gaze had darkened with earnestness as he'd told me he had feelings for me. That he was interested in me. And that second kiss, short but full of hunger. Full of promise.

I could have him if I wanted. He's left the ball in my court.

The only thing is, Madeline Woodward is not a risk taker. She plays things safe. She follows the rules.

There are no rules for this, though. No textbook to read. No instruction manual. If I took a chance, what would happen afterward? Where would it leave us?

Well, sitting here debating it endlessly isn't going to change anything. I grab my stuff and drive to the fire station, telling myself to stop worrying about it.

Yesterday, we'd practiced using a pike pole to breach a ceiling, which of course was more difficult for me since I'm not as tall or strong as the other guys. I'd completed the exercise, my upper arms and shoulders burning afterward since the hinged door we'd practiced on had weighed sixty pounds and we'd had to do the exercise several times in our full gear.

This morning is not much better as we go over more forcible entry methods and breaching walls, but it's the afternoon that does me in. Hunter and I work together on performing a modified hose load, him standing on the step at the back of the engine feeding me hose while I kneel in the hosebed, packing two hundred-foot stacks of hose side by side.

My arms and back are sore by the time we're finished, and I'm paying more attention to the ache than what I'm doing as I jump down.

A dumb, dumb decision.

My ankle rolls and I fall to the floor, hissing in a breath as pain explodes up my leg.

Hunter kneels beside me in a flash, his face full of worry. "What is it? What's wrong?"

My eyes squeeze shut, trying to block it out, but it doesn't work. "My ankle."

"Can you stand?"

"I don't know." I shift and a whimper escapes me as a fresh wave of hurt travels over me, though it's not as bad as a second ago.

"I'll carry you inside."

Before I can agree to it, he's whisked me in his arms and is halfway across the open bay toward the inside of the fire station. Um, okay. Guess this is happening.

Grizz stares at us open-mouthed from where he's supervising Silas and Harry practicing a forward hose lay. "What's wrong?" he calls out.

"My ankle. It's fine, don't worry." I don't want him thinking I'll get hurt easily every time I'm on the job. "Hunter, put me down," I whisper.

"Let Sebastian check you out first." He carries me carefully over the threshold inside, then bellows the EMT's name, who's thankfully on call today.

Sebastian comes down from the second floor a moment later, pausing when he sees us. "What happened?"

"I rolled my ankle," I explain, feeling ridiculous with all of Hunter's fuss. The pain's already subsided significantly.

"Can you check it out?" Hunter asks, his fingers flexing on the back of my thigh where he's supporting me.

"Put her down in there," Sebastian says, pointing to the break room.

Hunter carefully sets me down on one of the chairs, then pulls around another to support my right foot.

"Do you need me to get anything?" Hunter asks as Sebastian kneels next to my foot. "A medical kit or something?"

"Let's see what we're dealing with first. Madeline, I'm going to take off your shoe and sock, then pull up your pant leg, okay?"

I nod, wincing as my shoe slips off, jostling my foot. Beside me, Hunter grips my shoulder, then lets go when I stare at him pointedly.

"Did you hear or feel any kind of popping when this happened?" Sebastian asks.

"No."

"Good. There are no breaks in the skin, no serious swelling. I'm going to remove your other shoe and sock now for comparison."

He studies my feet, then asks me to wiggle my toes, which I'm able to do.

"How would you rate your pain on a scale of one to ten, ten being the highest?"

"Um, when it happened, maybe a seven. Now it's down to probably a three or four."

He nods. "I'm going to palpate it now. Tell me if anything hurts."

He touches my ankle at different points, sometimes holding it, sometimes letting it rest against the chair, but nothing hurts too bad, thankfully.

When his examination moves to my leg and up my calf, Hunter asks, "Why do you need to touch her there?"

"Hunter, let the man work," I murmur. He almost sounds . . . jealous.

"Some ankle injuries have associated tibia fractures," Sebastian says easily, unfazed by Hunter's underlying hard tone. "Everything seems okay, though. How about we see if it can bear weight?"

Before Sebastian can help me up, Hunter's there holding my hand for balance as I maneuver my foot off the chair and stand.

"It's not the most comfortable," I say as I ease more of my weight onto my right foot. "But it's better than I thought it'd be."

Sebastian nods. "Good. It doesn't seem broken or sprained. Probably just landed on it wrong. Rest, elevation, and ice can't hurt, though. Take it easy for the next week."

"Thank you so much," I tell him, and Hunter gives his thanks, too.

When he leaves, I ask Hunter, "Maybe I can use you for balance if I feel wobbly back out there?"

His brows knit together. "We're not going back out there. I'm driving you home."

I blink up at him. "You are?"

"You heard Sebastian. Rest, elevation, and ice."

"That was optional. There's still an hour of training left."

He makes a *pshh* sound. "It's freaking hoses, not rocket science. It's okay if we miss the last bit. Your health is more important."

I nearly laugh. My health? "I didn't even sprain it. I'll be okay."

"Please, Madeline. Can you rest it for tonight? I don't want you to seriously hurt yourself reinjuring it."

His tone more than his words gives me pause. He actually seems worried.

"Okay. But don't carry me out of here again. I don't want Grizz to think I'm weak."

Even if it was nice to be carried by him.

He concedes, but hovers close to me as we slowly make our way out, as if I'm going to collapse any second. I explain what happened to Grizz, who asks if he needs to fill out any worker's comp paperwork for me, but I wave him off.

"I'll be fine," I tell him. "Totally better with a little rest."

"And you need him to drive you home?" Grizz asks, glancing at Hunter.

"No, but he's insisting."

"I am," Hunter says, crossing his arms over his chest. Apparently, it's not up for debate.

Grizz shrugs. "Okay. See you next week."

Once we're out of the bay and direct sight, I grab Hunter's arm, letting him support some of my weight.

"I should have stepped off of the truck, not jumped. How stupid."

"There's no way you could have known."

He carefully loads me into the passenger side of his car, telling me we'll figure out about getting my car later, and drives, surprising me when he takes the turn to his house rather than mine. I don't say anything, though, secretly pleased he wants to spend more time together.

He sets me up on the couch, propping a pillow underneath my foot, and gets a gel ice pack from the freezer to position over my ankle. I let him fuss over me, watching him with amusement as he brings me a glass of water, then a bag of chips, and drapes a throw blanket over me in case I'm chilly. He hands me the remote and tells me to put on anything I want, but I draw the line when he sits on the living room floor, not wanting to disturb my ankle.

"You're going overboard," I tell him. "My ankle barely hurts anymore. You sitting on the end of the couch isn't going to make a bit of difference to it."

"I don't—"

"Sit on the damn couch."

He carefully lifts the pillow and my ankle, and situates them on his lap.

"So, anything I want, huh?" I wave the remote at him. "You're putting an awful lot of power in my hands."

"You have more power than you know."

I look at him, but he's looking at the TV. What's that supposed to mean?

"Pick whatever you want," he says, gingerly crossing his feet at the ankle on the coffee table, so as not to jostle me. "Seriously, I'm good with anything."

I take him at his word and put on my ultimate comfort show—*The Great British Baking Show*. I half expect him to balk, but he watches along with me, barely saying anything throughout the first episode.

Another three episodes and a frozen pizza later—because that's apparently all he knows how to cook—he's surprisingly into it, asking me all sorts of things.

"What's this marzipan stuff they keep talking about?"

I snuggle further under the throw blanket, the pillow that was holding my foot now being used by Hunter to lean against the side of the couch. My feet are on his lap, all toasty warm under the blanket, my ankle fine now.

"Honestly, I'm not entirely sure. I don't think we bake with it much here in the US. It must be something sweet, though."

"And it's different than frangipane?"

"I think so." I smile to myself, entertained by his interest in the show. He never would have watched this in a million years when we first started this training program.

He nods, tuning back into the show.

"So, you're into this?" I motion toward the TV.

He chuckles. "I mean, I'm not inspired to start baking. But it's not half bad."

I nudge his arm with my foot. "Come on. You like it more than that. I'm going to sign you up for the show."

"Do I have to fake a British accent?"

"Oh, totally. Let me hear it."

He clears his throat and says some nonsense about *cheerio* and *top o' the mornin' to ya*, which I think is more Irish than British, but it's so awful that it doesn't matter as I cackle with laughter.

"You're jealous," he says with a grin. "Especially because I'm going to get a Hollywood handshake and you're not."

I get my giggles under control. "Oh my God, I would die. Will you at least introduce me?"

He pretends to think it over. "I guess I could do that for you."

"It's only fair since I introduced you to the show. And look, I've made a convert out of you."

"Well, you like it, so of course I'd give it a try."

He goes back to watching the show, but his offhand comment sticks with me. Paul would have taken one look at a show like this and dismissed it. I know for a fact this normally wouldn't be Hunter's cup of tea, either. But he tried it, for me.

Something about it reminds me of that moment in my garage last weekend, when he said he wouldn't help anyone else out like that. Just me.

Another episode starts up and the thought crosses my mind that I should ask Hunter to drive me back to my car now so I can go home. His couch is so comfy, though, and the lights are dim and we're having a good time. Maybe after the next episode. It's a marathon at this point, after all. I can't interrupt that.

I sigh, getting more comfortable, but as the night wears on, I get a little too comfortable. The next thing I know, darkness surrounds us, the time reading one a.m. on my phone on the coffee table. Hunter's lifting me into his arms, just like he did at the fire station, as if I weigh nothing.

"What's going on?" I ask, although I think it comes out with more slurring than I intend in my half-awake state.

"We're going to bed," he says, carrying me down the hallway and into his bedroom. "We'll get your car in the morning."

Did he fall asleep on the couch, too? I have the presence of mind to realize he also must be half asleep. It wouldn't make sense to have him drive me now, then.

"Okay," I agree, not that I put up any kind of fight.

He lays me on his bed, and the last thing I think before I fall asleep again is that his comforter is just as soft as I thought it'd be.

Chapter Twenty-One
MADELINE

When I open my eyes again, it's still dark out, but with the faint gray light of early morning creeping around the edges of the window blinds. Hunter's next to me, his face peaceful in sleep. In my drowsy state, I mentally trace the slope of his forehead, down to the dark slashes of his brows and straight nose. I get stuck for a moment on his lips, remembering how they'd felt against mine, how good it'd been between us. I'd never expected that kind of chemistry with Hunter, of all people. Then again, my experiences with him have been nothing like I expected, either.

How caring he can be, tending to my ankle like that. How thoughtful he is, helping out with all those things around my house. How responsible he's become with all of our training and studying.

How he watched a show for hours only because I wanted to watch it. How he asks questions and listens to me, like he's interested.

How he makes me feel important.

My heart squeezes, realizing all those things I told him I find attractive in a guy are true with him.

Shifting to my back, I look up at the ceiling and tell my heart to stop it. That's not what this is. Hunter is . . . He's a player. He's not interested in anything long-term, even if he's hinted he's into me right now.

Christ, how many girls have slept in this bed, too? Woken up in this exact position, wondering about their life choices that brought them to this point?

A sad smile curls my lips upward. No, they're probably waking from a long night of pleasure, their bodies still sensitive in all the right places. An echo of my own remembered pleasure pulses within me, his rough voice in my ear telling me to ride him, his thumb teasing my nipple.

"What are you smiling about?"

I yelp, my hands tightening into fists as I look over at Hunter. "You're awake?"

My eyes have adjusted enough to the darkness by now to make out his grin. "Am I not allowed to be?"

"Of course you are. I wasn't expecting it, is all."

He stretches and something cracks in his back, then he turns on his side to face me. "So, what were you smiling about?"

"Nothing, it's stupid."

His grin grows wider. "Well, now you have to tell me."

Crap. It's like I'm throwing bait at him. "Fine," I huff. "You want to know? I was thinking about how many other girls have woken up in your bed like this." I pause. "After a very different kind of night, obviously."

I doubt any of them fell asleep on his couch after marathoning a baking show.

His smile vanishes. "None."

I nearly laugh, then realize he's serious. "You're lying."

"I'm not."

A beat of anger throbs below my breastbone unexpectedly. "There's no way you can tell me you haven't had girls in this bed."

An uncomfortable look crosses his face. "I didn't say that. Just that they haven't woken up here. I don't want them spending the night."

But he let me? And not only that, but carried me to his bed himself when he could have left me on the couch?

No, that's different. We'd both fallen asleep and were tired. He was being nice.

"So, what? You kick them out before midnight or something?"

He scrubs a hand over his jaw. "Nothing as merciless as that. But there's a mutual understanding that what we're doing . . . It's not the kind of thing where you spend the night."

"Because you don't want it leading to anything more?"

"Yeah," he admits.

"So, you take what you want and send them on their merry way?"

He shakes his head, even as his lips curl in amusement. "You're painting an awfully bad picture of me. And I'd never only take what I want. I'd make sure she had a good time, too."

That pulse between my legs aches again. "And if she didn't have a good time?"

"Then I'd make it up to her."

"How?"

The bedsheets rustle as he shifts. "You know how."

I'm silent, both wanting to imagine him doing that stuff to me, but not wanting to think of him doing it to anyone else.

"I can feel your blush from here."

"Stop it." I push his shoulder, not that it moves him at all. At least he broke some of the rising tension. "Well, that's very chivalrous of you, I guess."

"Did your ex do that for you?"

"Do what?"

"Make sure you were satisfied?"

I wet my suddenly dry lips. "It wasn't a priority for him," I admit.

"Because it wasn't important to him?"

"Right," I whisper, feeling stupid. It sounds so obvious now. Why be with someone who can't even be bothered to make their partner come?

"And with other guys?"

Heat travels up my chest and over my cheeks. "He's the only person I've been with."

Hunter goes so still, I can't even hear him breathe.

"You haven't been with anyone in three years?" he finally asks. I can tell he's trying to keep the disbelief out of his voice, but he doesn't fully succeed.

"I haven't."

The idea is probably unfathomable to him. How often is he with someone? How often does his *itch* need to be scratched?

"So, in the two years you were with him, he didn't make you come?"

My cheeks are scorching now, but I don't think he can tell in the barely there light in the room. "I didn't say that. It was just . . . rare. And I had to help things along . . . a lot."

His hand reaches out, sweeping over my cheek. "You deserved better than that."

I'm not sure if it's the gentle way he says it or the tenderness in his touch, but I get a little emotional. "Yeah, but it doesn't matter now."

"It always matters."

His hand moves to brush my hair back away from my face, and I close my eyes, reveling in the connection. He always knows exactly how to touch me.

"So, what do you do with unsatisfied customers?" I ask.

His hand pauses in my hair. "There are no unsatisfied customers."

A thrill runs through me, just as I think what a big ego he has. "How do you know?"

"I ask her if she came."

He'd asked me that. "And if she says no?"

"Then I ask if she wants me to finger her or go down on her."

He says it both casually and brazenly, like he's daring me to say something about it or shock me. Or maybe I'm simply shocked because it's so out of my realm of experience.

"And what's usually their answer?" I find myself asking, more curious than I ought to be.

He strokes my hair one more time, then removes his hand. "What would be your answer?"

"I'm not asking for me." That would be crazy.

"Really? Because I'm assuming your ex didn't do either of those things for you."

"He didn't," I confirm. What's the sense in lying?

"Are you curious?"

Maybe it's the sense of anonymity the darkness brings, or the growing ache within me at all this sexual talk, but, against all reason, I whisper, "Yes."

He moves closer, though still doesn't touch me. "So, what's your answer?"

About if I'd have him finger me or go down on me?

A nervous laugh escapes me. It must sound crazy. I *feel* crazy. Maybe I'm actually dreaming all this. "Either," I admit. What the hell? What do I have to lose after admitting to him I haven't had sex in three years, and that before that, it was with a guy who, in hindsight, didn't care all that much about me? "Both. Anything."

His hand moves to my hip, resting there, as if to see what I'll do. Waiting for me to tell him to stop.

But I don't. The truth is, I like his hand there.

"All you have to do is ask." That rough promise is back in his voice.

"You would . . ." I trail off.

He squeezes my hip. "Yeah, I would."

My thighs clench with the sudden rush of arousal that runs through me.

This is a terrible idea. Didn't I just tell him last week this wasn't happening? That we're better off not adding stuff like this to the mix while we're training partners? What if things get weird afterward? Or awkward?

I guess they'd only get that way if I made them that way, though. He seems completely casual about it. Sex isn't a big deal to him.

Not that what he's offering is sex. It's a sexual act, which is different. I think. I'm not really sure. God, I'm so inexperienced when it comes to stuff like this, compared to him.

And I've probably been sitting here for who knows how long debating everything in my head while looking like a slack-jawed idiot.

"Okay," I blurt out, going with my gut instinct.

Is it the responsible choice? Maybe not. But I'm in a hot guy's bed and he's offering to pleasure me. And not just any hot guy. It's Hunter. The guy I've come to trust. To seek out. To think about, day and night.

Oh my God, I really like him.

There's no more thinking as he covers my body with his own, his lips on mine, taking me back into oblivion. Into that place of pure sensation.

The way he kisses me over long minutes, as if he's desperate for me . . . is that the way he kisses everyone? Or is it just for me?

Okay, I need to get out of my head and stop the comparisons. I'll drive myself crazy otherwise.

I thread my hands in his hair, letting myself go. Don't think. Only feel.

He makes a low *mmm*, then breaks away, shifting to his left side. "Can I touch you?"

I nod, afraid to speak. It might come out a croaky mess, begging him for relief from this growing ache.

His hand sweeps over my stomach and underneath my shirt. Unlike last time, there's no teasing. He cups my breast, both of us sighing. It's not enough, though. I still have a sports bra on from training earlier.

He pulls me up and strips my shirt, then my bra. He hooks his fingers in the waistband of my leggings, and my panties come off along with them, leaving me completely nude.

His gaze devours me, radiating lust. The only reason I'm not covering myself is because he seems to like the sight.

"Christ, Madeline," he murmurs, then bends to suck a nipple into his mouth.

Oh my God, oh my God. I didn't know I'd like that so much. Didn't know someone could be that talented with their mouth.

He takes his time at my breast, in no apparent rush, but tell that to the rising lust within me. I make the mistake of looking down, where he's lapping at my nipple with the flat of his tongue. An inarticulate sound escapes me, and I grip his broad shoulders, wanting to feel his skin, too. He lets me take his shirt off, then he's right back on me, working at my other breast, his hand gently squeezing me.

I run my hands over him as far as I can reach, loving how attentive he is, how much he seems to enjoy this. I can't help but squirm against the bedsheets, wanting more even as I never want him to stop.

"Hunter," I say. "Can you . . ." I'm not sure what I'm even asking for. All I know is I need more.

He looks up at me, eyes glazed over with desire, then realizes what I'm asking. A wicked smile crosses his face.

"Fingers or tongue?"

Chapter Twenty-Two
HUNTER

Even in the dim early morning light, the widening of Madeline's eyes is unmistakable.

Not that my goal was to shock her, but she has to know what she's in for. I'm making her come, one way or another. The only question is how she wants it.

Anticipation thrums through me as I wait for her to decide. Honestly, I could probably make her come by sucking her nipples alone, if she gave me enough time. She's incredibly responsive, and her breasts are just as perfect as her ass.

Everything about her is perfect.

Her thighs split, one leg riding up to expose her pretty pussy, and she takes one of my hands, guiding it to the area. Guess that's her answer, then.

I slide my palm over her, then slip two fingers inside, unable to wait any longer.

"Oh, fuck, you're wet for me." Do I turn her on that much? My dick hardens even more at the thought. "So fucking sexy."

I draw my fingers in and out, until she's practically riding my hand with eagerness, then I return my mouth to her breast, swirling my tongue around her nipple.

Her legs splay open, hips thrusting to meet my hand. "Keep doing that," she says, her hands coming up to sift through my hair, holding me in place. As if I would go anywhere else when I have this insanely sexy woman under me.

I'm losing my mind with the way I want her. I've never craved someone so much, especially because it's *her*. Madeline. The girl that's invaded my life in the best way possible.

Carrying her to bed earlier had felt so right. So natural. It makes sense she'd be the only girl to ever sleep here with me. She's the only one I've ever wanted like this.

Focusing my attention on her clit, I grin against her breast as her hold on me tightens, her heels digging into the mattress.

"Like that, Hunter. Oh my God, like that."

I don't think she realizes what she's saying, what she's doing, as she rides my hand, a low groan issuing from her a few moments later. Her pussy milks my fingers as her orgasm rolls over her, and triumph zings through me. I love hearing her moan for me.

Releasing her breast, my lips travel up her chest and neck, and finally to those luscious lips, kissing her with reverence. She kisses me back, curling herself around me, one of her legs sliding over my hip.

"That was amazing," she whispers. "I loved every minute of it."

"And I loved doing that for you." Seriously, we could make a standing appointment for me to get her off every night. I'd be one hundred percent down for that.

"But you didn't get anything out of it."

"Don't worry about me." I don't want her to feel obligated to do anything she's uncomfortable with. I'm still reeling that I got her to agree to let me touch her at all.

"You said yourself how much I like fairness," she whispers, her hand snaking between us to cup me.

I hiss in a breath, her touch bordering on sensory overload directly on me like that.

She snatches her hand away. "Sorry. Was that not okay?"

"No, it is." I find her hand again, placing it back on me, and groan. "I'm just incredibly turned on."

Her lips curve in a smile. "Really?"

"Yes, really. You keep touching me like that and I'm going to come quick."

She seems delighted by my admission. Did her ex never praise her? Tell her what he liked? What turned him on?

Then again, the man didn't even make her come, so chances are no.

I pump into her hand for half a minute, my body doing all the work, waiting until she gets comfortable, until her touch turns bolder.

"Can I take these off?" I ask, motioning to my shorts and boxer briefs. "Not to have sex." I don't think she's ready for that. "Just to . . ."

She nods and helps me undress, her slim fingers sliding over me once I'm bare to her.

Christ, yes. Her touch is everything I imagined it would be.

I tell my hips to keep still, to not scare her off with demands, but I can't stop myself, groaning madly as my hips move of their own accord.

"Grip me tighter," I tell her. "Yeah, like that. And move your hand . . . Yeah, exactly. Oh, fuck, that feels good."

I kiss her as her hand glides up and down my dick, my hands drifting over her body, exploring her. I want to learn every curve, every dip and hollow, map every bit of her until it's imprinted in my memory. I can't guarantee she'll return to my bed after tonight. I have to memorize everything while I can.

Even if it may be our only time like this, she kisses me back with enthusiasm, stroking me just how I want it. Then again, I'd want anything with her. I can't believe she agreed to anything at all.

When a familiar tingle surges down my spine, I welcome it, wanting that release. I pull away slightly, taking in her beautifully nude body, the graceful fall of her hair over my pillow, the concentration on her face as she gets me off.

"You get me so hot." My hand joins hers, speeding up the rhythm. "I'm going to come soon, okay?"

She nods in understanding, and maybe it's wishful thinking, but I swear she looks excited. Regardless, it's what tips me over the edge, my movements going jerky as I come on her belly.

"Madeline, yes. Oh, God. Fuck, yes."

I can't keep track of the words coming out of my mouth, afraid I'll say something she's not ready to hear. Not about how much I want her, but how much she means to me. How I want her in my bed every night from now on. That now I've had her touch, I can't go back. She's what I crave.

That wouldn't go over well, though. She's so skittish, I can't scare her off. Not that I have the first clue what I'm doing when it comes to getting a girl to actually date me. I've spent so long doing everything I can to prevent that from happening.

When I'm finished, I tell her to stay there, and get up and dampen a washcloth in the bathroom. Bringing it back to her, I wipe the cum off her belly, a sick sense of possession running through me. A part of me wants to leave my mark, to let everyone know she's taken. She's mine.

Pretty sure the caveman routine won't impress her any, though, so I keep the primal thoughts to myself as I get rid of the evidence of our night together. Or, morning, I guess. There's not that much longer until I have to be up for work.

"So, are you satisfied?" I ask, laying back down next to her. I can't help running my hand down her side, wanting to touch her while I still have the chance. I have a feeling daylight will bring back that distance she keeps between us.

"Yes." She tucks her hands under her pillow, looking at my chest rather than my face. "We maybe got a little carried away, though."

If it had been up to me, we would have done a hell of a lot more. But I know the limits.

"I had a good time," I say instead. "An amazing time, actually. You're incredible."

She gives a soft smile, then yawns. "You're not so bad yourself."

"You want to go back to sleep?" I ask her. "I have about an hour until I have to be up for work, but you're welcome to stay here as long as you want."

"Hunter, I . . ." She pulls up the bedsheet, covering herself. "I think I should go."

And there it is. That distance I was afraid of.

"You want to grab breakfast?" I ask her. "Daisy's Nut House is probably already open. Or I could make you something here."

I may not be able to cook much, but I can handle scrambled eggs and bacon. Sort of.

She hesitates for a second. "That's sweet of you, but no. I just need a ride to my car."

Right. I forgot that's why she was here to begin with. "Sure."

I get out of bed and change, but she stays hidden under the sheet. I get the message and leave, giving her privacy, and head out to the living room, where I grab our dirty dishes from last night off of the coffee table and bring them to the kitchen to wash up.

She joins me a minute later in yesterday's clothes, her hair up in a messy ponytail. God, she's beautiful.

"Ready?"

She nods and I lead her out to my car, opening the passenger door for her. When she's situated, I round the car and get in, then back out of the driveway.

"I don't know if I've mentioned it before," she says after a minute of quiet, "but I love the way your house is decorated."

An unexpected flush of pleasure runs through me. "Oh, thanks."

"Did someone help you?"

"No, I did everything myself. Well, I did get help from Monroe & Sons with some of the renovation work I couldn't do alone."

"You renovated it?"

I nod. "It wasn't in great condition when I bought it. That's the only reason I could afford it to begin with. Even then I had to pull a lot of overtime for the down payment. But my home is important to me. I spend pretty much all my time here."

A small chuckle escapes her. "I wouldn't have pegged you for a homebody."

I shrug. "What'd you think I was?"

"Some extroverted jock party boy."

I laugh, something in me easing when she laughs, too.

"I guess it would seem that way to you. Especially since you moved away after high school."

"What changed since then?"

My fingers flex on the steering wheel. "Graduating, is all. Back then, I did football in the fall and baseball in the spring as an excuse to be out of the house. Same with partying all the time. It was so I didn't have to be home."

There's a long pause and then she asks, "Because of your family?"

Shit. This is not the conversation I wanted to have right now. I'm supposed to be convincing her to get closer, not driving her further away. She made her contempt of my family known that first day of the training program, and I don't blame her.

"Yeah" is all I say, leaving it at that.

"You never talk about them," she says.

"No. I don't."

I've been visiting them less and less lately and it's felt . . . good. Even with Mom's guilt-tripping.

She nods, the silence lengthening between us until it would be too awkward to say anything else.

When we arrive at the fire station, I park next to her car, letting the engine idle. "We still studying tonight?" I ask, sticking to a safe topic.

"Yeah. I'll see you at the library."

"We don't have to go to the library, you know," I find myself saying. "We could study at my place." And she could spend the night again.

She fiddles with her purse strap for a moment. "I focus better at the library. I keep doing things I don't mean to when I'm inside your house."

She says it with a self-deprecating laugh, but it still stings a little, anyway.

"Thanks for . . . everything," she says, opening her car door.

I wanted to kiss her goodbye, but there's no chance of that now as she leaves the car. We're back to training partners. To friends. The last hour was only a blip in our otherwise normally scheduled programming.

No, stop being so negative. Today was progress. She let me touch her everywhere, let me get her off. And she gave me a hand job, too. Can't complain about that.

I just have to figure out how to make it happen again.

Chapter Twenty-Three
HUNTER

"So, I found a website where we can make online mind maps for each of the textbook chapters," Madeline tells me, turning her laptop around to show me. "It's one of the dyslexia strategies I was telling you about."

I look around, but there's no one close enough to overhear us, as usual. The library staff have learned to leave us be over the last month.

"We?" I ask, looking at the screen. It looks like she made one for a chapter we went over today.

"Okay, me. What do you think?"

"When did you have time to do this?"

She waves off my concern. "Everything went right with the code I wrote today, so I had extra time."

I still don't understand what she means by *writing code*, even though she's explained it to me before, but I nod as if I do.

"Thanks. You didn't have to do this."

"I wanted to. It's part of tutoring you."

Her hands twist in front of her, a sure sign she's nervous. Because of this morning? Or something else?

I'm not sure what to even say about this morning that won't come off as me begging her for another night together.

"Well, if it's helpful," she continues, "I can make mind maps for the rest of the chapters, too."

"Yeah, sure."

"I was thinking I could make a case for you to get additional time on the written exam, too."

"Why?"

"Because of your dyslexia."

Is she serious right now? "Absolutely not."

"But—"

She stops herself when I give her a sharp look.

"It's not like I have it officially," I tell her. "I've only been armchair diagnosed by you."

Her lips purse. "I'd make an excellent psychologist, I'll have you know."

The tension in my shoulders releases. If she's joking, then she's willing to let it go. "No doubt. But you promised to keep it a secret. I don't want anyone else to know."

"Know what?"

The blood drains from my face as I swivel to my left. What the hell is my brother doing here in the library?

I glance at Madeline, but she appears just as startled as me at his sudden appearance.

"You keeping secrets?" Nate asks, picking up my firefighting textbook. "What the fuck?" he murmurs to himself as he thumbs through the pages.

I snatch it back from him and toss it on the table. "What are you doing here?"

Why would Nate be here? He hasn't stepped foot in a library . . . ever.

He pulls out a chair and plops down, making himself comfortable. "I've been calling you for the last hour and a half."

I keep my phone on silent when studying with Madeline. "Why?"

Nate looks pointedly at Madeline, then at me.

"Oh, this is my brother, Nate," I say to her. "And this is my . . ." I can't introduce her as my training partner. I still haven't told him about that. And as far as anything else . . . I don't know what we are to each other anymore. More than friends, but not dating. Shit, this is confusing. "This is Madeline," I end with lamely.

Nate leans back in his chair, a smirk on his face. "And what are you and my brother doing at the library, Madeline?"

This is one of those times I thank whatever higher power there may be that Madeline is as smart as she is, because she doesn't incriminate me at all.

"He's helping me with something," she replies vaguely, with a cool confidence I'm half-surprised she pulls off.

Nate jabs a finger at the discarded textbook. "With firefighting?"

His extreme skepticism is deserved, but she's silent, apparently not caring to elaborate further.

"How'd you know I was here?" I ask, wanting his attention off of Madeline. He doesn't have a tracker on my phone or something, does he? No, he's not smart enough for that.

"Word is you've been hanging around the library with a girl," he says. "Thought it was crazy when I heard it, but I guess not."

People are watching us? And talking about it? I knew it was a mistake to do this in public.

"So, why are you here?" I ask.

He stares at me for a moment, his face hardening, then tilts his head toward Madeline. "She cool?"

Oh, shit. It's something serious. I nod.

"We need bail money."

I scrub a hand over my face, knowing the answer already as I ask who for.

"Dad."

Of course.

Madeline's eyes widen, but she doesn't otherwise react. What must she be thinking?

"I know you've got money stashed away," Nate says. "You've got your own house. Your own car. A cushy full-time job with benefits."

Cushy? I work at a fucking sawmill. What does he think I do all day? He's the one home playing video games nonstop when he's not dealing.

Besides, I worked my ass off for the things I have. He's not entitled to any of it.

"I don't have money for you."

"Bullshit." He leans forward, getting in my face. "With all the overtime you claim to work, you have to have something."

Guilt passes over me. I've been telling Mom I'm working overtime the past couple of months so I don't have to go over there as often. In reality, I haven't picked up a single extra shift lately. All my free time is taken up with training and Madeline.

"I can't help you." I try my best to stay calm, not wanting to make a scene in the library of all places.

He shakes his head, looking at me like I'm scum. "Well, I'm not leaving until you do."

He's not going to let this go? Fine. Time to take it outside.

Which I should have done when he first showed up. Why did I let him say anything in front of Madeline? If I was worried about what she thought of my family before, this definitely isn't helping.

I stand and gather my things, then realize having all this stuff makes it look like I'm the one studying. I hand it all to Madeline, praying she doesn't say anything about it. "Here's your stuff."

She nods, her gaze steady on me, but I can't tell what she's thinking.

Nate motions between me and her. "Are you two together?"

He asks it casually, as if it isn't an incredibly loaded question. I want to say yes. Even besides my personal feelings and what we did this morning, it would explain why I'm here and helping her. I'd even stupidly told Lydia I was seeing her.

But I also don't want her anywhere on Nate's radar. I don't want him to remember her name, her face, anything about her. She doesn't belong anywhere near my family.

"Come on," I mutter, walking past him, but he doesn't follow.

"Hold up. Give a guy a chance to shoot his shot." He smirks at me as I glance back at him, then he turns to Madeline. "So, can I get your number?"

My hand is on the back of his shirt before I realize what I'm doing, yanking him out of the chair. "She's not giving you her number."

Whoa. Is that my voice that's so growly?

"Why not?"

"Because she's too good for you."

I steer him out, looking over my shoulder at Madeline. She's silently watching, that intelligent gaze flicking between me and Nate. She'd be a hell of a poker player.

Sorry, I mouth, but I'm not sure if she catches it.

Why would she ever give me a chance now? Who would want to get involved in this shit? I don't even want to and it's my family.

When we reach the parking lot, I pace in front of Nate's beat-up Civic. "So, how much did Dad have on him?"

Nate frowns at me, not answering.

Oh, now he doesn't want to be chatty?

"Was it just possession? Or possession with intent to distribute? That one's a felony, you know."

"Yeah, I know," he mutters. "Listen, we don't have to get into specifics, but he's been there since yesterday already. The arraignment was this afternoon and they set the bail at ten thousand—"

"Ten thousand?" I shout, stopping my pacing. I run my hands through my hair until it's standing on end. "Are you fucking kidding me? You think I have that much stuffed under my mattress or something?"

"Let me finish." He's calmer than I expected. "If we go to a bail bondsman, we only need to put up ten percent of the bail. So we need one thousand."

I snort. "And your precious Wraiths won't pay it? Shouldn't that tell you something about who you work for?"

He grits his teeth. "The money's tied up at the moment."

Were their assets frozen or something? Or is it tied up in product?

You know what? I don't even want to know. Don't want to be involved in this in any way.

"Come on, I know you have a thousand," Nate whines.

Yeah, I do. But that's not the point. There's no way in hell I'm spending that on Dad, even if he paid me back with interest. Which he won't.

"No," I tell him.

Nate's nostrils flare. "Stop fucking around."

"I'm not."

"If you won't do it for Dad, then do it for Mom. She's a wreck."

My jaw hardens. "Don't use her as a weapon."

If she only left Dad, I'd never have to see him again.

"Well, you can tell her yourself." He pulls out his phone and taps at the screen, then it's on speakerphone as Mom answers. "I found Hunter, but he won't help. Here he is."

He sticks his phone in my face, forcing me to take it. "Hi, Mom."

"Why won't you help your father?" she says without preamble. "Family helps each other."

Underneath the scolding, there's worry in her voice. Even so, I get stuck on her words about family helping each other. What exactly have they ever done to help me? I've had an undiagnosed learning disorder my whole life and they couldn't be bothered to help me with it. Didn't even pay enough attention to realize I had it.

And here Madeline is not only discovering it, but going out of her way to help me with it, too.

"I don't have the money," I tell her, which isn't a complete lie. I don't have the money *for him*.

I'll never have enough money for a man who thinks respect is earned through fists and threats. Who's more interested in what the Iron Wraiths think of him than anything else. Who thinks berating his child for being stupid is the height of comedy, for years on end.

"Besides, aren't you more concerned about why he's in jail to begin with?" I ask her.

"We can sort that out later," she says. "For now, we need to get him out."

What a load of crock. She's going to bury her head in the sand like she always does. Better to ignore and pretend something isn't happening than rock the boat.

"I have to go," I mutter, handing Nate his phone.

"We need that money," Nate calls out as I walk away.

"You're not getting a fucking cent from me!" I yell back, uncaring that Mom can hear, too. Maybe she needs a wake-up call.

I waver for a second on whether to return to the library, then decide against it, not wanting Nate to follow me. Same goes for my house, I guess.

So where the fuck do I go?

Chapter Twenty-Four
MADELINE

"Hi, honey," Mom calls out as I drop my bag at the front door. "Did you finish studying early?"

"Yeah."

"Come join me in here." The sound of the TV shuts off a moment later.

I let out a sigh, not wanting to keep her company at the moment. I still can't get Hunter's face out of my mind as he left, pleading with me not to say anything.

"I'm pretty tired," I tell her, peeking my head in the living room.

She waves me off. "Oh, you're always tired. You don't have two minutes for your mother?"

Here we go. I trudge over and sprawl on the opposite side of the couch, resting my temple in my palm. What am I going to do about Hunter? And not just about tonight, but this morning, too.

"You didn't come home last night," she comments, turning to face me.

I stare back at her, unsure what to say. Is she trying to play responsible parent?

"Not that you're not allowed to," she says on a breezy note when I stay silent. "Think of me more as a concerned roommate."

Roommate, huh? Roommates pay at least their share of the bills.

"Sorry if I worried you," I mumble, leaving it at that.

"Were you with Hunter?"

Is it that obvious? Then again, he's the only person I've brought around lately.

"We were watching something at his house and fell asleep on the couch."

She smiles, but it doesn't look like she believes me. Even if it's not the whole truth, she doesn't know that.

"What?" I ask her, the word coming out way more aggressively than I intended.

Her brows raise. "All I asked is if you were with Hunter. You don't have to get so defensive."

"You're just . . . always in my business." I look away, not wanting to see the hurt on her face that's sure to be there. I honestly don't think she tries to manipulate me with emotions, but the effect is all the same.

"I care about you, honey."

"If you cared, then you'd get a full-time job and take over the bills here instead of making me do it."

The silence in the room after my outburst is deafening, and when I finally can't take it anymore, I look at her, the shock there front and center. Behind it is distress, along with a good dose of bewilderment.

"I-I'm sorry," I stutter. "I don't know where that came from." It's like all of a sudden I went from zero to sixty. Maybe I'm on edge from everything that's happened today.

It takes her a moment to recover her voice. "Well, it must have come from somewhere. Sounds like you've had that bottled up for a while."

"Maybe," I admit. Wasn't I just complaining to Hunter about this not that long ago?

"Well, um . . ." She looks down at her hands in her lap. "Let's talk about it, then. I didn't realize it was an issue."

I can't help the sound of disbelief that escapes me. "You didn't realize me moving back home and paying the bills for the last three years was an issue?"

"I . . ." She falters. "I thought we had a good thing going. I make up the difference by taking care of the house and meals. It always worked for me and your father."

"I'm not Dad," I say bluntly. "Or your partner or your roommate. I'm your child."

She blinks a few times and rubs at her eye. "I know that. Believe me, I know that."

As harsh as I'm being, maybe it's necessary. I've let this go on way too long, afraid to confront her about it. But haven't I proved lately that I can stand up for myself? I did it with Hunter, and look how that's turned out.

Okay, maybe not the most comparable situation.

"I moved back here to help you out," I say in a softer tone, "so they wouldn't foreclose the house. But I can't stay here forever."

She nods. "I've been following that payment plan you set up for me to pay off my debt. I just need a little more time."

"And then you'll take over the mortgage?"

"Well, I don't know if I make enough for that. And I can't find a new job. Those kids need me at the school."

I resist the urge to ball my hands into fists, consciously relaxing my fingers. "I get that your work is rewarding." She works part-time as a teacher's aide at the elementary school. "But if it can't support you, you'll have to look for something else."

She makes a scoffing noise. "Honey, you can't tell me what job I can and can't have."

"Fine. Then I guess you'll have to move if you can't afford this house. Downsize. Call Aunt Lucy and see if you can live with her."

She blinks at me, as if I suggested she should go walking naked down Main Street. "I won't impose on her like that."

But she can impose on me? "So, what are you going to do?"

She smooths her hands over her lap. "Where's all this coming from, anyway? Why do you want to leave me?"

"Please don't try to guilt me." I say it as kindly as I can, but also firmly. "I'm not saying I'm moving out tomorrow, but I'm twenty-five. I want a space of my own." I think again about Hunter's home and how he's made it his own. I want something like that for me, too.

"You mean you want space from me."

Yes. But I've already pissed her off enough for one day.

"Think about what I've said." I get up from the couch. "We can talk about it more later."

I head to my room, shutting the door softly behind me. I should be halfway through an anxiety attack after that kind of confrontation, but instead, there's this lightness in my chest. Like I feel . . . free. I didn't realize how much all of that was weighing on me. How stuck I've felt here hiding in this house, letting life pass me by.

I used to have somewhat of a social life back in college. But when I returned to Green Valley, Mom needed so much of me. My money. My time. My emotional support. It's like she saved it up over the four years I was gone for college, only to spring it all on me at once when I came back. Things have leveled off now, but I never got around to connecting with others again.

Not until Hunter.

My chest aches again thinking about how embarrassed he was at the library. How ashamed he seemed of his family's issues. Does he think I'd judge him for his dad's mistakes?

And why wouldn't he? Didn't I throw that in his face the first day of the training program?

He still obviously hasn't told them about the firefighting thing. It's been almost two months now. I wasn't going to be the one to let the cat out of the bag, though. Why is he so intent on hiding it from them? He'd said they wouldn't like it, but why?

I have no illusions either that his brother was actually interested in me. More like he was trying to rile up Hunter. Guess those two are alike in that sense. And he did rile him. The way he'd said I was too good for him, all dark and serious. Did he mean that? Or was it a way to get his brother out of there?

And if he did mean it . . . was it intended only for his brother or him, too?

The butterflies occupying my stomach take another short flight, the same way they have whenever I think about Hunter and what we'd done this morning. It was totally out of character for me. I've never done anything like that in my life.

And while part of it had felt so right, it had also seemed to be happening so fast. Hunter and I aren't even dating. Paul and I hadn't done anything sexual until four months after we started dating, and we'd been friends for a year before that, too.

Yeah, and look how that turned out. The guy couldn't even make me come. Meanwhile, Hunter has definitely made me come. Twice now. Would it have been even better if I'd asked him to use his tongue? The crazy thing is, he actually seemed like he wanted to do it. Like the thought excited him. It had excited me, too, but I'd been too chicken to take the chance, as usual.

The same way I'd left him this morning, refusing to sleep in his bed any longer or go out to breakfast with him. Once the lust had worn off, it was all too real. I was out of my element.

Hadn't he said the other week there is no element, though? That I can always talk to him?

Easy for him to say. He doesn't over obsess about everything.

I pull my phone out of my pocket, looking at it. I should reach out to him. See how he's doing after his family drama. Plus, I owe him a conversation about this morning. I hadn't given him a chance to talk about it at the library earlier. I'd started in right away going over our chapters for the week.

Me: *Sorry about Nate earlier. Is there anything I can do to help?*

Instead of a text back, my phone rings.

"Hello?"

"Hey. I hate texting. Plus, I'm driving."

"Oh, okay." Now that I think about it, he always gives one-word responses to my texts. I thought he was just disinterested before. Now I realize it's the dyslexia thing. "Are you free to talk? You're not with your brother, anymore?"

"I left him at the library after he ambushed me. He called our mom and forced me to talk to her, too."

I hadn't seen either of them in the parking lot by the time I left there, but I'd taken my time packing up. "Do you want to talk about it?"

"Not particularly."

My shoulders drop, my ribs feeling tight. I guess it was stupid to think he'd want to confide in me.

"But I owe you an explanation after getting you involved," he continues. "And even if I don't want to talk about it, I will. With you."

There's that fluttering in my stomach again.

"Do you want me to come over?"

I shouldn't be inviting myself over to his house late at night. Past experience has proven I'm not to be trusted alone with him there.

He sighs heavily over the line. "I don't know if Nate went looking for me there."

And I don't really want to be here after that talk with my mom. "How about we go out for ice cream?"

There's silence, long enough that I'm afraid the call may have disconnected, then he asks in a half laugh, "You want to go out for ice cream?"

I laugh, too, realizing how dumb it sounds. "I don't know. Ice cream always cheers me up."

"Yeah, okay. You want to meet at Utterly Ice Cream in fifteen?"

When we hang up, I turn to my closet to look for something to wear, then dismiss the idea. This isn't a date. And what I wore to the library is perfectly fine.

When I pull up to the ice cream parlor on Main and Walnut, Hunter's Mustang is already parked out front. Inside, the teen behind the counter is scooping triple fudge brownie into a waffle cone. Oh, I love that flavor.

When I join Hunter at the counter, it catches me off guard when the worker hands the double-scooped cone to me.

"You got me this?" I ask Hunter.

He shrugs, as if it's not a big deal. "Yeah."

"How'd you know I like this?"

He gives me a look like I'm ridiculous. "Come on. I know you."

He's right. He does know me. I don't know why, but the simple exchange has me a bit blindsided.

He gets a peanut butter cup cone for himself, then leads me over to the tables in the corner, far enough away from the counter for some privacy.

"What else do you know about me?" I ask him.

He gives me a sidelong glance. "That you're probably overthinking this morning."

Damn.

"And that you want to know why my dad's in jail."

Also true.

Maybe best to tackle the second thing first.

"Did Nate tell you anything?"

He takes a few seconds to answer as he concentrates on his ice cream. "He wouldn't confirm anything. But it's a ten thousand dollar bail, so I'm assuming it's drug-related."

My eyes bug out. How can he say that so casually? "Ten thousand?" is all I'm able to manage.

"Yeah, but Nate only needs to put up a thousand. A bail bondsman will cover the rest."

"And did you give it to him?"

"No."

I take a couple of licks of my ice cream, debating what to say, but he beats me to the punch.

"You were right, you know."

I look over at him, unsure what he's talking about.

"About my family and the Iron Wraiths. My dad and brother deal for them. Guess Dad's luck ran out."

"Hunter—"

"They're both real pieces of shit," he continues, as if he didn't hear me. "My dad more so than my brother. Always let me know how much of an idiot I was growing up, when he felt like paying attention. How stupid I was."

I'm quiet, not wanting to hear this, but also desperate to. He never talks about his family.

"I just keep thinking . . . why didn't anyone ever figure out the dyslexia thing? If not my parents, then a teacher or something? It might have changed . . . everything."

"You'll kill yourself with the what-ifs," I whisper.

He nods. "Now he's been pushing me to join the Iron Wraiths the last few years, as if I'd want anything to do with them. Nate's followed him like a good boy, but none of them can understand why I wouldn't want to, too."

"Well, you have a good argument for why you won't now."

He rolls his eyes as he looks away. "I warned them. Mom, especially. She refused to even acknowledge they were dealing to begin with. I can't wait to hear what kind of excuse she makes up for him."

"I'm sorry you have to deal with all that."

He shakes his head. "Honestly, it'd be so much easier if he wasn't around. Maybe him being put away is a good thing. Then she'd realize what a drain he is on her."

"Have you talked to her about this before?"

"She won't listen. And I can't be sure, but I think he used to hit her if she talked back. So she doesn't talk back, anymore."

My heart aches for him, for the way he seems helpless to protect his mom.

"That must have been difficult to grow up in that kind of dynamic."

He scrubs a hand down his face, staring at his ice cream cone. "Shit. I didn't mean to start complaining about all this."

"No, I like when you talk to me."

One side of his mouth quirks up in a smile. "You really would make a good psychologist, huh?"

I laugh lightly. "Just call me Dr. Woodward."

He grins and works on his ice cream for a few moments. "Thanks for not saying anything to Nate. About the firefighting stuff, I mean."

"Yeah, of course."

"You're lucky you don't have siblings. They're a pain in the ass."

"I don't know. I always wanted a brother or sister. Being an only child can be lonely."

"Well, you wouldn't want Nate."

"Okay, maybe not him," I agree. "He seems pretty chaotic."

He huffs out a breath. "I've brought nothing but chaos to your life, haven't I?"

The way he says it, as if he's really down about it . . . "Well, a little chaos isn't too bad. It makes life more interesting."

"You don't have to try and make me feel better."

I nudge his arm. "No, seriously. Without you . . . honestly, I don't know where I'd be. I can lift weights now. And run without collapsing. I wouldn't have made it this far without you. And even besides all the training stuff . . ." I swallow, remembering that stuff I was thinking about at home, about connecting with others. "I'm so glad I've gotten to know you. I didn't realize I'd kind of shut myself off from others for a while."

He rubs at the back of his neck, and I swear his cheeks are flushed the slightest shade of pink. "Shit, Madeline. You trying to make me blush?"

I grin, unable to help myself.

There's a tinkling above the door as another customer walks in and Hunter stiffens beside me. Is it Nate? His mom?

No, it's . . . Lydia.

Chapter Twenty-Five
HUNTER

S hit.

Shit. Shit. Shit.

What are the chances Lydia, of all people, walks into the same fucking ice cream shop I'm at with Madeline? I've never even been here before.

Does she remember what we talked about at that party? What am I thinking? Of course, she does. I should be grateful word hasn't got back around to Madeline about what I said, even if the two girls don't run in any of the same social circles.

"You want to get out of here?" I ask, eyeing Lydia, who hasn't noticed us yet. She's with her sister and nephew, studying the list of ice cream flavors on the wall.

Madeline pointedly looks at her unfinished ice cream cone in her hand, then Lydia. "Yeah, okay," she says quietly.

Shit. She knows I want to leave specifically because of her. She probably thinks something's up between us.

As we stand, Lydia notices us, and she gives us a delighted smile as she walks over.

"You two look cozy," she says, giving us a once-over. "I see things are working out for you."

I give a noncommittal nod. "Yeah, we were just going." I only need her to not say anything for a few moments longer.

"So, what we talked about the other night helped?" she asks.

Madeline's gaze flicks between me and Lydia, that overactive mind of hers hard at work.

"We ran into each other at a party," I explain, not that it explains anything.

"And who knew I'd be giving relationship advice to this guy, huh?" Lydia shakes my arm and laughs. "Totally caught me off guard when he said you two were dating."

And there it is. I should have grabbed Madeline's hand and ran as soon as Lydia entered.

Madeline, bless her soul, doesn't display the extreme shock I thought she might. In fact, she hardly has any reaction at all. She simply takes another lick of her ice cream and gives Lydia a strange smile. "I didn't see it coming, either."

"It was good seeing you," I say to Lydia, even though it wasn't at all, and usher Madeline out, dropping the rest of my cone in the trash. My appetite is gone, my mind going a million miles a minute trying to figure out what to say.

"So . . . when were you going to tell me we're dating?" she asks when we get to our cars. There's amusement in her tone, along with a healthy splash of bewilderment.

I pace between our cars, my chest tight. "It's not what it sounds like."

"It's not?"

I lace my hands behind my neck, not knowing how to explain this. "Okay, it is. But I only said that because she wanted to have sex with me."

Okay, now she's shocked.

Shit. I shouldn't have said that.

She shakes her head, as if she's stunned. "I guess I'm more surprised you turned down a girl propositioning you than anything else," she jokes. At least, I think she's joking.

"She's not the only one lately," I say, thinking of Josie at the bar the other week.

Her eyes widen again.

Fuck. What is wrong with my mouth? Why can't I say the right thing?

"I'm messing this all up. What I meant to say is I don't want to sleep with Lydia or Josie or anyone else. I only want to sleep with you." No, that's not what I meant to say, either. "I mean, I want everything with you. I . . ." I swallow hard. "I really like you, Madeline."

Her mouth falls open as she blinks rapidly at me.

Fuck. This is not going well. It's like I'm in one of those dreams where I'm pantsless in front of the whole school and they're all pointing and laughing. Not that she's doing those things, but she's also not responding.

How the fuck did this happen? I wasn't going to confess anything to her tonight. We were just having that really great personal talk in the shop, and then Lydia ruined everything.

"Madeline, I . . ." How can I make this better? "I know I don't deserve you. That you could do way better than me." No, that's making things worse. "But I promise I'll always treat you right. I'll always make you feel like you matter. You're so important to me and you're all I think about and . . ."

I trail off, not sure if I'm making things any better.

"What are you saying?" she whispers after what feels like forever. "That you want to actually date me?"

Was that not clear? "Yeah."

"You said you don't do girlfriends."

"That was before I met you."

Her lower lip trembles. Did I upset her? Completely read her wrong? I'd thought she'd been into what we were doing this morning, but maybe she'd only been into it sexually. Maybe she's not interested in anything more than that.

Maybe all I'm good for is a hookup.

The punch to my gut has my knees weakening as I back away from her. "Forget I said anything."

"Hunter—"

"It was a long shot." I bump into my car, then fumble to find the door handle. "I understand if you don't—"

"Hunter, stop." She places her hand on my door to stop me from opening it. "I'm overwhelmed, not rejecting you."

I look at her, really look at her, and any thought of fleeing leaves my mind.

"Fuck, baby. I'm sorry."

When I open my arms, she's in them in an instant, and I hold her close. Her head resting against my chest is the most natural feeling in the world. Her arms wrap around my middle and we stay like that for I don't know how long. I'd stay like this all night if it means I get to keep holding her.

"Why are you overwhelmed?" I finally ask.

"Because you mean so much to me, too."

Her words and accompanying squeeze do more than she knows to reassure me. Even so . . . "Then why do you make it sound like a bad thing?"

She shakes her head against my chest. "It's stupid," she mumbles.

"I'm sure it's not."

She releases her hold on me but doesn't meet my eye. "I don't want to lose you."

My brows knit. "You won't. I'm not going anywhere."

"I mean . . . if you change your mind."

I blink, taken aback. I've never heard such raw vulnerability from her before. That tight control she used to cloak herself in has completely unraveled, leaving her bare.

I lift her chin until she meets my gaze. "You think I'll change my mind?"

She tries to turn her head, but I won't let her. Her face turns pleading instead. "I don't know."

"What makes you think I would?"

"Hunter . . ."

"I'm being serious. I want to get everything out in the open. To reassure you. Because there's nothing that's going to change the way I feel about you."

She sways toward me, her expression changing to longing for an instant before she squeezes her eyes shut. "I just don't understand how I could hold your interest when you know what you're missing with all those other girls. I'm not as sexy or adventurous or kinky or the million other things you're probably used to."

That's what has her worried? I nearly laugh in relief. "First of all, you're wildly overestimating my sex life. And there's nothing to miss. They were empty, meaningless encounters."

"Then why'd you have them?"

"Because I didn't know what I was missing."

She finally opens her eyes, the deep brown of them penetrating me. "Missing?"

I grip her shoulders. "You. I was missing you. Any other experience isn't comparable. This morning, all you did was put your hand on me and it was the hottest thing I've ever felt."

Her gaze flicks over my face. "You're serious?"

"Of course I am. And if you want to talk about comparisons, I could argue that you dated someone for two years. How am I supposed to compare to a relationship as long as that?"

She shakes her head before I'm finished. "No. The way I feel about you . . . You're right. It doesn't compare."

"So, what would make you feel better?" I ask her. "You want me to get *Madeline's Bitch* tattooed on my forehead or something? To keep all the girls away?"

She laughs, just like I wanted her to, the tension in her loosening.

"Maybe a temporary tattoo," she says, biting her bottom lip.

"I'll do it. Don't tempt me."

She smooths her hands over my chest. "In all seriousness, don't ever get a tattoo for me. I'd hate it."

"Duly noted."

"And no funny business at the fire station. I want them to take me seriously, not just be someone's girlfriend."

My breath catches. "So you'll . . ."

She nods, looking equal parts nervous and excited. "I trust you. And I want to be with you."

How in the world did all the shitty things that happened today lead to this? If Dad hadn't gotten busted and Nate hadn't shown up looking for bail money, we never would have gone out tonight. And if Lydia hadn't run her big mouth, we never would have had this conversation.

The universe works in mysterious ways, but I'll take it if it leads to this.

I kiss her, holding myself back, wanting to take her right here against my car in the middle of town. "Please tell me you'll come back to my place."

"There's nowhere else I'd rather be."

I force myself to break away while I still have the willpower. "I'll meet you there, okay?"

The drive back to my house is the longest it's ever been, but I get there first, probably because I treated a few stop signs more as suggestions than commands. When she finally arrives, I can't help myself as I press her against the back of the front door, my lips on her neck, my hands on her ass pulling her closer.

"I want you," I murmur, stripping off her top.

Her hands slide over my hair, my neck, my shoulders, every place they touch like a brand, marking me as hers. I only want to be hers.

Unhooking her bra, I slide the straps down, revealing her perfect breasts. Her nipples are beaded, eager for me, and I give them each a strong suck, ready to play with them for a while.

"Hunter." She's panting already. "We're not even in the bedroom."

She's right. Against the front door for the first time isn't very romantic.

Picking her up, I carry her through the house and to my bedroom, tossing her on the bed. She reclines on her elbows, observing me as I grab my T-shirt at the back of the neck and slide it off, then toe off my shoes and socks. My gaze is all over her, from her bare breasts to the way she keeps rubbing her thighs together, seeking relief.

"You look like you're the big bad wolf watching me like that," she murmurs. "Ready to eat me alive."

"Oh, I'm most definitely going to eat you up." I pull her to the end of the bed, removing her sandals. "I'll huff and puff and make you come so hard, you'll see stars."

Her breathing grows heavier as my palms slide up her legs, to her inner thighs.

"I want to go down on you so bad." I unbutton her jeans and slide the zipper down. "That good with you?"

She nods, her eyes wide.

I fully undress her and pause a moment, taking in her beautiful body. I will never get enough of this sight.

Hooking my arms under her thighs, I pull her even closer, to the edge of the mattress, and kneel next to the bed. I part her legs, spreading her wide until she's fully open to me, and bend my head to lick teasingly along her pussy.

Her hands grip the comforter and a whimper escapes her as I lap at her.

"You like that?"

"Yes," she breathes, angling her hips up to give me better access.

That's my girl.

"You taste so fucking good."

I nestle into her, the honeyed taste like ambrosia, and set a leisurely pace. My dick is straining against my fly, but I ignore it for the moment, wanting to make her first experience one to remember.

A thrill of possession runs through me knowing I'm the first to do this, the first to taste her pussy, the first to put her needs first. She deserves it, and I take my time worshiping her. I discover what makes her moan low in the back of her throat, what makes her thighs shake, what makes her arch her back as she offers herself to me, wanting more.

I give her everything she wants, until she's panting, saying my name with reverence. She just needs a push to reach the other side.

My hands glide over her inner thighs and to her pussy, my thumbs parting her folds. Focusing my tongue on her clit, I add in a finger, then two, working her until she cries out. Her fingers tear at the bedsheets as her hips buck against my face, and I keep at it as her orgasm rolls through her, drinking her down.

When she finally goes limp on the bed, I back off, kissing my way up her body, exploring all the dips and valleys I mapped out last time with my hands, this time with my lips. I can't get enough of the taste of her, pride filling me knowing I worked her up that much.

When I reach her mouth, she kisses me back hungrily, twining herself around me. "That was incredible."

"Baby, that was only the beginning."

Chapter Twenty-Six
MADELINE

I'm floating on a cloud named Hunter. The things the man can do with his tongue . . . Holy Christ. And the way I'd lost control there at the end, my hips pumping with a mind all their own into his face, a loud cry escaping my lips. If it had been anyone besides him, I'd be embarrassed beyond belief.

But Hunter's my boyfriend now. The thought still feels fuzzy, like it's not real. Like we're playacting something for tonight.

But there's also no one I've trusted more. Somewhere along the way, he became my closest confidant, the person I feel most myself with.

He stands and shucks his pants and boxer briefs, leaving him fully nude. I shamelessly gawk since it was much darker the last time we were like this. His cock is long and thick, and I totally get now why he was considered such a sex god in high school. If he's hung like that and it's been this good so far . . . what will it be like when he's finally inside me?

"Are you on birth control?" he asks, breaking my train of thought.

"Um, no. But I can get on it."

"Whatever you feel comfortable with," he says, rounding the bed and opening one of his nightstand drawers. "We'll use condoms for now."

Ripping open the foil package, he rolls one on, and I pick up the discarded wrapper.

"These look awfully familiar."

A sheepish smile crosses his face. "I may have spent a small fortune on that prank."

Serves him right. "It was pretty good," I admit. "Also ridiculous."

He kneels on the bed, then positions me so my head is on the pillow. "You didn't save them by chance, did you?"

I nod. No sense in throwing away perfectly good condoms, even if I had no plans for them.

He grins wickedly. "Because you wanted to use them with me."

I laugh, loving that we can be both hot and heavy, and playful and teasing together simultaneously. "You know full well I didn't."

He leans over me, nuzzling my neck. "Glad I changed your mind, then. I'm sure we could put them to good use now."

"Oh, definitely."

His hands run over me, leaving pleasurable shivers in their wake. "You ready for me? Or do you need another minute?"

"I'm ready."

He covers me with his big body, a satisfying weight that ignites desire within me again. His hand snakes between us and he enters me with two fingers, working me up for a few moments before he replaces them with his cock. He lifts my thigh, opening me further to him, and fills me slowly.

My fingers grip his broad shoulders as I blow out a breath. The pressure is more than I was expecting. "Holy shit."

He immediately stops. "Is it too much?"

"Just give me a minute."

He kisses me, my body relaxing by degrees, and he brings a hand to my breast, thumbing my nipple.

I moan, my hips shifting, and he slips further inside.

"I know what you need," he says, pulling out of me.

I'm about to ask him where he thinks he's going when he pulls me to a sitting position, then shifts me atop him, so he's sitting against the headboard with me straddling him. He props me up further so my breasts are face level with him, and my breathing picks up in anticipation. His cock slides along my seam, his hands on my waist, but he doesn't enter me yet.

He leans forward, capturing a nipple in his mouth, and I arch my back instinctively, loving the delicious zing of pleasure that races through me.

"You go wild every time I touch you here," he murmurs against my breast, then nips at me.

Oh God, I like that.

I murmur some kind of unintelligible agreement, wanting him to do it again, and he does, knowing what I want. He sucks me gently, teasing me with that talented tongue, and when it gets to be too much, he feeds the length of his cock into my pussy, now slippery with fresh arousal.

Rising up and down, my movements are slow at first as he still kisses my breasts, but when he moves his lips to my neck, I pick up the pace. His hands grip my waist, guiding me in the rhythm as he drives into me from below, our breaths growing harsher over the long minutes.

"Christ, I've never seen anything as sexy as your tits bouncing in my face while you ride me."

I look down at him, at the slack-jawed lust on his face, and a wave of desire rushes over me. I can't believe I turn him on that much. That being with *me* is the hottest experience he's had.

Because he loves me.

Wait, no. He never said that. He said he really *likes* me. There's a difference.

Do I wish he'd said the other L-word? Maybe. Because the truth is, I'm falling for him. Hard. Especially after his confessions. It's as if I've finally been given permission to feel all these emotions I've kept buried deep. My desire for him. The way I've come to admire the person he is, rather than who I first thought he was. The way he cares for me, listens to me. He'd said earlier he wants to show me I matter. He actually remembered I said that at the bar about what attracts me to a guy.

My rhythm falters, overwhelmed momentarily with the feelings rushing inside of me, and he nips at the shell of my ear, shifting me in his lap.

"Want to try another position?" he asks, his voice all dark promise.

I nod and let him position me on my elbows and knees, ass tilted toward him.

"Fuck, you are so sexy." His warm palms skim over my ass, startling me when he gives a light slap.

Okay, definitely exploring that another time. It felt a little too good.

He slides his cock inside me from behind, the sensation so much fuller from this angle. A moan escapes me, and I brace my knees so I don't slip as he draws in and out, faster and faster, working up to a punishing rhythm that has me breathless.

The stirrings of a second orgasm swirl low in my core, surprising me. I've never come twice in such a short period, even when I'm by myself.

Then again, I've never been with Hunter.

"I love you from this angle," he says. "Your ass is goddamn perfect."

My heart skips a beat before I process the rest of his sentence.

"That day in your bedroom," he continues, "with the workout video, I couldn't stop looking at it."

I knew he had been checking me out. "So, I wasn't crazy accusing you?"

He chuckles, his hands squeezing the globes of my ass as he pumps into me. "No, you weren't. I was the one crazy wanting you when I knew you couldn't stand me."

"And look at us now."

He slows down his rhythm as he leans over, his chest to my back, and brings my head to the side to kiss me.

"I'm so grateful you took a chance on me," he murmurs. "That things worked out the way they did. Because I couldn't imagine my life without you now."

My chest glows with warmth. All those weeks ago, I'd never have guessed he'd say such sweet things. That he'd make me ache with want, not just physically, but emotionally, too.

He pulls out and flips me on my back, entering me smoothly once more. "I want to see you when you come again."

I'd tell him he's too cocky for his own good assuming he'll make me come again, but he's right.

"I'm close, too," he says. "You turn me on so much. I can't wait to come inside you. Do you know how many times I've thought of this exact moment?"

"You have?"

He nods, bending down to caress his lips along my neck. "You've been the star of my fantasies for a while now."

My body thrums with excitement at his confession. "You have for me, too," I admit.

He leans back to look at me, his gaze alight with curiosity and lust. "Please tell me you've touched yourself while thinking of me."

I nod, trying not to be shy, but it's hard when you're divulging one of your most personal secrets.

"What'd you imagine?"

If I wasn't so far gone already, there's no way I would tell him this. But in this moment, turned on as I am, the words slip out.

"The way your tongue would feel on my pussy. How good it would be."

"Yeah?" he croaks out, his movements becoming more frantic.

Oh my God, am I seriously turning him on?

"And the way you would fill me up with your cock."

"I fill you up good, don't I?"

I nod. "And I just had another fantasy."

"Tell me," he says, his voice brooking no argument.

I inhale shakily. "I want you to slap my ass again."

"Oh, fuck," he calls out, his hips going jerky. "Oh God, Madeline, I'm coming."

The sight of him in the throes of passion sets me off, too, and I groan as the wave washes over me, taking me under.

I love the way he keeps us tightly joined until the end, his grip like iron on me, like he never wants us to be apart. Or maybe it's only me feeling that way. That I want to be with him always. It's as if being with him altered my DNA somehow, like he's a part of me.

And I never want to let him go.

When our breaths are steady again, he pulls out and leaves to clean up in the bathroom, but he's back soon, rearranging us on the bed so we're under the covers, my body half-draped over his. He runs a hand over me, almost absent-mindedly, like he needs to keep me close.

"You'll stay the night?"

I'm not completely sure if it's a question or command, but I nod, anyway.

"I'm the luckiest bastard in the world." He turns his head to kiss my forehead. "I somehow landed the most amazing girl I've ever met."

A flush of pleasure spreads over me. "Hunter . . ."

"Oh, that's right. You don't like compliments."

"What?"

"You get all flustered every time I give you one."

"I do?"

"Uh-huh. But you better get used to them. Because I want my girl to know how much I'm thinking about her."

His girl. I love the sound of that.

"Hey, the last time I complimented you, you got a little flustered yourself, mister."

"When was that?"

"At the ice cream shop. I told you how much I appreciated you being my trainer and how glad I am we've gotten closer."

He squeezes my hip. "Yeah, I wasn't expecting that."

I run my hand over the light dusting of hair on his chest, the way I'd wanted to that day we got caught in the rain and he stripped his shirt off. There's something that's been on my mind since the library. "You said earlier you don't deserve me. Why would you think that?"

He shifts, his hand on my hip, tightening and releasing. "Don't worry about it."

"Hunter . . ."

He chuckles lightly. "Can't just get up and walk away from the conversation, huh?"

With both of us naked in his bed? Uh, no.

"Part of being with someone is answering to them. Even if we don't always want to."

"I know." Still, it takes him a bit to say anything more. "You're the kind of girl who doesn't need anyone."

Okay, I wasn't expecting that. "I don't understand."

He sighs and brushes the hair back from my face, tucking it behind my ear. "You're so smart. So capable. You run circles around everyone else."

I wait for him to elaborate, but he doesn't. "And that makes you feel bad?"

I told him before I'm not dumbing myself down so he can feel better about himself.

"No. It's one of the things I like about you most. Especially because you don't play the damsel in distress. But it's like . . . what do you need a schlub like me for, you know? If I hadn't been here to help you with training, you would have figured it out on your own. You even said yourself you don't need me as much as I need you."

"I didn't mean—"

"I know you didn't. But it's the truth. And there's so much more, too. You're beautiful and caring. You have this wicked sense of humor you hardly let anyone else see. You're so committed to your ideals and you know who you are. I wish I was more like that."

I don't know what to say, unaware he even saw me like that, but I shake my head. "I think you don't see yourself clearly. And you've said before there's no keeping score. We're a team. Not just with the firefighting stuff, but now with everything else, too."

I look at him, past the handsome exterior to the soft underbelly he doesn't show anyone else. He hid behind bravado and sarcastic quips for so long, but underneath it all is a man who needs more reassurance than he lets on.

"I usually go under the radar," I say in a soft voice. "But with you . . . You see me. And that means everything. You said earlier you want to show me that I matter to you, and you do. Those things I told you at Genie's, about what attracts me to someone . . . You fit the bill on all of it. When you're not driving me completely crazy, you make me laugh. You're always doing things for me, without any kind of expectation in return, which I appreciate so much. You push me out of my comfort zone, which I need, and after you stopped purposely trying to piss me off, you know when to stop."

He chuckles, some of the tension in him receding, which I'm grateful for.

"I don't want you to ever feel like you don't deserve me," I continue, "because you do. Life may have dealt you a shitty hand with some things, but you've turned it around. You've worked hard to own a beautiful home that you've made into a haven for yourself. You're doing so much volunteering your time and effort for your community with this firefighting thing. You have a girl-friend who feels so lucky to have you in her life. There are so many things I admire about you." I think back to that day at the fire station when we'd had to tell Chief McClure why we were in the training program. Hunter had said he wanted to feel good about himself for a change, as if he didn't before. And that he didn't want to be like his father. "You're a good person. You're worthy."

He's silent, other than something that suspiciously sounds like a sniff, but I don't comment on it. Hunter's not the vulnerable type, and I don't want to embarrass him.

He finds my hand and brings it to his mouth to kiss my palm, then twines our fingers together. "I wasn't expecting that, either," he finally says, his voice a bit watery.

"But you believe me?"

"I think that's going to take some time," he admits. "Not because I think you're lying. But because of how I've always seen myself."

"Well, if you need me to make a list of all the wonderful things about you, just let me know. Oh, I have one more."

"Yeah?"

"Mm-hmm. You're sort of good looking, I guess."

He laughs, freer sounding now.

"If you squint really hard," I add, glad he laughs harder at that.

He brings me in close and kisses me, long and slow. "Who knew my main selling point would be on the bottom of your list?" he murmurs.

"Well, not the bottom. Maybe the middle."

He gives me another quick kiss before leaning back. "To be honest, I'm glad it's not at the top. That I have some other redeeming qualities."

"Of course you do."

A banging on the front door has us both startling.

"Expecting late night visitors?" I ask.

His face darkens. "No. Stay here, okay?"

He gets out of bed and slips on his boxer briefs and jeans before leaving. I pull the sheets over my nude body, then get dressed, just in case. I search on the floor around the bed, only finding my underwear and jeans, then remember my shirt and bra are by the front door still.

Crap.

Chapter Twenty-Seven
HUNTER

Peeking through the peephole, my stomach sinks as I spot Mom on the other side of the door.

She bangs again with her fist. "I know you're there," she calls out in her gravelly voice. "And I'm not leaving."

Fuck.

I open the door and look down at her. "I thought we already discussed this."

She pushes past me and into the house. "I stopped by earlier and you weren't home. Now there's another car in the driveway. Who's here?"

"Don't worry about it."

And for the second time after saying that tonight, I'm promptly ignored. "You've been avoiding us like the plague lately. What's got you so—"

She stops and bends down, picking up a bra off the floor.

Oh, shit. I forgot I half-undressed Madeline out here earlier.

"Getting laid is more important than helping your family?" she asks, zero amusement in her tone.

I snatch the bra from her and toss it toward the couch. "I said don't worry about it."

A wrinkle forms between her brows. "You leave me no choice when you're too busy with your latest piece of ass—"

"She's not a piece of ass," I interrupt, my mouth getting away from me. "She's my girlfriend."

Her eyes widen, and I immediately curse myself for saying anything about Madeline to her. Really, though, how long could I keep it hidden if Madeline and I are together now?

Then again, I've kept the firefighting stuff a secret this long . . .

"A girlfriend sounds pretty serious. When were you going to tell me about this?"

I block out the hurt in her voice as best I can. "We've been friends for a while, but the dating part is new." As in, tonight new.

"So, you have time for her, but not your family?"

"Will you stop with the family shtick?" I ask her. "This isn't *The Fast and the Furious*."

She appears confused, so I elaborate. "I've never gotten along with Dad. He's a bully and I can't stand him. The only reason I come around is for you. And since you're not the one in jail, there's nothing for me to do."

Her nostrils flare. "You'd abandon your father like that in his time of need?"

I can't keep inside the laugh that escapes me. "His time of need? This situation is entirely of his own making. If he wasn't dealing—"

"We don't know that for sure."

I shrug, tired of sugarcoating things for her. "You're delusional if you really think that."

The truth is, she's been telling herself lies to keep the peace for so long, she might actually believe them at this point.

She shakes her head. "Where did I go wrong with you?" she murmurs.

"Wrong with me?" Is she fucking kidding? "Where did you go right? You've always cared more about making sure Dad stays happy than anything to do with me."

"That's not true," she snarls in a low voice. "I've defended you. And this is the thanks I get."

"What exactly did you do? Huh? I'd love to know."

She stares at me, but doesn't say anything.

"Because if he yelled at me, all you did was say I shouldn't have upset him. As if I was doing anything other than existing around him. That if he backhanded me, you said it was my fault for getting too close to him when he was drinking. That I should have known better. That if he went on one of his endless rants about how goddamn stupid I was, you said I should have gotten better grades."

"Well, you should have," she replies petulantly, ignoring everything else I said.

"And did you ever offer to help me with anything in school? Did you know it turns out I have a learning disorder? An actual fucking disability? If you'd paid the slightest bit of attention, you might have realized it. Might have gotten me the help I needed. But no, you were too busy catering to Dad."

Her jaw trembles for a moment before she firms it. That's right. Can't show weakness. Dad would sniff it out in a second. "And what was I supposed to do?" she shouts. "Choose between him and you?"

"Yes!" I cry out, throwing my arms up. "If that's what it took. I was your child. You were supposed to protect me. But you didn't have the guts."

She backs away, as if she's trying to run from it all over again. "It was an impossible choice. I did what I had to, okay?"

"You don't *have to* do anything when it comes to him. You could leave him. He's a shitty father and husband and person all around. Let him rot in jail. He deserves it."

"You don't mean that."

"I absolutely do. And this conversation's been a long time coming. I'm tired of dancing around it. You're welcome to come over here, but I'm not going home, anymore."

She blows out a breath. "Fine. We'll visit—"

"No. No *we*. *You* can visit here. Not Nate if he's going to continue being a copycat of Dad. And definitely not Dad. I'm tired of acting like everything's okay when it's not."

She sneers at me. "You really think you're better than us now, don't you? Living in your nice house with your nice car and your new girlfriend. But you're not as good as you think you are. You're an O'Connor. And you can try and run from it all you want, but—"

"You can leave now," I tell her, opening the front door. "I don't have the bail money."

Her lips purse mulishly. "If you give me it, I won't bother you about your dad anymore."

"No."

She stands there stubbornly for another minute, but when she sees I'm not budging, she huffs out a breath. "Your father was right about you," she mutters as she leaves.

Her parting jab has its intended effect, and all of the pain I kept at bay throughout her visit comes rushing at me all at once. I shut the door and sag against it briefly. What the fuck just happened? Did I really let loose on all the things I've wanted to say for years?

I get myself under control and turn the corner toward the hallway that leads to my bedroom, only to stop at the sight of Madeline there, wearing my discarded shirt.

"Did you hear all that?" I ask, though it's a stupid question. Of course she did. Even if she'd stayed in my room she would have. We were practically screaming at each other at parts.

Her serious gaze pierces me through. "I wanted to make sure you're okay."

I shrug. "Yeah, I'm fine."

Her head cocks to the side, her expression shifting to one of skepticism. She doesn't have to call me on my bullshit answer because we both know it's bullshit.

I shrug again, my shoulders suddenly feeling like boulders as they curl forward. There's a building pressure behind my eyes I can't seem to get rid of. "I think I just lost my mom," I whisper, and then Madeline's there, holding me in her arms.

I tuck my head into the crook of her neck, too tall to do this comfortably, but I don't care. Nothing has ever felt as good as being in her arms like this.

She strokes a hand down my back. "I'm proud of you."

A chuckle escapes me, though there's no humor in it. "For what? Screaming at my mom?"

"For standing up for yourself. It's a difficult thing to do."

My arms wrap around her middle, hugging her tight, and as she keeps stroking my back, something in me loosens, my eyelids hot, then wet. She doesn't say anything as her neck dampens, though she must feel it. I want to apologize, but I'm afraid it'll come out a mess. She'd already got me earlier telling me I'm a good person. That I'm worthy of her.

I'm not, but maybe I could be one day.

I pick her up, her legs wrapping around my waist, and carry her back to bed. I spoon her from behind, her body tucked into mine until she falls asleep. It takes longer for me, though, my head caught up in the fact that I essentially cut my family off for good.

But even with the guilt and feelings of disloyalty, there's also a sense of freedom along with it. That I'm not tied down by them anymore. So much of the last couple of months has been about reinventing myself, and this feels like the last puzzle piece. If I'm not a part of their dysfunctional mess, I can be something different. Something good. *Someone* good, like Madeline said.

I tug her tighter to me, my hand resting on her stomach. For once, the future looks . . . bright.

Chapter Twenty-Eight
MADELINE

The next two and a half weeks fly by in a blur, Hunter and I eating, sleeping, and breathing firefighting training. We run through all the CPAT exercises on our own, even borrowing some equipment from the fire station to make sure it's as authentic as possible. The office manager says we're the only ones who ask, so we get first dibs at using the weighted vests we'll have to wear during the test or practicing with the twenty-four-foot ladders at the station, since neither of our cars can transport them home.

I do what I can, finding the ways that work best for me as someone shorter and lighter than the rest of the team, but all that matters is I pass the eight events in less than ten minutes and twenty seconds. Such a small amount of time for something so important.

For Hunter, I scour the internet for all the practice tests I can find, and we take them night after night, poring over the answer keys afterward to figure out how we can improve. He's probably sick of me quizzing him endlessly, but he doesn't let on if he is, patiently answering my relentless questions.

Late at night, after all the practicing and studying are done, is my favorite time, though. We put those condoms he stuffed in my locker to good use, and I get a crash course in what it means to be the object of Hunter's desire. He takes me on every available surface in his bedroom, his bathroom, his living room. Bending me forward over the back of the couch and fucking me from behind. Eating me out in the shower. Even one memorable time on the kitchen counter as I'd been prepping dinner. I'd had to sanitize everything and completely start over afterward, but it'd been worth it. I love how much he wants me.

And even more, it's as if he's awakened this other Madeline I didn't know existed. One who finds sex fun and incredibly hot. Who enjoys giving blow jobs instead of it being a chore. Who isn't shy to have someone see every part of her. It seems it only took being with the right man to unlock all that.

The night before our final exams, I'm a nervous wreck. "Did you see this email?" I ask Hunter, waving my phone at him. There's no way he can read my screen from this distance, but I still do it, anyway.

"You know I don't check my email," he says, gathering the dishes off the coffee table from dinner earlier.

That's right. The idea is unfathomable to me, but I guess he's made it this far without it.

"They want to do a live fire exercise to assess our teamwork skills on Sunday. I guess they had some issues previously with the full-time team that made them think it'd be a good idea."

He shrugs. "Okay, no problem."

"No problem? We haven't prepared." I push down the gnawing sensation in my stomach, despite having just eaten.

"We did that live fire practice the other week."

"But that was individual practice, not teams, and from a distance. This will be closer, it sounds like."

He sets the dishes in the sink and walks over to me, placing his hands on my shoulders. "You sound insane. It'll be fine. And if it's teams, it's even better because Chief McClure will definitely partner us up."

Right. He's right. We've found a great rhythm working together at the station.

I blow out a long breath. "Okay, sorry. Should we get some last-minute study practice in? I can quiz—"

He shakes his head. "You need to relax tonight. Here, come on."

Leading me to the couch, he turns me away from him, then rubs the tense muscles of my upper back until I melt under his touch. His hands move lower, down my spine, working their magic until they're practically on my ass.

"Hey, you're just trying to seduce me." Not that I've put up any kind of fight.

"Is it working?"

I don't have to see his face to know he's grinning.

"Maybe."

He leans forward, running his lips over my neck. "Anything I can do to sway you further?" He presses a kiss behind my ear, shivers running over me at the intimate contact.

I bite my lip, wavering. I really did mean to study tonight. Maybe he's right, though. A night off would do us some good, to be refreshed in the morning. What's that saying? All work and no play . . .

Oh, who am I kidding? I just want him to touch me.

Reaching behind me, I place my hands over his, then guide them to my front, to my chest. He groans low in my ear as he slips under my shirt and quickly unhooks my bra, then molds his palms over my breasts, squeezing gently.

I arch into his touch, loving how he draws soft circles around my nipples until they're beaded with arousal, and moan as he plays with me, working me up. I squirm, needing relief, and when none is forthcoming, I sneak a hand between my thighs, rubbing softly over the fabric of my leggings.

My head falls back against his shoulder, a groan ripping from me as the lust within me ratchets higher, and that's when he seems to take notice of what I'm doing. He lifts me onto his thighs, his chest to my back, and whispers, "Don't stop." There's unrestrained excitement in his voice. "I'm going to undress you, but don't stop."

He slides my shirt and bra off, then hooks his thumbs in my leggings and panties, dragging them down my legs and over my feet, leaving me nude on top of him. He spreads my legs wider, giving him a clearer view from over my shoulder of what I'm doing.

"Oh, fuck, baby. That's hot." His hands return to my breasts, thumbing my nipples into tight peaks. "Keep playing with yourself like that."

I let myself rest against him and draw my fingers in and out of my pussy, half focusing on the bundle of nerves growing tighter and tighter with want, and half on the way he fondles my chest, his breathing growing rough with desire.

"You're so sexy," he murmurs, pressing a hot kiss to my shoulder. "You drive me out of my mind wanting you. Tell me what you want. What'll get you there."

"Your tongue on me," I murmur. "I want to come on your tongue."

"Thought you'd never ask."

He maneuvers himself from underneath me and kneels in front of the couch, scooting me to the edge. Trailing kisses up my inner thighs, he parts me and buries his tongue in my pussy, a wild zing of pleasure running through me.

I'm helpless to do anything other than experience the full force of his ministrations as he alternates between long, slow licks and fast flicks with his tongue. My hands sift through his hair, keeping him close, never wanting him to stop even as the pressure builds, higher and higher.

When he sucks on my clit, I'm done, spiraling over the edge on a wave of sensation. My thighs quiver as he continues to lap me up, and when I'm finished, he presses one more kiss to my pussy and leans back, rubbing his hands up and down my legs.

"You relaxed yet?" he asks with a grin, knowing full well I'm a boneless heap over here.

I nod, taking in his smug smile. The sudden urge to do the same for him strikes me. To taste him. To have him come on my tongue the same way. "You need some relaxing, too?"

Interest alights in his gaze. "I'll never turn that down from you."

I motion for him to stand, his groin eye level with me on the couch. "Unzip your pants."

His brows pop up, but he does what I say, the sound of the zipper pulling down making a thrill of anticipation run through me.

He tugs his jeans down a little, until his erection straining at his boxer briefs is on full display. I run a hand over him, teasing him through the soft fabric, and he lets out a low noise of satisfaction.

Reaching through the pocket in the front, I pull out his beautifully erect cock, stroking one finger along the underside. It bobs toward me, wanting more, and I look up at him, at the need already on his face. I lightly circle my fingers around him and he shudders, looking down at where I'm stroking him with barely there passes.

"Fuck, Madeline. You have any idea how sexy you are?"

"I am?" I ask coquettishly, and lean forward to give a soft lick to the head.

"I've created a seductress," he murmurs, his hand resting on the back of my head.

I guide his cock into my mouth, smiling to myself as he groans loudly, his hips subtly rocking in the rhythm he likes. Closing my lips around him, I lick and suck, building him up, loving the way he curses under his breath, the way he gently adjusts me to take him in further, the way he says my name like it's a benediction.

There's a sort of power in the act, and though it may seem like I'm the one submitting, it's him that's at my mercy. I release him with a pop, and trail kisses down his length, staring up at him with all the lust I'm feeling.

"Christ," he mutters, swallowing hard. "How do you keep doing this to me? Every day I want you more and more. It feels like it'll never end. Like I never want it to end."

I know exactly what he means.

"And you just keep opening more doors. When you touched yourself, I thought I was going to come then and there. I can't wait to watch you masturbate again."

A flush spreads over me, half in self-consciousness about my actions in the heat of the moment, half in anticipation at how excited he seems. With him, I've done things I've never dreamed of doing. And the thing is, I love doing them.

Only with Hunter, though.

"Should I touch myself again?" I murmur, sliding my tongue over his cock.

His hand tightens on my scalp for a moment. "Please."

I snake a hand down and enter myself with two fingers. I'm slick with arousal already from coming earlier, and I moan softly as I find my clit, rubbing it.

"You like that, baby?" he asks, guiding his dick into my mouth again. "When you finger your pussy while you suck me off?"

I tremble at the vivid image his words bring, and nod, working him up as I work myself up, too. I keep eye contact with him, at his hungry expression, his gaze flicking between where his cock disappears in and out of my mouth, and lower, to where my fingers do the same in my pussy. I lose myself in the taste of him, in the feel of him sliding through my lips, in the smell of musky arousal filling the air. I'm so turned on, dripping for him, and my second orgasm looms close on the horizon. Coming twice in a row is the norm now, and my body anticipates it, knowing what's in store.

"God, I love your mouth," he murmurs. "Love—"

My belly jumps, wondering how he's going to finish that thought, but he groans instead, his hold turning possessive as he comes in my mouth. I swallow him down, relishing the way he loses control, how he turns to putty, panting heavily at what I do to him.

"Oh, fuck," he mumbles as he finishes, and I lick him clean. "Here, let me . . ."

He drops beside me and kisses me deeply as he replaces my fingers with his own, drawing in and out of me with urgency. His other hand grips the back of my neck, holding me to him as his tongue slides in my mouth, claiming me as his.

That's what it feels like, at least, with the way he surrounds me. No one else could ever have this kind of effect on me. Could ever make me feel like I . . . belong to them.

A cry rises in my throat, and he swallows the sound as I break in his arms, clinging to his shoulders, my body tense with need until I finally relax again, bringing him down with me as I stretch out on the couch.

His cock rests on my thigh, dangerously close to where it shouldn't be, and I think again about going on birth control. About feeling him fully inside me, nothing between us. As much as I've loved us together with a condom, how would it feel for him to fill me up as he comes?

A shiver runs over me, and he pulls the throw blanket off the back of the couch to cover me, thinking I'm cold. I snuggle into it, not saying anything, and make a mental note to schedule a doctor's appointment soon.

I have a lot of things I need to do soon, actually. Between studying and training for the volunteer firefighter exams, and the happy bubble Hunter and I have created the past few weeks at his house, I've hardly been home. I've slept every night in Hunter's bed, wrapped in his arms, and even brought my computer here to work during the day at Hunter's insistence. It's a wonder what not being interrupted at home has done for my productivity. Even when he gets home from work, he respects my time and only gives me a kiss hello before making himself busy doing something else until I'm done.

I'd invited him earlier today to my weekly Friday afternoon virtual get-together with Adelaide, which had delighted her to no end, but the one thing I haven't done is invite him back to my house. Before opening that can of worms, I need to talk to Mom about everything that went down a few weeks ago. Now that we've had some time to cool off, maybe we can have a more constructive conversation.

I let myself bask in the comfort of lying next to Hunter for a few more moments, then turn to face him. "I should probably go home tonight."

His brows punch down. "Why? Did I do something? Are you mad?"

I keep my smile at bay. "No, and stop being ridiculous. But you know I don't actually live here, right?"

He finds my hand underneath the blanket and entwines our fingers. "Yeah, but I like you being here."

"I like being here, too. But I have to talk to my mom at some point."

He nods, understanding. I'd told him everything that went down with her, though it obviously doesn't compare at all to what happened with his own mother.

"I'll be back tomorrow, after our exams." I kiss him one last time and find my clothes on the floor, getting dressed while I still have the willpower to leave.

He looks like one of those big predator cats lounging on the couch, watching me with hooded eyes, the hazel in them sparking a bit like amber.

"Don't look at me like that," I say as I retie my disheveled ponytail.

"Like what?"

"Like you're contemplating pouncing on me to keep me here."

His lips quirk up one side. "That doesn't sound like me at all." He reaches out, running a palm down my outer thigh. "I just . . . I've been really happy lately. Like I didn't know what happy was before we started dating. And I don't want anything to change."

My heart melts a little, loving how open he's being with me. It's on the tip of my tongue to tell him . . . No, it's too soon. We haven't been dating that long.

"Nothing's going to change," I whisper, leaning down to kiss him again. "I won't let it. Not with how happy I've been, too."

He slides his hand over the back of my neck, kissing me deeper, but I pull away before I get too sucked into it.

"I really have to go."

He half pouts, half grins, and I laugh, then take my leave.

It's time to get this over with.

Chapter Twenty-Nine

MADELINE

Mom's in the living room watching TV when I unlock the front door, but shuts it off when she notices me, which is eerily similar to our last confrontation.

"Hi," she calls out. "Didn't know you were coming home tonight."

I can't tell if her tone is passive-aggressive, or if I'm imagining it. I need to stop being on the defensive.

I take a seat on the opposite end of the couch from her. "I thought we should talk now that we've had a chance to think about things some."

"Have you been avoiding me?" she asks, picking at some lint on the couch cushion.

"I've just been at Hunter's." Really? I'm already going to start out with evading the truth? "We've been studying and training nonstop. The exams are tomorrow."

"That's right. You have nothing to worry about, though." She reaches over and pats my hand. "You're your father's daughter. Firefighting's in your blood."

I'm fairly sure that's not how it works, but I keep my mouth shut.

"And how are things with you and Hunter?" she asks.

I'd texted her to tell her we're dating the day after we'd made things official. She'd never forgive me for keeping something like that from her, even if we're not on the best of terms right now.

"We're great. Almost . . . too great it seems like sometimes. I keep waiting for the other shoe to drop."

She smiles softly, a tinge of sadness to it. "When you find the right person, everything falls into place."

Crap. I didn't mean to remind her of Dad.

"I'm happy for you," she says, tapping the back of my hand. "Really. I've always wanted you to find your great love."

I bite my lip, suddenly nervous. "You think that's what he is?"

Her smile this time is more genuine. "Every time he's around, you can't take your eyes off of him. Why do you think I asked him to do all those things around the house?"

"Um, so we wouldn't have to pay someone to do it?"

"No, so you'd have a reason to spend more time together."

She can't be serious. Hunter and I had spent nearly every day together for weeks at that point.

Well, whatever. If she's happy to have played matchmaker, then I'll let her think she did.

"So, about the house . . ."

She nods. "I've thought a lot about what you said. And while I think you could have put it a little nicer . . ." She gives me a pointed look. "You also had some valid points."

She fiddles with the bottom button on her shirt for a moment, seeming to collect her thoughts. "I've thought of us as a team for so long, braving the world together after your father's death. And I was so lonely when you were away at college. I lived for your school breaks when you would come home."

"You're guilt-tripping me again," I chide softly.

"Right. I'm sorry, that wasn't my intention." She returns her hand to her lap. "All of that to say, I've loved having you here again the last few years, but I understand you can't stay forever. And it wasn't right of me either to depend on you like that after I got myself in all that financial mess."

"I didn't mind helping out at first," I tell her. "But it's time you took things over again. And I'm sorry how harsh I was the other week."

"Thank you. Well, I talked to your Aunt Lucy about it. She's open to me moving in with her."

My brows raise in surprise. That was quick.

"Not anytime soon, mind you," she adds. "I'll have to go through this whole house top to bottom first and figure out what to do with everything."

Oh, God. That alone will take months. She refused to get rid of anything of Dad's when he passed, and brought it all to Green Valley with us.

"There are a few things to fix up with the house, too, before trying to sell it. Maybe your new man can help with that."

"Yeah, he will." I already know he won't say no.

"And you'll still be here until I'm ready to sell?" There's a nervous note in her voice, like she's waiting for me to say no. "We can split the mortgage and utilities fifty-fifty. And I . . . I'd give you a portion of the sale, too."

I scoot closer, wrapping my arms around her shoulders. "I'll be here. And we can figure out the details later. I'm just glad you listened to me."

"Of course, honey."

She hugs me back, and a wave of nostalgia washes over me. She's right that it's been me and her for so long. But I'm also ready for something new. Something more.

And for the first time, I think I've found it.

* * *

SWEAT TRICKLES down the back of my neck and I ache desperately to wipe it away, but I can't. I'm covered head to toe in turnout gear, a sticky, sweaty mess in the Tennessee summer heat.

I can't focus on that now, though. It's almost time for Hunter's and my turn for the forcible entry.

If I'd known yesterday what today's live fire exercise would be like, I would have savored the exams a little more. The written part had been in sweet, sweet air conditioning, and even the CPAT hadn't been the overblown beast I'd turned it into in my head. With as many times as Hunter and I had practiced the events, I'd finished with a solid fifteen seconds to spare. Hunter thought he did an okay job on the written part, too, but we won't get the results for a while.

In the meantime, we'll keep training, but won't be allowed to go out on actual calls until we officially pass. And today's a pretty good wake-up call as to the potential realities of what things will be like during a real situation. Everything we've done so far has been a one-off practice, but it's all put together today.

Hunter and I are paired up for the day, as expected, and our job during the first session was to lay hose as the other members of the team entered the large shipping container–like structure brought in to the fire station parking lot to simulate a burning building. Once they'd broken open the door, it had been our job to extinguish the flames. The heat had been more intense than I thought it'd be, even with all this gear on, and I suspect it would have been worse if Hunter hadn't been in front to shield me.

Now, it's our turn to forcibly enter.

I grip the axe in my hands tightly, afraid of dropping it, and listen for Chief McClure's command. Everything is slightly muffled with all this headgear, but his booming voice is hard to miss as he instructs Hunter and me to start.

We rush forward, and I feel like a kid playing dress up with how big this gear is on me, but I forge ahead, waiting as Hunter wedges the Halligan bar into the doorframe. I hit the end of it with the flat head side of my axe to force it in further, praying I don't miss and hit Hunter by mistake. That would be all I need.

Hunter pulls at the bar, leveraging it like he's supposed to, but it still takes another try until it cracks open. We both connect our low-pressure regulators to our facepieces until air from the tanks on our backs flows through, turn on the flashlights clipped to our gear, then head inside.

The heat is as bad as last time, maybe worse now since the sun is higher in the sky, and the smoke is a black, choking cloud that's impossible to see through, even with the flashlights. If we hadn't watched Silas and Harry do this earlier, I'd have no idea where the next door is.

Hunter and I switch tools as instructed, and I wedge the Halligan bar into the locked interior door. Theoretically, this one is supposed to be easier, but it still seems plenty difficult to me. Hunter strikes the end with the axe, the metal bar vibrating in my hands, and though it jams it in further, I can't get the leverage I need to force the door open, even putting all my weight into it.

After the fourth try, Hunter shouts, "Do you want me to do it?"

"No, I'm supposed to."

Behind us, one of the controlled flames roars to life, and Rodney and Waylon spray at it from the doorway. Shit. We were supposed to have broken this door down already.

Hunter moves in closer, blocking the worst of the flame's heat from my back. "We're out of time," he says. "Let me help you."

He puts his hands over mine, tugging on the bar with a force I could never dream of. I probably look like a ragdoll with the way it shakes me, but it does the trick, the door breaking at the lock. Hunter kicks it open and we make our way in further, Rodney and Waylon right behind to get the flames ahead. I swear, the fire hadn't seemed so close when we'd been extinguishing it earlier, the heat coming in waves.

It's so freaking hot in here. No air, only smoke. Sweat pours off me now, but it has nowhere to go, trapped in my clothes under the turnout gear. It stings my eyes, but I can't wipe at my face, the face shield in the way. And I can't remove that or I won't have breathable air.

"Madeline."

I blink and Hunter's there in my face. When did he get there? Was I out of it for a moment?

"You okay?" he asks, but I can't tell if he's worried. There's no nuance to anyone's voices right now, only shouting to be heard over the fire and these damn masks and helmets.

"Yeah!" I shout back, and he points ahead and to the right, where we have to use pike poles to breach the ceiling for ventilation.

How is he moving so quickly? Isn't he exhausted, too? It gives me a newfound respect for the physical job he does daily. He must be used to sweating like this, but I'm definitely not.

Squinting closely at the room ahead, there are slivers of light coming from above. Those are the two spots in the top of the structure we have to work on.

I pick up my pike pole, and even though it's only ten pounds, it feels a hell of a lot heavier at the moment. Hunter immediately gets to work, pulling and pushing at the metal surface to create an exit for the growing heat in the room. I start on mine, but it takes forever just to allow one little shaft of light to poke its way through. Meanwhile, Hunter's made a hole the size of a bowling ball.

Behind us, someone shouts something, and I turn around, my eyes widening as a flame licks its way into the area. Rodney and Waylon are struggling to contain the growing fire and Chief McClure and Grizz barge in, taking over the hose for them.

There's a tug on my arm, and Hunter guides me forcefully over to the furthest corner, away from the flame.

"I need to finish the ceiling!" I yell at him, but he doesn't let go of me.

"I'll do it!" he shouts, then turns to do it himself.

I want to yell at him that it's my responsibility, but the chief and captain are right there. If the point of this is to assess our teamwork skills, I can't argue with Hunter in front of them.

Meanwhile, I'm relegated to a corner while he does all the work.

My eyes sting again, but this time it's not sweat. It's frustration and hurt and a good dose of self-pity.

Hunter finishes the task as fast as any pro firefighter, and the flame is quickly contained. I march past him, our part of the exercise finished now, and disconnect my regulator as I exit the structure. I rip off my gloves then my face shield, fire hood, and helmet, being careful not to damage anything while also wanting it off as fast as humanly possible.

Someone touches my arm and I whip around, finding Hunter there, a questioning look on his face as he removes his shield.

"Not here," I mutter, mindful of Harry and Silas at the equipment table that's been set up. I place my headgear on the table, then unbuckle the straps that hold the air tank of my breathing apparatus to my back. I slip that off, too, then stalk off toward the fire station. I just need some time to—

"What's wrong?"

Hunter's there again, and I know he's being kind by checking up on me, but all I can think of is the way he completely took over during the exercise. How I couldn't seem to finish anything myself.

"What the hell was that?"

Chapter Thirty
MADELINE

"What?" He seems completely confused. He probably doesn't even realize what he did.

"You hijacked the whole exercise," I whisper-yell, not wanting the others to hear us. "You didn't let me do anything."

There's a thickness in my throat I can't get rid of, and it has nothing to do with the smoke in the air.

His forehead wrinkles. "I helped you a little."

"No, you did it for me. How do you think that makes me look to the team? To the captain and chief? You made me seem weak."

He stares at me silently, and I know what he's thinking, because I'm thinking the same thing.

I am weak.

Even after all that training, I'll never be as tall as him, or as strong. I'll never be as good of a firefighter.

"I get what you're saying," he says softly, his tone making me want to wring his neck, like he's calming a wild animal. "But I wasn't trying to make you look bad."

"Well, you did. I would have got it on my own eventually."

His jaw tightens. "And how long would *eventually* take? We didn't have the luxury of time inside a burning building."

He has a point, but that's not the point. "It was a controlled fire."

"Which was quickly becoming out of control with those two dipshits at the hose. We don't know what could have happened, even if it was supposed to be controlled. It's still a fucking fire."

"You put me in the corner!" I shout, my anger exploding out of me. It's not only toward him, though. It's toward myself, too. That experience wasn't what I thought it'd be at all.

"You froze up. I called your name and you didn't respond."

He did? All I remember is staring at the fire coming toward us.

"And I'm not going to apologize for trying to get us out of there safely. When the woman I love is in a dangerous situation, I'm going to do everything I can to protect her."

His breathing is slightly elevated, but other than that he seems composed. He either doesn't realize what he said, or it isn't a big deal to him.

It is to me, though.

I've been wanting him to say it for weeks, even as I wondered if it was too soon to feel this way. Then again, nothing about our relationship has been conventional. And I can't deny that what I feel for him . . . is love.

Even if I'm mad at him.

I swallow hard, the words coming out shaky. "You're not off the hook because you said you love me."

He blinks at me. "What?"

Oh, so he didn't realize he said it. "You said you love me."

"I did?"

Disappointment sinks hot in the pit of my stomach. He must not have meant it. Was it a slip of the tongue?

"I mean, I do," he clarifies. "I love you. But I didn't mean to tell you like this." He motions around us. "Here, where we're all sweaty and gross."

My heart beats harder, faster even than when we were in that fire. "When did you mean to tell me?"

He rubs at the back of his neck, suddenly nervous. "You know, over a candlelit dinner or something."

A candlelit dinner of frozen pizza? I don't say that out loud, though. The man has other redeeming qualities than his cooking skills.

"That sounds really romantic."

"Yeah?" He looks up at me, and though his hair is plastered to his head with sweat and there are trails of soot over his face, he's never been more handsome to me.

I nod. "I love you, too."

The grin that breaks over his face has my heart fluttering like mad, ready to break free as he comes in close and slides his hands around my waist, kissing me thoroughly.

My arms instinctively wrap around his shoulders, loving how he consumes me, how he makes me—

A loud *ahem* has us drawing apart. Chief McClure is there, staring at us in disbelief. Beyond him, Grizz mouths, *What the fuck*. Harry and Silas are watching from a distance, also with identical expressions of incredulity.

Shit. This is exactly what I didn't want to happen. Then again, it was bound to come out sooner or later.

Hunter keeps his arm around my waist. "We're dating," he says, shrugging, as if that explains everything.

Chief McClure eyes us warily. "Didn't you just hate each other?"

"You made us play nice and now we're in love."

Again, an extreme simplification, but Chief McClure only blinks, then shakes his head. "Okay, well, I came over to talk to you, Madeline."

Me? Am I in trouble? Am I kicked out because Hunter finished the tasks I was supposed to do?

Hunter squeezes my hip in reassurance, then walks away. Grizz falls into step with him and asks, "How long have you two been sneaking around behind everyone's backs?"

I can't hear Hunter's reply as Chief McClure moves to fill my vision.

"Have to say, I didn't see that coming," he says.

Well, whatever he has to say must not be too bad if he's making small talk first. "It was a bit of a surprise to us, too. But thank you for making us work together."

He barks out a breath of laughter. "Yeah, sure. That's not what I came over here to talk to you about, though. I wanted to address your performance."

My lips press tightly together. Right.

"How do you think you did today?"

Great. He's going to make me say it? "I, um . . . I think the first session went okay. I'm good at laying hose and assisting with the attack line."

He nods, as if he agrees with me, but that's not the issue.

"And then during the session just now . . . Well, I struggled a little with the Halligan bar. Getting the leverage I needed was difficult. And I was getting the hang of the pike pole, but then the fire came in . . ."

For the first time today, I'm thankful for the sweltering heat. Maybe he'll attribute my red cheeks to that instead of shame.

"Today made it all pretty real, huh?"

"Yes."

"Everyone's first time is more difficult than they think it'll be."

Not Hunter. He'd jumped into action with no problem.

"I'm glad we had the chance to practice" is all I say.

He nods. "You never know how you'll react until you're in the thick of things. In my training academy a million years ago, I watched a grown man run away crying the first time we were put in a situation like this."

Oh, Jesus. Well, at least I didn't do that.

"Thankfully, no one here did that," he says, echoing my thought, "but this is why we do training drills. It shows us what areas we need to work on. It also shows us what our strengths are." He looks over his shoulder, toward the group of guys by the equipment table, Hunter among them. "Your boy there was cool, calm, and collected."

He was. If I hadn't been partnered with him, what might have happened? And as mad as I was that he took over, he's right that we were out of time. I had my chance and I . . . I failed. Maybe it wasn't anger I was feeling, so much as jealousy.

"I've watched his confidence grow the past couple of months since I assigned you two together. I think you've had a lot to do with that."

"I'm proud of him," I whisper, my throat tight. Really, I am. His success is mine, too, even if I'm feeling a little envious at the moment.

"I am, too. You need to stop the comparisons, though."

I meet his eye, a serious gravity in his gaze.

"You're not Hunter. You're not any of the guys here. It's important for you to have the basics down, but remember we're a team. Not everyone gets to be the hotshot hero carrying people out of burning buildings."

If he's aiming for this to be a pep talk, it's not exactly working. "So, you're saying I should be happy to be on the sidelines?"

He purses his lips. "Maybe I'm bungling this. What I meant was you should play to your strengths. I'll bet you can calculate pump pressure on the fly faster than any of the rest of them. You can identify all the hazmat symbols in your sleep. You could help in an extrication where the rest of us are too big to fit into a space. The firefighters assisting behind the scenes are just as important as anyone else. The ones on the frontlines can't do their jobs without them."

I nod, knowing he's right. I knew going into this I'd have my work cut out for me. And, to be honest, that fire had been scary. I'm not sure how soon I want to revisit something like that. Focusing on assisting could be a blessing in disguise.

"I understand," I tell him. "And thank you for talking to me about it."

He nods. "You think my talk with the Clewis boys will go as well?"

"Um . . ."

"Yeah, that's what I thought, too."

He heads inside the fire station and Hunter returns to me, running his hands up and down my arms. Guess the cat's out of the bag now, so there's no reason to remind him not to do that. It's actually been kind of exhausting to hide our relationship here the past couple of weekends.

"Everything okay?" he asks, a wrinkle between his brows. "Did he say anything about what happened in there?"

"He didn't mention it outright, but he implied I should focus on stuff other than being on the frontlines."

"Shit, I'm sorry."

"No, it's okay. He's right. And someone has to do the prep work and behind-the-scenes stuff. That can be what I'm good at."

He eyes me skeptically. "You're accepting this way too calmly."

A laugh escapes me. Yeah, I'd normally fight like tooth and nail over a setback like this, but the live fire exercise had introduced a whole new perspective I wasn't prepared for. "The stuff I do on the sidelines would help protect people like you in the thick of it. That's more important to me than trying to prove I'm someone I'm not."

The corners of his mouth quirk up. "You want to protect me?"

"Of course I do. I love you."

He bites at his bottom lip, heat flashing in his gaze. "Yeah, I'm going to need you to say that again in bed tonight. A lot."

Warmth curls in the pit of my stomach. "I promise."

Life with Hunter will never be dull, that's for sure.

And as I've discovered lately, that's just the way I like it.

Epilogue
HUNTER

Six Months Later

"A little to the left."

Madeline's mom directs me toward the opposite wall and I pick up the full-length standing mirror, moving it over until she tells me to stop.

"Actually . . . I like it where it was before."

"Mom." Madeline groans from her spot at the closet, where she's unzipping a garment bag and hanging everything up. "He's not your lackey. You were supposed to decide where everything goes before we helped you move."

Behind her back, Vera mimics her daughter, and I hold in my laughter. That would not go over well.

"Babe, it's fine," I tell her. "We have all afternoon."

"Yeah, but we still have to get my stuff out of the house, too. We only have a week left."

She acts like she has a ton of stuff left to move, when we both know she's pretty much been living at my house already for months.

"Yes, dear."

She looks over her shoulder at me, trying to look severe, but she can't hide the way her lips tip up at the corners. "Don't *yes dear* me. Am I the only one taking this seriously?"

"Yes, dear," Vera and I say in unison, and everyone busts out laughing.

Vera hugs her daughter tightly around the shoulders. "Don't worry so much. We'll get it all done. Especially with your strapping young man here."

She crosses the room to squeeze my arm. I'd take it as flirting if I didn't know she acts that way with everyone.

"I'm going to check on the stew," she says. "Your aunt's so excited to have me cook for her all the time."

She sounds genuinely excited to move in here, which has me breathing a sigh of relief. Madeline was worried about being on the short end of a long guilt trip regarding her mom having to move, but she hasn't run into as many problems as she thought she would. And luckily, the house sold within a month of putting it on the market. We're only waiting on the final closing now.

Which means Madeline can finally officially move in with me.

Not that much will change, but I want her to feel fully comfortable in her new home and not like she's a guest. Thankfully, she says she loves everything just as I have it, so there are no plans for major redecoration, but I'm still prepared to do anything she wants.

Madeline finishes hanging the clothes and walks over to me, smoothing her hands down the front of my shirt. I'll never tire of her touching me so comfortably. The only time she doesn't do it is when we're on a firefighting call together. She says we should be *professional*, even when I need to reassure myself she's okay. She mostly stays away from the main action, preferring to help with the pumps and hoses, but you never know what could happen.

"Have you heard back from your mom?" she whispers, probably not wanting Vera to catch wind of it.

I shake my head. It's been radio silence since that blowup at my house six months ago, although I did find out Dad's still in jail. I guess they never got the bail money, and he'd likely have to serve time anyway if it was a serious drug offense.

I invited my mom over for dinner recently, wanting to extend an olive branch after we've both had a long time to cool off, but she hasn't responded. I thought she might be over it by now, but maybe not. I've done my part, though.

"I'm sorry," she says, wrapping her arms around my middle to hug me tight.

"It's fine. It was a long shot, anyway."

She looks up at me, probably to act all therapist the way she does sometimes, but is interrupted by the text alert on her phone.

"Oh, Adelaide said she was going to send me an idea for the guest bedroom since we're moving my old bed in there." She taps at her screen, then rolls her eyes. "Oh my God, look at this."

She turns her phone toward me, where a little girl's princess unicorn fever dream room is on the screen, with liberal use of pink glitter and rainbows.

"Hey, I might still have some of that glitter I pranked you with. We could use it for this."

She playfully smacks my arm. "You do that and I'm not moving in."

A grin crosses my face. "Fair enough. We'll save it for a future kid's room or something."

She leans back, confusion on her face. "What?"

I shrug. "You know, in the future. We'll eventually have to turn the guest bedroom into a nursery if we have kids."

Her mouth opens, then shuts. Opens . . . then shuts again.

It's rare I can turn her speechless, but that's not always a good thing.

"Have you not thought about that?" I ask tentatively.

"You have?" she responds, not answering my question.

"Yeah."

She steps back, an air of alarm over her. "We've only been dating six months."

My first thought is concern that we're on vastly different steps on the relationship timeline before I dismiss it. She loves me. She's committed to me. The same as I am to her.

"So? I'm not saying let's try for a baby right now. I want us to get married before that."

Her eyes widen further. "You've thought about us getting married?"

"Have you not?" I ask again, feeling like a broken record.

"Yeah, I have," she admits. "But I didn't think you had."

"Baby." I cup her face, drawing her in close to press a kiss to her lips. "You and me are forever. The when's not so important, only that it happens at some point."

She nods, her eyes still wide, but she smiles, too. That beautiful smile that still knocks me out. "Okay," she says shakily. "But let's focus on getting the rest of my stuff in your house first. And then, sometime in the future, we can talk about . . ."

She doesn't finish her sentence, but she doesn't have to, especially with that look of love on her face.

"I love you," I whisper, kissing her again.

"Love you more," she whispers back, stepping into my arms again to kiss me deeply.

And as long as I have her, that's all I need.

About the Author

Allie is also the author of the Crescent Pass series, the Bishop Brothers series, and the Suncoast University series. She lives in sunny Florida with her husband, daughter, and two cats. A librarian by day, she spends her nights writing happily ever afters. She enjoys reading, playing video games, and all things Disney.

Follow for all the latest book info and news:
Website: alliewinters.com
Newsletter and bonus epilogues: alliewinters.com/extras
Instagram: instagram.com/alliewintersauthor
Facebook: facebook.com/alliewintersauthor

Find Smartypants Romance online:
Website: www.smartypantsromance.com
Facebook: www.facebook.com/smartypantsromance/
Goodreads: www.goodreads.com/smartypantsromance
Twitter: @smartypantsrom
Instagram: @smartypantsromance
Newsletter: https://smartypantsromance.com/newsletter/

Also by Allie Winters

Also in the Lessons Learned series:

<u>Under Pressure (Lessons Learned #1</u>)

Mia knows stress. She's dealt with it her whole life. So when she gets an opportunity to run a psychology study to help her get into grad school, it should be no problem dealing with the prickly guy she suddenly finds herself paired with.

The one she had a secret crush on last year. The one who refuses to let anyone close. The one she's discovering by the day may have a softer side than he lets anyone else see…

Tyler knows stress. He's grappled with it for as long as he can remember. And just because he has to share credit with this girl on his new psychology study doesn't mean he has to be friends with her. Except she somehow keeps worming her way into his life. In school. In the boxing gym.

In his bed.

But everyone knows it's safer to keep to yourself. You can't hurt anyone that way. Even if it means giving up the best thing that's ever happened to him.

As things heat up in the Stress Lab, will this match be able to work together without disruption, or will this growing attraction between them eventually… combust?

<u>Not Fooling Anyone (Lessons Learned #2</u>)

The deal is simple—pretend to be Ethan's girlfriend for a psych study and we each get a nice payday. Despite him being a dumb jock who willingly gets punched for fun at my dad's boxing gym, I can handle it. I've mastered the art of keeping others at a distance. Especially after… Well, never mind that.

Except, I didn't count on him not understanding the definition of boundaries. Suddenly, we're having to fake being in love all over campus to keep up the ruse. And when he tries to slip under the barriers I've worked so hard to create? Yeah, that's not happening. Even if it turns out he's surprisingly understanding… and funny… and charming… and smarter than I ever would have given him credit for. Not to mention that muscled body from all that boxing…

No, that's irrelevant. I may have misjudged him, but that doesn't mean I'm interested. He has no idea what kind of baggage I'm carrying. A relationship is the last thing on my mind.

Even if I'm not fooling anyone.

****

The Crescent Pass series is a contemporary small-town romance trilogy that follows the Taylor family siblings as they find love in the Pacific Northwest.

A Forest Between Us (Crescent Pass #1)

- Owen -

Harper Calloway is the one who got away.

Gorgeous. Vivacious. Witty. Everything my introverted self could never be. And though that single night five years ago is all I had with her, there's no forgetting the girl who steals your heart.

So when the woman in question shows up on my doorstep demanding an annulment for a drunken Vegas wedding I don't fully remember, it seems like a sign. A second chance to make good on that connection I've never felt with anyone else.

Except she doesn't have any interest in reconnecting, even as things between us heat up the longer she stays in town. What will it take to convince her I want forever?

- Harper -

Owen Taylor is not who I expected.

Protective. Thoughtful. Humble. And the sexy lumberjack vibe he's got going on? Who knew I was such a sucker for that?

I didn't come to Crescent Pass to start anything up. My life is in Chicago, not the forests of the Pacific Northwest. But the longer I stay here waiting for an annulment, the harder it is to resist this rugged mountain man who shows me for the first time what it's like to be understood. Cherished. Worshipped.

We both knew from the beginning this couldn't last. So why has he gone and stolen my heart?

A Mountain Divides Us (Crescent Pass #2)

- Kristen -

Eli Andrews wasn't supposed to be anything other than a temporary roommate.

On paper, it all makes sense. I rent out a room to him to earn some much-needed cash when my work hours get cut. I'll stay on my side of the house and he'll stay on his. Away from me and my kids.

But he wasn't supposed to be tall and gorgeous and make butterflies flutter in my stomach. He wasn't supposed to be helpful and charming and supportive in a way I didn't know I needed. He wasn't supposed to waken that part of me that's laid dormant for so long, an attraction building between us the longer he stays. I wasn't supposed to fall under his spell.

Or into his bed.

For years, I've made sensible choices. Ones that are best for me and my kids. Ones that don't involve sexy blue-eyed strangers who are only in town for a month.

Eli Andrews isn't staying in Crescent Pass. But tell that to my heart.

- Eli -

Kristen Taylor wasn't supposed to be the woman of my dreams.

On paper, it doesn't make sense. She's a widow with two kids, while I'm the guy who avoids relationships. Only, when plans fall through and I'm stuck on a job with nowhere to stay, she's the one who comes through for me.

But she wasn't supposed to be so easy to get along with. She wasn't supposed to show me what a family could really be like. She wasn't supposed to make my heart pound.

Or tempt me beyond belief.

For years, I've kept to myself. It's safer that way. No one to disappoint or hurt you in return. Besides, I'm not staying in Crescent Pass.

So why can't I get her out of my head… or my heart?

A Fire Within Us (Crescent Pass #3) releases in 2024!

***

The Bishop Brothers series is a contemporary romance trilogy featuring three sexy billionaire brothers who find love in Manhattan.

Resisting the Billionaire (Bishop Brothers #1)

- Gabriel – When I'm forced to make a deal with my father to marry the woman of his choosing for a business deal, I never expected to find someone I connect with. Someone who doesn't fawn all over me because I'm the heir to a billion dollar fortune. Someone who sees the real me. And someone I can't get enough of in turn.

There's only one problem—I can't have her. She's the wedding planner.

- Mackenzie - It's the chance of a lifetime—plan the wedding of a billionaire's son that'll put my event planning business on the map and get me out of debt. A no brainer, right?

Except the bride wants nothing to do with this arranged marriage. And as the groom and I get closer, the professional lines between us keep blurring until there's something there neither of us can deny. With my business on the line and our chemistry off the charts, I'm torn whether I should keep resisting the one person I never expected to fall for.

Marrying the Billionaire (Bishop Brothers #2)

- Serena - Marrying the man of your dreams after crushing on him for the last decade should be cause for celebration. So why am I crying alone in the honeymoon suite on my wedding night? Because there's just one problem—it's a fake marriage. Purely for appearances as part of a business deal between our fathers' companies.

But I can't sit idly by pretending this is only a platonic relationship, especially as sparks begin to fly between us. So what will I have to do to convince my stoic Prince Charming I want him for real? And what will I risk along the way?

- Archer - The plan is simple—act like a husband in love publicly after I foolishly got myself involved in this fake marriage, and behind closed doors keep things separate. But the longer we continue this charade attending events and staging selfies, the more I'm unsure what's fake and what's not, especially when things start to heat up in private.

As the successor to my father's billion dollar company, work has been my life. Focusing on my job has never been harder, though, when there's a temptress living in my guest bedroom. What are the chances this business deal of a marriage could turn into the real thing? The last person I ever expected to fall for is… my wife.

<u>Seducing the Billionaire (Bishop Brothers #3)</u>

- Connor - It's all on me now. The billion-dollar company I just inherited from my late father. The public eye waiting for me to slip up. The pressure of keeping it all together.

At least there's one bright spot in my life—my new assistant, Emma. My dream woman come to life if I didn't know better.

It's too bad the paparazzi would have a field day if they discovered something going on between us. I can't afford for anything to jeopardize my new role as CEO of Bishop Industries.

Even if she is temptation personified.

- Emma - It was supposed to be a simple assignment. Become Connor Bishop's new assistant and convince him to buy my father's company, Montague Media. So how do I do that? By any means necessary, according to my dad—including seduction. Otherwise, I lose everything.

But no one told me how hard it would be to seduce a billionaire who insists on acting like a perfect gentleman, especially when real feelings begin to emerge. At what point do I stop the charade and tell him who I really am? Before or after I fall in love with him?

***

Check out the Suncoast University series – Four steamy new adult romances that will have you swooning.

<u>Let Go (Suncoast University #1)</u>

- Charlotte - Putting yourself out there? Getting close to others? No, thanks, I'll pass. It's safer to keep to yourself. I've learned that lesson the hard way. So when I accidentally tell the muscled hunk I've been secretly drooling over all semester how I really feel about him, it's not like I meant for him to take an interest in me. I don't want a boyfriend. Not even when it turns out he's so much more than just brawn.

My goal for so long has been simple—get into grad school. And when I get a dream TA position at the beginning of the new semester that will help me achieve just that, I'll have to forget about him now that he's my student. Easy, right?

- Luke - I can't get her out of my head—the shy, sexy brunette that's trying so hard to keep me at a distance. I can be patient, though. Anything to break through that reserve and get under her shields. But just when I thought I've succeeded, she's off-limits. Say hello to my new TA. Even though I'm hot for teacher, there's no way she would risk this opportunity. Right?

<u>Watch Me (Suncoast University #2)</u>

- Samantha - I need a place to stay ASAP when my living arrangements fall through before college starts. And I shouldn't have any trouble resisting my new roommate... despite how much I find myself connecting with him.

- Levi - I have absolutely no interest in the beautiful blonde living in the room next door. She's not my type. Not even when it turns out she's nothing like I expected.

She's only here for the summer, so it shouldn't be a big deal to act on this attraction before she leaves. It doesn't have to mean anything, right?

<u>No One Else (Suncoast University #3)</u>

- Evan - I messed up. I admitted to the girl of my dreams I'm in love with her, only to have her run away. Why don't they ever warn you things like that happen?

Now that we're paired up for a class project, I have to figure out a way to keep things from being weird between us. I can't lose her again.

- Natalie - We shared a kiss the night after I broke up with my boyfriend of three years. A heart-stopping, panty-melting kiss I still dream about. But I wasn't ready then for anything more.

Now that I am, he's unavailable. What will it take to get us both on the same page - and stay there?

<u>First and Only (Suncoast University #4)</u>

- Jake - When my dreams of going pro are crushed by a career-ending knee injury, I have to figure out how to use brains over brawn for the first time to graduate college. Enter Eden, my new Biology tutor. Except she doesn't want to be paid in the usual way.

She wants me to give her relationship tutoring to attract a guy she likes. But this shy, awkward brainiac is turning out to be so much more than I expected. In the words of a scientist, will this equal exchange turn out to be more than the sum of its parts?

- Eden - Hot guys don't fall for nerds like me. It's just a fact of life—one I've come to accept like gravity or thermodynamics. So even though others think Jake's interested in me, I know it's just this tutoring deal we have going on. I show him the electron transport system and he shows me how to kiss. Simple as that. There's no sense in getting my hopes up, even as I realize this ex-jock and I fit together in a way I never thought possible. Rarely does an equal exchange turn out to be more than the sum of its parts. Even when I desperately want it to.

Also by Smartypants Romance

9 781959 097907